THE PAWN

Acknowledgments

Thank you, William, Zak and Ellie for believing in me and supporting my new career in writing.

Corinne, Sharon, Suzie and Claire for listening to my never-ending chats about how my novel was advancing.

I'm indebted to Jon Stewart for his technical skill and ability to guide me through my dilemmas and assist me with the overall formatting process. To his wife Margaret, who was forever encouraging me to achieve my goals.

You have all been there for the guidance I have longed for.

Prologue

Check mate! His hand slid across the board to put the pawn into position. It's taken 6 whole years to finish the game, to finish the detailed planning and execution of every move needed to see his success begin. It was staring right in front of him, that prize winning move, one in a thousand chances. The moment of self-adulation filled his head with feelings he had never felt before in his life. A sense of victory welled within him.

Who would ever have thought that a pawn could take down the King. Small and insignificant to all the rest of the pieces. Yet here he stands, triumphant amongst his fellow rivals on the board, who he conquered and successfully vanquished with precision.

The next game he plays would be his own, briefed and guided by God his saviour. With rules and instructions that have been meticulously penned by his fair hand. There won't be conditions with his game or constraints as a player to immediately achieve his objectives. There won't be wooden carved out miniature figurines to knock into oblivion, no unhelpful knight to show him the way or a Queen to bellow out orders. He will play like the pawn, manoeuvring around the board, undetected and being the last piece standing.

He will need his instructions, numbered counters, his dice and a few components to help him accomplish his moves. *The smaller objects can be transported in my pocket*, he mused. His opponents would be his playing pieces. They would have no idea they have been successfully selected to participate in such an exhilarating game. Such lucky, honoured players. They would be real to touch and with his instructions written down, easy to remove from play. The participants will be delighted to have been chosen and selected from the thousands of gamers who reside in Choctaw County.

***

He sat waiting in his vehicle. The broken heaters were making loud noises, the pressure of air trying to flow through. 'Damn vehicle,' he cursed, knocking the dash as if that would rectify the vehicle's problems. The fuel pressure gauge was faulty, there was a stench of lingering sulphur in the damp air as he sat slouched down in his seat. He was low enough not to be seen by those staggering out of the bar, but in a position where his first opponent of the game, wouldn't be obstructed.

Evening was drawing in, daylight had diminished, making the visual on his objective harder to see. He would soon disappear in the darkness, which made the perpetrator anxious. He couldn't wait to put everything God had instructed him to do, read his own notes he carefully transcribed over the last 6 years, into action, into play.

The doors of the bar opened, he saw him, Evan Thomas. He had seen this drunken act from his first opponent on numerous occasions, as he sat every evening, for the last year watching, observing his every move. He was meticulous with his own instructions and rules. Sit, observe, follow the opponents, but don't touch.

Tonight though, was the next step in the game. He had thrown his gaming dice already back in his favourite room and it landed on **4**. How he longed to play and take down his enemies, his long-term oppositions, moving cautiously and skilfully without being noticed, winning each time he rolled his dice.

He had spent years designing and crafting his pocket full of trappings. He was a master of his own guile and knew the game was going to be extraordinarily complex, but he was ready. God would be with him throughout, encouraging him to make righteous decisions and moves. Now to move forward enough paces to be able to reach his first opponent. *Let my game begin..*

Chapter One

Darkness engulfed her aching body. Daylight had vanished too quickly for her. She was lost in an unfamiliar forest of overwhelming quietness. The cold bitter air was the first thing she felt. Her legs were numb, her torso was shivering uncontrollably. Her hands were cut with deep lacerations where she had scraped her way through the side of the shack, he held her captive in. The young girl's fears started to escalate as the memories of the last 48 hrs, came flooding back. She struggled to process what was happening. *He'll find me, I know he will,* she thought desperately.

The air remained still and quiet. Emily could only hear the sound of her heart beating frantically. The trees that stood tall and engulfed her weak body, were dead calm and the sound of leaves falling, were eerily frightening. Emily knew this was her last chance to get away from him and his sadistic torment. She didn't know why he had chosen her; she was just a teenager minding her own business. Her thoughts were cut short when she heard the sound of rustling leaves behind her. She held her breath, praying to God, he wouldn't find her in the dark. Emily could hear the sharp noise of his breath wheezing in the air and tried to stand up, but her feet were numb to the bone. Her last bit of determination got her to her knees. She was going to get away, see her family again, hug them all and never let them go. Then in a split second, her whole world went dark.

Clara had been following this perpetrator for the last hour, but lost sight of him when his pick-up veered off up a slip road. Special Agent Clara Strong, a field agent in the FBI and her work partner Special Agent Carlos Ferendez, were put on this case over two months ago.

One victim had already succumbed to the killer's actions. Clara was not going to let that happen again. She wasn't ready for his deviation and had to spin her vehicle around to pick up his trail. She had temporarily lost sight of him. He had Emily and she wasn't about to let her die. Clara didn't have time to call for police back up, she had to keep her eyes focused on the task ahead and was going to get this son of a bitch at any cost.

Dust filled the road to the east of her, visibility was almost zero, when she could just make out the taillights of his vehicle. He suddenly screeched to a halt and jumped out with the girl, dragging her into his wooden shack. Clara noticed Emily wasn't moving. 'Shit,' she murmured.

She sprung from her vehicle and pulled out her Glock 17. The moon light casted shadows on the plethora of obstacles in the front yard. Large rusty old machinery entrenched into the ground, visibly fallen apart over the years from pure neglect, made Clara's job difficult.

Reaching for her maglite, she switched it on to manoeuvre around. She should have called it in, asked for backup. Clara knew this would come back to bite her, but there was no time, she wouldn't let an innocent girl die because of protocol. Time was something she didn't have and wouldn't wait for. She peered in the window to the front of the shack. Dirt rimmed the glass; she could just make out some movement inside. 'Gotcha,' she whispered. Clara poised her arms in front as she moved quietly towards the front porch, clutching her weapon, turning the door handle gently.

It opened so she covertly moved inside, her Glock still pointing forwards. The room was in total darkness, she shone her light in all directions. Her eyes were scouting for the perp, but the place was empty. She heard banging coming from the room above. Her heart pounded with the realisation of his location. *He couldn't have dragged Emily upstairs in such short time,* she thought. *He must have hidden her downstairs, where the hell is she?*

Every step Clara took, was one of extreme pressure. She couldn't afford to make a noise, otherwise it would be all over. Emily's life would end, and it would be her fault. She advanced across the room, trying not to knock over the pile of boxes balancing precariously to her left. The room was filthy and cluttered, with a foul smell of faeces dominating the air, making Clara gag. She put her hand up to her mouth and nose, so she wouldn't make a sound.

The noise above shifted direction. Her maglite following the noise. He was making his way back downstairs. There was an old wooden door hanging on two old hinges, straight in front of her. She lowered her hands, with her weapon still firmly in her grip, to lift the door. Slowly and carefully, she raised it up, pulling it towards her. The wooden structure bore down upon her with force, smashing her back against boxes, throwing her to the ground.

The perp saw her gun lying by her feet, he went to grab it. As he bent down, Clara kicked up her foot, causing an almighty blow to his jaw. He flung back whimpering like an injured animal. She clambered back on her feet, exerting all her force to thrust him into the furniture behind. The side of his forehead bounced off the wooden desk, splitting open. Falling sideways onto the ground, he was knocked out cold. Blood spilled on the floor. She had got him.

This monster would rot in jail for the rest of his life. She got to her feet, kicking him hard in his face, splitting his mouth open to match his bloody head. Months of pent-up frustration had got the better of her. Clara reached for her handcuffs and cuffed his hands behind his back, as he lay helpless amongst the animal faeces that was strewn across the floor. *He won't be waking up for a while,* she thought, wiping his blood from her boot, climbing over the clutter littering the floor, to find Emily.

***

Clara slumped her head down on her desk, 'What the actual...'
'Strong, in my office now!,' Executive Assistant Director Miller screamed, his head rushing with fury. He was in his late 50's, but his work had put years on him. He was a tall, thin, haggard looking man, with a posture that stooped at a 45-degree angle. Clara always suspected it was due to the numerous times he bent forward, to shout at his task force members, including her.
Today was one of those days. She knew how to react to all the expletives that bawled from Miller's mouth. Clara had to stay quiet and be professional. It was hard, but she knew she was treading on very thin ice. Director Miller could be fastidious to a point of no return, but shrewd and proficient all at the same time. He was a hard man to judge and get the better of, today she wasn't about to try.
She pushed her chair back with so much force, the coffee machine sitting behind her danced like a ballerina, performing the best pirouette of its life. She picked up her badge and strolled towards his office. 'Shut the door, sit down and explain yourself. What the hell were you thinking, and you can cut the bullshit?'
Clara sat down on the black plastic chair and it teetered around. *Please let this be a warning and nothing else,* she thought nervously, trying to calm herself. She refused to look Miller straight on. Instead, she stared at her shoelaces under the table. They were covered in soil from the yard she shouldn't have proceeded to go into, without calling for back up. That's why she was sitting in Millers office, which was filled with an assortment of filing boxes and stacks of paper-filled trays in every space possible. They all contained information on cases past and present. Her name was

probably documented in the majority of them. But here she was, waiting for the dressing down of her career. She wasn't disappointed. He knew exactly what had happened and didn't give her the chance to explain.

'You didn't just put yourself in danger, but also the hostage the bloody creep had inside his house. He could have ended her there and then. Do you ever stop and just think about the consequences behind your actions? What if you had got yourself killed, how would I have explained that one to the Director, who by the way hates the sight of me. Don't even answer me! Just get out of my office, go home and don't show your face in this bureau until I decide what to do with you! Leave your badge and weapon on my desk. And close the bloody door behind you!'

'Damn protocols,' Clara said furiously to herself, picking up her phone from her disorganised desk. She knew it was her attitude to following procedures got her into trouble and not acting like a professional FBI agent. She was fine with that; she always got the job done, had a high record of closing cases putting perpetrators behind bars. Rules were there to sometimes break, especially if she had no other option to outwit the perp. It was another cross beside her name. Surely, she had run out of luck.

Clara walked through the parking lot of the bureau in a raging mood. She could feel her indignation rising. Every word that was launched at her in that office, blocked her train of thought. She was ready for a stiff drink.

It was getting dark and cold, so she jumped in her vehicle, slammed the door, which was already temperamental and turned the key. 'Shit, start you piece of crap!' The old 3 litre V-6 Ford Taurus was sold to her by a guy one of her colleagues recommended. He had bought copious amounts of cars from him over a short period of time. That should have been a red flag to her. Flushed with cash she wasn't. She turned the key again. It wasn't going anywhere. She thumped the steering wheel, *could this day get any worse?* She debated, trying one more time. Nothing happened, apart from the drops of rain that started to slide slowly down the windscreen. Clara was at a point of blowing her own gasket, she took out her phone and ordered an Uber.

***

'Can you just drop me off here?' Clara asked the driver. He pulled his plush new car over to the side of the road. She was glad to get out as it smelled of some expensive cologne that was overpowering. The fresh air was needed after today's events.

Downtown Main Street was charming with all its unique boutique shops, restaurants, which served the most delicious recipes for miles around. It had dozens of one-of-a-kind gift shops, which sold eye catching items, for a price that was a bit too expensive for Clara's liking. The shop windows all lit up with lights as The Fall was in mid swing. The few trees along the sidewalk were turning with the season and passers-by drank their pumpkin spice lattes. Christmas decorations already starting to take over, as though there was no time to spare. Durant City in County Bryan, Oklahoma, United States serves as the Capital of the Choctaw Nation, and to Clara it was home. She didn't hang around to take in the scenery; instead, she chose her drinking house and swiftly walked inside. It wasn't the first time she had frequented here; she had lost count of how many times Frank the bar tender and owner had filled her empty whiskey glass up for free. Getting out of the relentless rain she walked straight to the bar.

Inside was decorated in old wooden panelling from floor to ceiling, with dark green worn-out leather chairs, filling the seating booths in all directions. The atmosphere was relaxing, with dimmed mood lighting around the bar area, which Frank said made folks stay and buy more booze. You could hear a few games of billiards being played towards the back; the nine-ball being placed carefully in the middle of the racks. To her relief, her favourite stool at the bar was unoccupied. She removed her sodden black mac and slid her petite bum on the seat. She waved her hand to get served, her best friend behind the bar came over, 'Frank I need a drink,' she said in an exhausting tone.

Clara began to relive her day to Frank, how her life just keeps going from bad to worse. She desperately needed some luck in her life. Frank was an amazing listener; it came with the job. He stood behind the bar listening attentively, wiping a glass with a cloth that was beyond clean. 'Another one Frank,' she requested.

'You've just had a bad day; you always bounce back.' He hung the semi-clean glasses onto the racks above her head at the bar and carried on serving customers. The bar was busy, partly due to the pouring rain, plus Frank's bar was easily the best in the street. People were coming and going for the rest of the night, yet Frank always kept his eyes on Clara. He cared about her, deeply.

A few drinks for Clara were never enough. Frank knew this and was concerned as the evening started to come to a close. She was getting the wrong sort of attention from two men occupying seats to the right of her, they had been buying her whiskey most of the night. She hadn't bothered to look to see who they were, she was just grateful that the drink kept flowing. 'Clara that's the lot for you tonight,' Frank announced.

'Just one more whiskey Frank, just one for me and my pals,' she retorted, resting her head on the bar as though all of her strength had subsided.

'Nope and it's not because I'm a bad guy, so don't get defensive. You've had your lot, you need to get yourself home,' he said in a gentle, caring manner.

Frank and Clara had been friends for just over 4 years. Their relationship was purely platonic. She never thought Frank was the marrying type, and she could tell he was dismissive towards relationships as a whole. They were a perfect match. He was a handsome guy, with eyes a deep ocean blue and dark hair slicked back in a man bun. She didn't understand why she didn't think of him in that way. To be honest she didn't understand relationships at all. Maybe it was because every time she was in his company the booze got the better of her. The lack of sleep, mainly from overthinking, made her groggy, cranky and damned right impossible and fogged that part of her emotions. She carried too much underlying baggage. Her difficulties she experienced as a child, continued to take up space in her adult mind and her present relationships were non-existent. Life for Clara was hitting rock bottom.

Outside in the rain, Clara struggled to button up her mac. Her blurry vision from the complementary Jack Daniel's was taking over, she was getting frustrated. She only lived a few blocks from the bar, on South Ninth Avenue and West Texas Street. The journey home could be executed with her eyes shut, which most nights she did. Her drinking habits were something she kept to herself. Clara wasn't exactly the favourite at the bureau, she could imagine Miller's face if he ever found out. Her strides were unsteady, with the raised sidewalk meeting her feet at various intervals.

The first noise behind her was muffled, she dismissed it quickly. The next time she heard it, a combined voice made her pay more attention. *It's just my screwed-up imagination, ignore it,* she thought. She tried to quicken her pace nevertheless, but her feet weren't playing. Her apartment was only a block away now and she would soon be in her bed, sleeping so deep that she didn't even care if the next morning came or not.

The two guys at the bar decided to follow Clara home. Their generosity with the flowing alcohol had been for an underlying reason. She was an easy target; drunk, alone and very pretty on the eye. The younger one ran up alongside her, coming from behind and started talking to her, making sexual suggestions and stepping in her way to distract her. The older, unshaven guy blocked her in by walking to the right of her. 'You wanna see an ol' guy smile, pretty?' his breath smelled like the bottom of a whiskey barrel.

'Get the hell out of my face!' She tried to screech.

'Come on pretty lady, I'll be good,' the old man retorted, with a smile on his face that would have sent chills down anyone's spine.

Clara stumbled, losing her footing, going over on her left ankle. That was the perfect time for the two perpetrators to lunge forward, grab her and take advantage of her drunken state. The alleyway was dark, the rain persistent, soaking her body right through to the bone. There was no one around to help, to come to her aid. The alcohol obstructed Clara's cognitive thinking, she couldn't kick start her brain. *What's happening? What the fuck are you doing?* She felt sick, her body being pulled in all directions, hands were touching her in places she knew were private. All the FBI training she had endured for 20 weeks at Quantico Headquarters was lost in this moment. Defensive combat was where she excelled. She was top of her class, she knew how to assess, evaluate and defend, so why could she not find the strength now? Her voice would not come, it waited for orders so it could spring into action and help, to play a major part. There were no words spoken.

Clara sensed a partially blinding light shining in her face. She tried to put her hand up to protect her eyes, but the forces around her stopped this from happening. Her eyes burned; she could feel herself falling. She had no control over her own flesh. Her body fell to the wet ground, she blacked out, lying still and unresponsive. Rain poured hard against her collapsed body as she started to hear distant sounds of her name being called, 'Clara! Clara speak to me!'

***

The morning's sun shone into her bedroom apartment. She was disoriented, her eyes flickered open, slowly and cautiously. Her head felt like she had been pummelled with a baseball bat, her stomach was convulsing in pain. A hand lent across her body holding a glass of water. 'Here, sit up and drink this.' She slowly turned her head and saw a figure close to where she was lying. She couldn't focus properly at first, so she tried to slide herself up the bed and get her bearings. Clara was home, she was in her bed, in her apartment, but how? Her eyes procrastinated, she looked to see who was sitting beside her, in her bedroom.
'Frank!' She said with so much effort it made her cough.
'Lie still Clara, you've been through a bad ordeal, try to rest. I'm not going anywhere, sleep as much as you can. You need to regain all of your strength. We can talk when you wake and feeling better.'
'But Frank, what happened to me, why are you here?' Clara's words started to weaken, she soon drifted back off to sleep. The afternoon was a long haul for both Frank and Clara. He sat by her bedside the whole time, nursing her episodes of sickness that came and went, every hour and on the hour. Time eventually transitioned into evening, when Clara started to stir in her bed. She slowly opened her eyes, head still pounding, feeling like it was on fire. Sitting up and stretching for the glass of water on her bedside table, she took a small delicate sip. It was ice-cold, sending a sharp pain up into her head.

'Evening,' he said, as he strolled over to her from the kitchen area. 'Feeling better?'

'Yeah, thanks. What the hell happened to me?' She asked fearfully.

'The two guys buying you drink last night decided it would be a good idea to walk you back to your apartment. They... they attacked you, Clara. I knew I hadn't seen the two of them at the bar before and when you left, they both intentionally got up and walked out. I said to Harry I needed to see where they were going and for him to lock up. I got in my car, followed behind them. And there you were, falling all over the place; they saw you were an easy target.' his voice was shaky, angry, but emotional.

Clara didn't know what to say in response. She was overcome with a sense of shame and embarrassment at the thought of being intoxicated. She knew alcohol wasn't the answer to her problems. It made her feel low, and her behaviour became erratic. She turned her head away from Frank, she felt guilt rising inside. This was not the first time Frank had been sitting by her side, nursing her from the destruction alcohol caused.

He was her best friend; she had let him down again.

There was an absence of noise for a while. Neither of them wanting to say anything else. They both knew the situation she had put herself in was dangerous and stupid. The room was still, a presence of unease engulfed the apartment. Clara lay still on her bed with the tenderness of Franks touch upon her hand. He gave it a squeeze to let her know he was always there for her, no matter what. Clara's cell phone suddenly rang, shattering the silence and startled their thoughts. Frank picked it up, passing it to her.

It was her boss Miller. 'Strong, I need you back at the bureau, now!'

Chapter Two

The Bar was on the corner of E.Smith Street and South Mulberry Avenue in the town of Butler, County Choctaw, Alabama. It was named in honour of Colonel Pierce Butler, a soldier who was killed in the Mexican American war. It was here Evan Thomas would make his last walk home and his last strides on this earth. He would inhale the cool air into his lungs and expel it for the final time. He didn't know that yet. That was part of the fun, the excitement, the thrill of the chase.

He watched his prey stagger around the corner of the bar. *The same route, the same time, the same lack of decency, this is going to be easy,* he thought. Evan was the number 4 on the dice. That was an important number to the predator. It indicated energy, knowledge, cleverness and confidence with an individual who had good leadership skills. That was him, he had thrown the 4 and it reflected on who he was, not Evan Thomas. Landing on 4 meant he was good at keeping secrets, love creativity and have a sharp memory. The last thought was so true. He was a bona fide expert when it came to remembering. That's why he was here, watching, waiting and to be triumphant with his first kill.

He stepped out of his vehicle, not bothering to lock it. His hands were cold from the night air. He wouldn't allow himself to wear woollen gloves, they would leave traces of fibres, he knew how forensics pinpointed the smallest piece of evidence from a crime scene. That was rule number 1 when he penned his game. His pace was in step with his precious prize, he could feel his own heart rate changing when his prey either staggered, fumbled around or sped up. *The palpitations i'm experiencing could be my own anxieties,* he thought, but that would be a sign of weakness and he wasn't a weak person, he was the strongest he had ever felt in his entire life. He wasn't about to give into weakness at such an early stage of his game. That thought had to be eradicated from his mind, it had to be thrown into the fire of eternal damnation.

The sidewalk wound in front of the town's church, with its cemetery lights flooding the grounds like a perfect display of ornaments. The old church itself, stood in partial darkness, looking lonely and desperate, as though it was waiting for its congregation to keep it company. Evan slowed his pace down and hesitated for a split second. It was as though he was slowing down in respect to those beside him, lying below the ground. The killer thought this ironic as he knew Evan Thomas would soon be joining them. A disturbing grin covered his face.

Evan stumbled forwards a few paces and started to whistle. He continued walking past two houses set back from the sidewalk. Their yards full of halloween decorations, which glowed in the moon light. Ghost and ghouls floated in the porch ways of the two adjoining houses. Desperation to beat one another with the innovated ideas they had for The Fall. Pumpkins glowed and flickered as the candles inside were coming to their end. Orange, brown and red leaves scattered the yards, covering some of the lower ornaments like a coloured textured quilt.

'Shush, be quiet, folk will hear you,' the perp mumbled in a deep frustrating tone.

He didn't want anyone else to play and interfere with his strategy. Evan was his and his alone. He had waited far too long for this moment, too long for someone else to just show up and impede his game.

To his surprise the whistling stopped. He protruded a wide grin, his body filling up again with that same self-adulation feeling he had when he moved the pawn to knock the king. The pavement veered off to the right, leading up to a dead end and a woodland. Trees engulfed the path on both sides, the streetlights were becoming a distant memory. The moon light was almost too perfect. It reminded him of lights in a show, shining down on the stage, ready for the crucial act to take part and for the audience to scream. Scream loudly in absolute horror at the scene they were about to observe and for them to turn their heads away from the performers, as it was becoming too gruesome to watch. He had no doubt he would sit and watch, his soulless eyes firmly on the stage. He was used to death and blood. It gave him a sense of belonging.

He knew this was the route Evan would take. He religiously took the same way home after his drinking bouts with his buddies at the bar. The visual thoughts were making his blood stir with envy, his stomach heaved with the memories of never being part of that unit, that closeness of a family's bond or the love of…He stopped himself. How could he even think about anything like this at such a pinnacle moment in his life. He put his hands over both ears, shaking his head vigorously. 'Stop, leave me be!'

He had a plan, things to do. It wasn't hard to work it out, especially if you had the patience of a killer. Planning was everything, right down to the very last detail. *He wasn't anything special,'* thought the perpetrator. He knew he had to die, he deserved it. Whenever he tried to get close to Evan, he was constantly ignored and rejected. The feelings of rage and towering anger overwhelmed his body. He quickly diffused everything racing around in his head, except for the kill.

The dead end continued into dense woodland. There was a path Evan had cleared with his numerous short cuts to his home, which sat on its own at the other side of the forest. His stately looking house towered above the trees and sat in grounds that were highly manicured. The perp had seen his house on many occasions. It had two imposing statues, he remembered, either side of the front door, which looked to be horses rearing up on their hind legs. *How pretentious,* he mused. Tonight though, Evan wouldn't make it that far. He wouldn't be kissing his wife with his stale breath, tucking his twin girls into bed or falling over the dog that slept near the front entrance, lying there every night to greet his master home.

Darkness was masterful. The American elm trees stood tall, with their arching branches creating shade during the day from the sunlight. Their bark was grey and deeply burrowed, the elliptical green leaves of the trees were turning into yellowish-brown, they were dominating the moonlight in the skies. The noise of a large bat was heard as it flew across the cold crisp air, finding its way amongst the trees to hunt for its midnight meal. The woodland was quiet, except the sound of crunching leaves, which was made by the footsteps of Evan Thomas, with every leaf falling precariously onto the ground. *He is going exactly where I want him too, he is so predictable, and he has to die because he is a cruel man. He cares for no one, and I will have eternal life when he is sacrificed and given to God. God will punish him accordingly and he will look down on me and reward me for my generosity,'* he informed himself, with so much faith welling up inside him, he thought he might burst. The time was upon him, the act of sacrificing was now.

A loud, disturbing scream was heard in the distance, it was a torturous hunt, but it worked. The perp ran towards his prey, shining a small light onto the distressed victim, created by his traps. 'Stupid idiot!' He guffawed.

'Help me, I'm bleeding, my feet are trapped, call for help!' He was shouting out in excruciating pain. 'Get them off me. I can't feel my legs, help me.' He swayed from side to side, drunk and trapped.

'I can't see you; I can't help you now if I can't see you. I can hear someone in pain and begging for help, but I can't see them. You don't see people either, do you Evan?' He said, smiling contentedly and repeating his words over and over again.

Evan was losing blood fast. The jagged metal spikes of the hunting traps had clenched just above both ankles and were gripping onto him with so much intensity. He tried pulling them with his hands in desperation, as he sat on the damp ground, amongst the pile of leaves encircling him. He was drunk, trapped and bleeding to death.

The panic was apparent, this excited the perp. He stood in silence watching for a while, inhaling the air of his triumph, which he had created that day. He had been careful and meticulous of course. No one noticed his presence. He blended in perfectly, positioning his trappings within an inch of where Evan's previous footsteps had walked. The leaves were his friends, they helped him play the game and disguised all of his carefully picked components.

'Now if you play nice and call me by my first name, I will help you,' he grinned, shining the small light up to his own face again.

'You! Why are you doing this? Get me out of these, help me!' Said Evan, struggling to put a coherent sentence together.

'Help me…. who?' He stood waiting and listening to the agonising groans coming from the ground. 'I'm waiting Evan… no? You don't know who I am? That is so unfortunate, because if you had a conscience, noticing I existed, then you would know, but due to your lack of respect for people, it seems to have got you in a mess, how sad.'

'I do know you; I've seen you before, help me please!!' he wailed in agony, rolling onto his side with both traps still fully gripping the bone. 'Please Tom,' he was desperate for a name, the right one never came. The sound of his voice slowly diminished into the leaves, he jerked his body with small movements, desperately trying with his last bit of strength to be free from these contraptions. He wasn't going anywhere.

Evan's body lay still in the night. He sat watching, admiring his work. *Could I have placed the traps any better?* He thought, smiling as he already knew the answer. The corpse lay before him in a pile of leaves. It's as though Evan was sleeping and his soul now had been given to God to discard with, in his own powerful way.

The blood-soaked pants unhurriedly oozed thick red liquid to the ground. The executioner gazed at his victim's face. Evan's dark brown eyes were empty, but not to him. They were looking at him for the first time. *Now you see me, I'm right here.*

The weight of Evan was stretching the killer's physical abilities, but this was in his planning, he knew how to raise him up to a standing position, below the Elm branches on his own for the whole world to see. The chains were hanging just above, firmly screwed into the thick branches. They weren't visible to anyone, but then this piece of woodland was never used for recreational enjoyment. Nobody frequented here, except Evan. This was why it was the perfect place to kill.

Slipping on his latex gloves, he walked calmly to the bottom of the tree trunk and reached for a rope fastened around the side and over the branches above. He pulled on it hard, causing the chains to tumble down, just missing the floor and they swung frantically like a child's swing. He lifted the corpse, wrapped the link chain around the body and neck, pulled back on the rope, which was still curled on the branches. He had made a hoist, it worked perfectly. Evan's lifeless body swayed in the dark. The small light angled up to his face. He couldn't have brought a flashlight, that was too bright to do his evil doings, and may have disturbed the animals and birds. He had to be silent and stay low key.

His brown eyes were still open and soulless, staring with an expression, which the killer thought was unpleasant. He moved his hand slowly around Evan's dead face, stroking it tenderly, placing his fingers near his eyes. The other hand slid into his pocket, reaching for his knife. He knew how to perform this part of the game. He had practiced on his family's livestock when he was a child, out in their back yard. They were normally still alive though. This part he knew he couldn't make any mistakes, he had to keep his gloves on. There was no room for him to be caught at his first kill. Others had to be taken out with his skills.

The rush of his own blood, driven by adrenaline, pressed into every vein in his body. He felt alive and strong. His world was starting to feel accomplished; this was the crowning of his new life. He reached into his other pocket with his bloody hand, pulled out his leather pouch, which contained his handcrafted dice and counters. He dropped the dice onto the wet leaves. He was thrilled with the outcome. It landed on 1. *She was nothing but a whore and deserves to be punished,* he thought scrupulously. He picked up his dice and placed it back into his pouch. He slid the counter out; number 4 carved deeply into the centre. It was perfectly made from wood, a circular shape with its deep red number, catching the eye of the holder. He carefully slipped it into Evan Thomas's pocket with a note wrapped around it to tell the authorities, "His game had just begun." He brushed the fallen leaves and sticks away beneath his feet, creating an arrow shape and hummed as he walked back out into the open air.

Chapter Three

Frank offered to give Clara a ride to the bureau as her vehicle was still sitting in the parking lot, with an air of melancholy surrounding it. To be honest Clara did like the old wreck. She had spilled her feelings to it on one or more occasions, especially when she was having one of her bad days. It knew all her secrets, that's the way she wanted to keep it. Her thoughts were concealed within the tin on wheels, which was abandoned by her through her own ill temper. She knew she had to get a grip on controlling her emotions and to be abstinent from alcohol, permanently.

What did Miller want with me? I'm going to get fired. Fuck, I've screwed up my career, my life. Get a grip Clara, she snapped out of her thoughts as Frank pulled up outside the main door. 'I'm really sorry Frank, I've been a godawful friend, I don't deserve you, I'm a screw up and my life is a shambles.'

'Clara, listen to me, look at me. You obviously have underlying problems you won't share with me, maybe you can't, but you have to get help and support from someone. Drinking isn't the answer, you're too young for that shit. You're top of your game, your bosses know that, so whatever they are gonna say to you in there, keep your cool and we can work through it. I'll wait here for you.'

Gratifying feelings overwhelmed Clara; she gave him a look of adoration. He was the brother she wished she had. That was a burning, agonizing emotion that pounded her heart uncontrollably. She contemplated for a split second then pushed it to the back of her mind. 'I would be lost without you Frank. I don't know how to repay you?' She reached over, kissed him on his cheek, exiting his Honda.

The air outside was bitterly cold, she ran into the main entrance. Her department was on the third floor. The elevator was the best option, she was still feeling fragile and dog-tired from the previous nights' ordeal. Clara felt too depleted to face the winding stairwell that would lead her to her fate.

As she sheepishly walked towards Miller's office, she tried to tidy herself up and look positive, but most importantly, professional. Her long blonde hair was tied up in a ponytail, her blue trouser suit wasn't as crisp as she would have preferred, but it would have to do. He did call her unexpectedly after all and late at night. The part Miller didn't know was the copious amount of alcohol she had consumed 24hrs previous. Her mind started to race, she knocked on his door and walked in. Clara was startled to see Miller wasn't alone in his office. He had company, her stomach began to churn. Some of the Jack Daniels was still in her system and her body began to shake. She dug deep to find some self-restraint. *Control yourself Clara, stay calm and look alert.*

'Sit down Strong. This is Special Agent in Charge, Adam Perez from the Behavioural Analysis Unit in Quantico,' Miller said with his autocratic leadership, style voice. He allowed no room for Clara to participate in the conversation. He sat on the side of his desk, dominating her, she was sitting in that godawful plastic chair she resented. Every time her petite backside had the pleasure of its company, she got a dressing down and an ear bashing. She braced herself ready for the onslaught of her career.

'There's a problem and we, that is The BAU and I, think you would be the best candidate for the job. You'll be working under the supervision of SAIC Perez,' Miller said firmly.

'A problem? What kind of problem?' She was totally confused and had no idea this was why she was summoned here at such a late hour. Her forehead crumpled as she looked up at her boss.

'There's been a murder in Alabama this evening, and we need you to go down and see what the situation is. Special Agent Perez will be over seeing the investigation.'

'But why have the FBI been called in sir? Can't the Sheriff's office deal with it? We aren't called in just for a murder,' Clara Questioned. Complete puzzlement engulfing her face.

'It looks like it won't be the unsubs only victim. He has left this one badly cut up and Sheriff Harris needs some assistance to catch this son of a bitch. I need you down there Clara.'

'Will my partner Ferendez be joining us?' She waited with anticipation for an answer from Miller. She wasn't in contact with her FBI partner, of 3 years, since she got reprimanded in this same office 24hrs prior. Had he complained to Miller about her actions over the Emily case? She thought they worked well together and had each other's backs. Clara was feeling paranoid about situations she wasn't privy to. She knew the alcohol could send these thoughts flying out of control.

'He won't be joining you this time; we haven't got the manpower to let you both go down. You'll be working under the supervision of SAIC Perez.'

Clara looked over to Adam Perez, who sat in silence, watching Clara's every move. He had origins of Spanish or Portuguese, with brown shapely eyes. His jaw line was sharp, covered with a short cut beard and moustache. He was handsome and clean cut. His suit was well tailored, he looked like he had come from a wealthy background. She feebly smiled, cutting her gaze short, turning back to Miller. 'Why are you sending me, I thought I was suspended until further notice?'

They need someone who is familiar with the area and who knows their way around. It's in Butler town.'

Her whole body went cold, she was in a state of trepidation. She knew she couldn't go back there, not back home, not to where her problems began. She stood up, feelings of dread and panic set in. *Remember what Frank said, stay calm and be professional or something along those lines,* she thought, inducing her memory.

'I'm not asking you Special Agent Strong, it's a direct order. I suggest you go home and pack. You'll be heading down tonight with SAIC Perez. You will be sharing the drive down, so grab yourself something to eat and try sobering yourself up. I don't have to remind you Strong, you are treading on very thin ice, so listen to SAIC Perez and work together. No fuckups!'

With that, Miller showed the two agents to the door. Did she reek of booze? How did he formulate she had been drinking? Her cheeks blushed with embarrassment and overwhelming shame.

***

The eight-hour journey was laborious. Two strangers who had just met, travelling in one vehicle. She asked Perez how he had arrived at Durant Bureau, so quickly after they got the call in from Sheriff Harris. His dad lives on West University Boulevard and North Tenth Avenue in Durant, he was visiting him, as he did regularly, to make sure he was doing alright, due to being on his own. The call came in just as they were about to have a takeout to celebrate his 74th birthday. His dad understood, he always understood.

She navigated the SUV through some sparse areas, whilst her work companion fell asleep beside her. He still had his suit pants on, buttoned up-shirt and a tie, which Clara grinned at. *He was probably more of a pen pusher and uses textbooks for references, rather than using his own intuition to solve murders,* her annoyed head thought. Travelling along the West Pushmataha Street, she saw signs for Butler. Apprehension rose within her as she drove the last part of their journey.

She remembered where the Sheriff's office was situated, Mulberry Avenue, East Alabama. It wasn't an overpopulated place and the main roads crossed dead centre of the town. That's where the Choctaw County Courthouse stood, with the Sheriff's department affiliated to the grand structure. The building was built around the late 1800's with its tall imposing columns at the front, to create a balcony for the once wealthy members of the town. Within the Courthouse grounds stood the Confederate Monument in honour of all Confederate soldiers who fought between 1861 and 1865. It was to achieve a separate and independent country based on what they called, 'Southern Institutions', the chief of which was the institution of slavery. The Union from the North won the American Civil War against the Confederates. It was an important milestone in the long process of ending legal slavery in the United States. It stood proud despite the outcome, and it honoured those that lost their lives, thanks to politics.

The Courthouse grounds were surrounded by trees, with their leaves turning a rich burnt orange. The parking lot wrapped itself around the perimeter of the building, which Clara noticed had ample spaces, she drove into the first one she came to. The SUV's engine switched off; Perez jumped up. 'We're here,' she said in a tiresome tone.

They headed towards the main doors, ascended up steps and through three decorative bricked archways. They had reached their destination. Tired, hungry and working on fumes, they proceeded inside and found the entrance foyer covered in large protective sheets and paint cans, which were sprawled precariously around the floor. The two FBI Agent's glanced around, trying to work out which direction to head. There were signs on the walls, but were covered in plastic wrap so densely, nothing was legible.

'Are you folks, okay?' A man's voice echoed from the other side of the large foyer.

'Yeah, we're looking for Sheriff Harris's office,' Perez shouted back. The man was dressed in overalls and in the midst of painting the handrails, that curved decoratively up and around to the level above. He was in his 30's at least, with a pensive look upon his face.

'Just head straight through those double doors, turn right at the end of the corridor and y'all find y'selves heading in the right direction. The Sheriff's office is to the back of the building.'

'Thanks,' Clara responded.

They adhered to the painter's words, following the corridor until they came to Sheriff Harris's department. They were greeted by a young lady officer who had been given desk duties. 'Can I help you?' She asked nervously, as though she was undergoing a verbal examination.

'I'm Special Agent in Charge, Adam Perez, this is my partner Special Agent Strong. We're from the FBI and are here to see Sheriff Harris.' The girl looked to be out of her depth with this statement, then looked down at her desk, trying to find an answer.

'It's okay Hannah, I'll take it from here,' a gruff, burley voice said from behind them. 'I'm Sheriff Harris, please to finally meet you. I appreciate the quickness of your arrival. I know you must be extremely exhausted; can we get you some coffee, water, some kind of refreshments? He gestured for them to follow him into his office.

'We're fine Sheriff, but thank you,' Adam Perez said quickly in response. Clara wasn't about to say no to a coffee fix. She needed one, fast.

'I'll take a black coffee if there's one going Sheriff, I want to get straight into this case and I don't want to stop later and waste time,' Clara knew this answer would sound professionally justified. She glanced over to Perez; he gave her an annoying look.

Harris shouted out to Hannah, ordering two black coffees and a handful of pastries to go. 'If you are okay, I'll drive you over to the crime scene. The victim, a white male, name of Evan Thomas, he was 39 years of age, married, father to twin girls and owned a bar in town. A pair of young'uns found him. They are still over at the hospital being looked over for signs of shock. It's not a pretty sight. We've never encountered anything on this scale before. And there's more, he, they, whoever is responsible, intends to carry on. That's why we need your expertise to catch this monster as quick as we can, before we have to visit another poor goddam family.'

They went back out through the front entrance foyer, coffee and breakfast in hand. The room reeked of different types of paint; Clara was starting to get one of her headaches. She always did after copious amounts of Jack Daniels.

Chapter Four

Sheriff Harris drove the very short distance along West Pushmataha onto South Academy Avenue, reaching E. Smith Street within minutes and turning right, up the dead-end lane situated on the edge of the woodland. Strong and Perez jumped out, following Harris through the yellow police tape and along the path Evan had made over the years.

'I know you've probably seen your fair share of corpses, but this one, well you'll see for yourselves,' Harris said solemnly.

'Hasn't the body already been taken to the coroners?' Perez asked.

'No, it's becoming a complex job to get him down from the hanging contraption he's tide up to, without compromising evidence. It's a godawful sight, even our coroner was lost for words,' Harris replied, shaking his head in complete disbelief at the whole situation.

Clara felt a sickness rise up from her stomach into her throat. She hadn't eaten enough in the last 24 hrs, feeling slightly weak at the knees, even after Hannah's pastries back at the Sheriff's department. Tiredness wasn't helping matters either, she kept giving herself a shake to come back to life. Perez, however, was alert and efficient. She was relieved he was here, taking the lead until she got her act together. Clara knew her job was bordering on the line and needed to prove to her boss Miller at Durant headquarters, she was competent.

The dense forest opened out slightly revealing where the victim Evan Thomas hung. His body swayed like a puppet on strings, his ankles still in the traps that had been set for him. Clara looked up, gasping at the disturbing appearance of his face. His eye sockets were dark empty pockets, blood rimming the edges, the realisation the eyeballs had been violently removed made

Clara feel lightheaded. The scene was so horrendous she turned and ran to a nearby tree, throwing up her only bit of food she had digested that morning.

Perez walked over to her with a look of confusion. 'Are you ok Agent Strong?'

'I'm fine, I just.... I just felt lightheaded from the night's drive and lack of food. I'll be fine,' Clara retorted. She straightened herself up and used a tissue to wipe the residue from her mouth. Her head was still spinning, but that was a problem she wasn't about to share.

Her eyes were focused once again on Evan Thomas in chains. In the short time she had been a special agent, this exceeded all other crime scenes. The trauma this victim endured before his death must have been merciless beyond comprehension. *Who would perform such an act on another human being, and leave him in full sight of any passer-by?* Thought Clara.

'When did the young couple find him?' Perez asked Sheriff Harris.

'They said they left their friends party around 1am, decided not to go straight home, if y'all know what I mean! They wanted to find a private place to get acquainted and chose here, due to its proximity from the main street. Neither of them can drive, so they found a close walking distance to nest. Too bloody young, to be at that and then...' He paused to catch his breath, 'and then the two poor buggers find this. That will haunt them for the rest of their lives,' Sheriff Harris shuddered at the thought of the scene that took place in the early hours of the morning.

'We'll have to get their names, speak to them both, individually. We can do that straight after we've processed here,' said Clara, looking at Special Agent in Charge Perez. She was waiting for a retort, but it never came.

The coroner in charge of processing the scene was older. He was in his 50's, of medium height and quite bulbous around his midriff. The forensic suit fitted him snuggly; he wasn't the quickest with his movements. Clara kept her distance with the rest of them, observing the horrific scene displayed in front of her. She wasn't about to trample all over the ground.

Her eyes caught sight of something to the side of the victim's feet. The form of an arrow shape in amongst the leaves. She got her cell phone out and put up her compass. 'If that's north then the arrow is pointing northwest,' she mumbled to herself. She reached for her pad, jotting the findings down. 'Sheriff Harris, what do you make of all this?'

'I can't say I've ever seen likes of it. Who in God's name would carry out such a heinous act? The traps, his eyes, the marking on the ground, the note saying he has only just begun, and the coroner found a small wooden counter in the victim's pocket, with a red painted number 4 on it, what does that even mean?' He said scanning the area of the scene.

'Could the counter be the victim's own property? Did he gamble in town?' Special Agent Perez asked.

'Not that I'm aware of. I didn't know him. I should have, it's a small enough town. My deputy has gone over to the family with one of my women police officers to break the news. His wife will have to eventually formerly I.D him, but Jesus Christ, how the hell can you ask a widow to identify her husband in that state,' Sheriff Harris rubbed his head and walked away. He dealt with crime and deaths before, but this one had him flummoxed.

'There's nothing we can really do here at present,' Agent Perez perked up, 'We can go and talk to the couple who found him. We'll get the details from Sheriff Harris and head over now.'

The Sheriff informed them they were still over at the hospital in Butler. He called over to the coroner to let him know they were going. Two other police officers stayed at the scene, they looked reluctant, but knew it was their job. No one would ever be able to forget this day. The FBI agents and Sheriff Harris jumped back into his vehicle, driving them back to the police headquarters, where they could pick up their own vehicle. Clara remembered where the hospital was situated. It wasn't a huge building, nevertheless it was big enough to serve the purpose it was built for.

S.A.I.C Perez offered to drive. The SUV was signed to the two of them, which meant they were both mobile. Clara jumped into the passenger seat and her stomach churned with anxiety. Butler hospital was where she was born, 28 years ago. Thoughts of her home life flooded her mind, she tried to supress them, she was too tired to fight her demons, too weak from not eating and still slightly hungover from her previous drinking session. She thought about Frank, her best buddy back home. *I must phone him later to say thanks, tell him I'm grateful he is in my life. Without him I have no one.* Her thoughts drifted, SAIC Perez looked at her for directions.

A green picket fence lined the path on both sides, which lead up to the main doors. The summer flowers that grew on the grounds of the hospital, were slowly dying off to let the next season foliage bloom. It had the air of a large residential home rather than a hospital. The foyer of the building was freshly painted in a brilliant white, providing a feeling of cleanliness. The two FBI agents went straight to the reception desk, introducing themselves. The lady sitting at the hub of all the action, kindly pointed the agents in the right direction.

'If you interview the young girl separately, I'll take the guy. His name is..' SAIC Perez looked down at his notes, 'Adam Hayes and she is Isabella Chen.'

They entered the hall adjacent to the room the two were occupying. Agent Perez knocked attentively on the door, walking straight in without consent. Isabella and young Adam lay in their beds, which were situated side by side. They were quiet and subdued, but slowly sat up at the arrival of the unknown guests. 'May we come in, we are from the FBI, I'm Special Agent in Charge Adam Perez and this is Special Agent Clara Strong?'

'The FBI?' Adam Hayes mumbled with confusion and obvious tiredness.

'We understand you both unfortunately found the victim in the forest, in the early hours of this morning,' SAIC Perez stated.

They both nodded their heads, grief expressions on their young faces. 'Are we in trouble?' Hayes asked, looking as though he had been the guilty person to commit the heinous crime.

'No. We just need to ask you a few questions while its fresh in your minds. I know that sounds callous, I don't mean to be insensitive to the horrific scene you both incurred, but we do need to gather up as much information, at such an early stage. The more we know, the more we have to work with,' Perez explained in a calm, professional manner. The two young lovers nodded their heads, glancing at each other. 'Would it be okay if I took you outside Adam, had a private chat? It's only a chat at this stage, but we will need you to talk to the local police and give them your statements.'

'We've already told the police everything we know. They were here earlier and took our statements. It was deputy Sheriff Jeremiah Dubois and a policewoman; I can't remember her name,' he replied.

Clara's head spun round to look at Adam Hayes. *Did he just say Jeremiah Dubois? It can't be, not after all these years.'* Memories once again filling her head, instead of concentrating on her job.

'That's fine, they may want to question you again, after such a shock. Memories can be forgotten and blocked. It's not until later your brain can properly process things,' Perez said softly, as though he was befriending them so they wouldn't close up and say nothing.

Adam Hayes slid round on his bed, slipped his shoes on to follow Agent Perez outside, leaving Clara with Isabella. She had noticed the young girl wasn't saying anything and had remained quiet since their appearance. *She is going to be a hard witness to open up,* Clara thought to herself. 'Isabella, I'm Agent Clara Strong, I can't begin to imagine how you must be feeling right now. Have the dr's checked you over?'

Isabella moved her head, just enough for Clara to get an answer. 'Hopefully they will be sending you home soon. Are your parents picking you up?'

Again, the slight movement of Isabella's head informed Clara of the answer. Clara guessed her parents were very good living and this whole situation wasn't a daily occurrence. Talking to the police for Isabella, looked like a completely new concept. 'Did you notice anyone else before you entered the forest, Isabella? Was there anyone acting suspicious or hanging around on E.Smith Street or along the dead-end road?'

'I....I didn't notice anyone; Adam and I were talking about the party, we were..' Isabella's sentence stopped short of finishing.

'Isabella, it's important you try and tell me everything that happened, I'm not here to judge you for your night's events, I'm only here to give the family of the victim some sort of justice. Do you think you can help me with that?' Clara asked in a gentle tone. She could feel her energy levels dropping even lower and didn't want to sound harsh and angry at her witness's lack of information.

'We were kissing and being.... you know, so we really didn't pay any notice of anything. We went into the forest because Adam thought it would be fun, he switched his cell light on and.......and...then.' Isabella's body started to shake, her eyes teared up and the droplets started to flow down both of her pale white cheeks. She wasn't in a stable position where she could respond to the questions that were being raised. Clara made a decision there and then to stop.

'Okay Isabella, thank you for your time. There will be support put into place to get you through the trauma you have endured, for Adam too. Here's my card, if you need to talk about anything or you remember something, even if you think it's insignificant, please don't hesitate to reach me. I will let you rest and hopefully you will get home soon. I know it's no consolation now Isabella, but you will find inner strength to drive through this and overcome, Christ, even thrash these memories. Life will go back to normal; I promise you,' she knew her speech wasn't totally true. When things looked black, Clara always tried to imagine a silver lining. She thought Isabella needed a few of those right now. Jack Daniel's was Clara's silver lining, she knew it wasn't the answer to her problems.

Clara gave the poor girl a sympathetic smile, exited the room and made her way back to the main foyer of the hospital. She knew the worst thing she could do at this point was to push for too much information. Isabella's brain was probably overloading with thoughts of what she saw. Total consternation and loneliness of not being able to express and put into words what she was processing, along with a multitude of other feelings. *Why did they have to fool around in that particular forest? That decision will haunt them for the rest of their existence! Damn life and it's abominable cruelty. It's impossible to suppress violence and death. The human race doesn't deserve to be on this planet. Maybe we should just let each other kill one another off until the last man is standing,* Clara's thoughts were deeply personal, she wanted to scream out loud.

Agent Perez was making his way back through the main doors with his witness. He shook the young guy's hand, patting him on his back. Clara noticed he had a calming persona, wondering if this was an act to get on the good side of people or if he really was a well-mannered agent.

'Any leads?' Agent Perez asked.

'No, she's still in shock. We won't be able to get her to remember anything right now. I've given her my card, so it's totally a waiting game. You?'

Agent Perez also had no luck. His witness provided the exact same story. So far, they had nothing. They decided to contact Sheriff Harris to see if the coroner had finished processing the scene, managed to procure the body of Evan Thomas and take him to the morgue for a better examination.

The coroner's office, by chance was located to the rear of the hospital. Sheriff Harris explained to the two FBI agents, the route to take by foot. This was such a small town and owning a vehicle wasn't totally necessary, however Clara knew other towns were a good distance away and public transport was a rare find. Thoughts of her home life emerged in her head, she quickly erased it from her mind, concentrating on the case at hand. She was adamant her own issues, which she was always fighting against, wouldn't be dealt with or discussed with anyone whilst she was here in Alabama.

Patrick Cameron's office had a newly made sign above the double doors that entered into his domain. He was the town's coroner, medical examiner and forensic pathologist, with years of expertise. As a medical examiner he could perform death investigations, complete autopsies, interpret toxicology and other laboratory testing results. The locals considered him as a modern streamlined approach to death investigations. They believed there weren't enough deaths in Butler and the surrounding towns to employ more than one main head person. Hence, when interviewed the combination of medical certificates was a must. At the age of 52 years old he was a highflier in his profession.

The doors opened just as the two agents were approaching. Patrick gave them a slight smile, inviting them into his dissection room. 'I saw you on the monitors,' he said dryly. 'Please don't touch anything as I'm still in the process of testing.' He handed them both a face mask, insisting they wear them every time they entered his morgue.

The smell of death was instantaneous, the decomposition process was well underway. Various gases created by microorganisms were created during the secondary stages and the smell in the room indicated this was happening as they entered. The putrid smell was filtering through their face protectors. Clara grappled against the gagging motions that were occurring in her upper body. Agent Perez was unfazed by the whole situation.

Evan Thomas lay face up on the cold metal slab. The postmortem had already begun, as he had a 'Y' incision on his upper torso. Dr Patrick Cameron's room was extremely organised, with test tubes labelled, bagged up, ready to be examined. Shiny metal instruments hung from racks on the wall, the smell of disinfectant was weak against the smell of death. The room was cold and eerily dark and had the presence of a torture chamber from an old movie. It was clinically clean however, and Clara and Adam knew not to touch.

'Would you have anything useful to help us with our investigation? Was he drugged for instance? I can't see how our victim, who was a big unit of a man walked into such a set up. Traps! Chains!' Agent Perez said with perplexity.

'The toxicology results have yet to conclude this line of questioning,' his tone was sharp, Clara gave Adam Perez a quickening glance. 'These tests may reveal the presence of one or more chemical poisons and should be carried out at the first stage, because post-mortem deterioration of the body, together with the gravitational pooling of bodily fluids, will necessarily alter the bodily environment, toxicology tests may overestimate, rather than underestimate, the quantity of the suspected chemical,' he said in a lecturing tone. The agents had a good understanding of how it all works, but didn't want to interrupt him, getting on his wrong side at their first meeting.

Patrick was interested not only in the direct cause of death, but also in trying to reconstruct the circumstances and events which led to the death of Evan Thomas. Whatever the immediate cause of death, he must also ascertain whether the death was an accident, a suicide or a homicide. This one was a foregone conclusion. He had already carried out a physical examination of any broken bones, skull depression, signs of strangulation, external examination of the clothing worn by Evan, but knew he needed to investigate in more depth.

His findings so far consisted of, the scene of death, signs of disorder, positioning of the deceased, the presence of possible evidential materials, such as the counter and note found. Determination of the direct cause of the injuries, such as the hunting traps, physical force and he was waiting on results of the toxicology samples from his assistant examiner. He wanted his report to be accurate and detailed.

'Do you have a rough time of death?' Clara chipped in.

'At this preliminary stage, the chain of evidence leads me to believe he found himself walking into the traps, which were buried, hiding beneath the layers of leaves on the ground. Bled out, I would estimate at least 40% of his blood supply, because his symptoms would worsen at this point, his pulse rate weaken, and breathing becomes shallower. Death can occur within five minutes from significant external bleeding. He had no fight in him at this point I would say, and his body lay in a fetal position on the ground, then hoisted to his feet by the perpetrator. Signs indicate his eyes were removed postmortem, which I estimate to be between 22hrs and 01.00hrs.' His words were blunt and matter of fact. 'The traps are proper hunting traps, the chains used are extremely high-end Alloy grade 80 and would be associated with industrial use. There are other items I still need to test, but that's your lot at this point.' He turned and walked out without any more words. He was done communicating for the day, giving the FBI no more information.

Chapter Five

His head was in a place of euphoria. He had just experienced so much pleasure and excitement. His game had started. The feelings were intense, he didn't really know how to deal with them or how to process them in his head. They were new to him, yet very real. A snigger sound presented itself from his mouth. He had done it, he had achieved and conquered his first opponent and it felt exhilarating. The water poured into his mug from the kettle, his hands were as steady as they always were. The night's events were very successful, he knew he had played it to perfection, not leaving his own trace behind. Knowing he was very efficient made his heart race. He smiled to himself as he stirred his coffee and reached for a snack. The act last night itself, was hungry and thirsty work, he needed refuelling. His head swivelled from the table to look outside. He noticed the air looked crisp, and it felt like a new world to him. New beginnings were commencing, they were crystallising, thanks to the years of planning he meticulously laid out, together with the help of his almighty, powerful God. He slurped his coffee and fixated on the trees outside the window. They were losing their foliage, but he knew when spring shows its beautiful self, they would produce new life. His insides chuckled sardonically, as he thought about the life he was starting to make for himself, which too, was going to be new and beautiful.

How had my first victim been so stupid and walked home by himself in the dark, in the woodland that was out of sight to most residents? He thought he was untouchable and surrounded by so many protectors. Where were they last night? Why had they not been there with him, to save his life? I tried so hard to be his friend, for him to recognise who I was, to ask me how my day was going or offer to buy me a drink. But no, he had to ignore me all my life and they allowed it to happen, his anguish started to build up inside as he thought of his childhood, his youth, his life, his Parents. He took another gulp of his drink.

Growing up with strict standards and Christian beliefs had a detrimental effect on him, he became ill-equipped to navigate a society with different rules. The abuse he endured affected his self-esteem, he had no self-worth. He was a nothing, a ghost, a mistake his parents didn't want to deal with. They thought he came from the devil himself, child of Lucifer that shouldn't be allowed to be of this world. His struggles were shameful. Schooling was traumatic, being laughed at and tormented when he was unable to spell the basic of words. Others teased and taunted him for being stupid and worthless. There was one boy younger than him, who tried to befriend him, but others bullied him too for his actions. He wanted help from his parents, but they scarcely noticed his existence, predominantly shouting out verses from the bible, as though that would eradicate him from this planet and universe.

The absence of love from his parents when he was a small boy burned his heart, his insides felt empty, which intensified as he developed into a teenager. He knew then that nobody wanted him. There was social contact for sure, but it was solely negative behaviour towards him, he became unattached to the circle of people, he so desperately wanted to belong to. He knew his actions as an adult, were encouraged by God, who spoke to him in his head and guided him into the light of eternity. He trusted his Lord in times of trial, he knew if he continued seeking his honour, with all that he had, and maintained a pure conscience before him, then he would be rewarded. God spoke to him frequently, he became his divine friend, trusting his judgement and the path that was being set before him. This grown man, sipping his coffee from a hand decorated mug, closed his eyes and thanked his Lord.

His late afternoon break was coming to an end, the daylight outside already fading, he needed to get back to his work. He became excited, uplifted by the prospect of another sacrifice, another kill, which the before mentioned, and had instructed him to do. He would carry out his great work, tower above all those who wronged him. Confidence in his game transcended and his achievements would be mighty. He knew how to pen the rules, he had taught himself over the years and was exceptionally creative in his written language. The words presented to him were recorded, every last detail using pen to paper, his favourite instrument and material. He hated the modern world of computers and high-tech gadgets. They had no purpose on this earth, with their passwords and login confusions. The idea of even owning his own cell phone, made his skin crawl. These were antisocial devices he would say to himself, people ignoring one another and creating immoral actions. They should all be destroyed and with the constant changes in technology, they amplify anxieties, *especially mine,* he thought.
Quickly he returned his thoughts to his next opponent.
She was very pretty, she knew it. Her figure was slender, too slender for his liking. He liked a wholesome woman, someone that wouldn't break so fast at his first touch. Her beautiful red hair flowed naturally, curling at the ends. Her face was flawless with a glow that could be seen for miles. Her emerald, green eyes twinkled regardless of the lighting. She was beautiful, she had an ethereal beauty, which always gave her a spiritual presence. He was captivated by her, but he knew she sadly had to die. His whole life she had left him to defend for himself, pretending he didn't exist. There was a short time where she was his confidant, his safe place and someone who tolerated his existence. *Then the whore got pregnant and left me to battle my own skirmishes, abandoning me like the others, as though I was trash. Her and her new fucking baby. Well*

to hell with her now. Eleanor Parker you are going to pay for your sins, and I will be rewarded once again. This world doesn't need whores like you, sleeping and having relations with your own Pa, words in his head made his chest expand and he felt mighty.

He had started with number 4, Evan Thomas. This powerful number signified what was solid, what could be touched and felt. He knew it had a relationship to the four points of the Cross, making it an outstanding symbol of wholeness and universality. He knew if you believed in angelic messages, seeing the biblical number 4 could be a message from God to determine what's missing from your life in order to make it feel more complete, or to finally complete something you've been meaning to, in order to take the next step on your spiritual path.

The beginning of his game felt powerful, it gave him strength he knew was purified by his saviour. Eleanor was number 1 on his dice, He had rolled it at Evan Thomas's feet when he was dangling and oozing blood. *He could have ruined my professional craftsmanship, dripping his ungodly gore everywhere. Even when he is no longer of this life, he is still selfish and egotistical.* He shivered with discontentment.

His thoughts moved contently to Eleanor and his game plan. Number 1 was a symbol of priority. Ultimately, God is always first. He stood, still clutching his empty mug, staring out the window, remembering the first scripture in the bible, Genesis 1:1. 'In the beginning when God created the heavens and the earth, 1:2 the earth was a formless void and darkness covered the face of the deep, while a wind from God swept over the face of the waters. 1:3 Then God said, "Let there be light;" and there was light.' How fitting this was for his plan to sacrifice her, for God to reward him once again.

His second opponent he had to eradicate, Eleanor Parker, lived by the lake and had recently married the love of her life, William

Parker. They met at Troy University, Troy Alabama, where they both completed their bachelor's degree in teaching and completed their chosen subjects. Eleanor loved the arts, whereas William turned towards the mathematical side of teaching. They fell in love within the first minutes of meeting each other, continuing to communicate when they had to go their separate ways to complete an internship, to gain first-hand experience in the classroom. That was almost four years ago, when Eleanor was 28 years of age, William one year older. They used to laugh at William's immaturities, his sense of humour which was contagious. His presence always, in Eleanor's eyes, lit up the room at parties and social events. That's what she loved about him, that and his very handsome, boyish good looks. Her heart was grabbed and stolen by this beautiful human being, who she now called her husband.

They didn't want to start a family straight away. They had plans to move to Butler, teach at the same elementary school, then when their careers had established, they would think about having their own children and build a life together. That time had unexpectedly arrived. Eleanor felt sick in the mornings, vomiting numerous times, but she had passed it off as a stomach bug. It continued to persist, so she decided to visit her local care physician. The news was extremely shocking, yet she was on cloud nine. They had been taking precautionary steps not to conceive, as they didn't think they were completely ready to be parents, not just yet. William's emotions, when Eleanor came home from the physician, were a combination of cartwheels and fireworks. He was truly elated to think he was going to be a father. They embraced each other with tears of laughter and worry. Parenthood was on the horizon, the physical act of caring and being responsible for another human were overwhelming. Smiles developed softly on both of their faces. They were ready.

But he knew everything about her. He knew how she liked her coffee in the morning, how her toast had to be slightly burnt then cooled down, before she buttered it with lashings of peanut butter. He knew how she was in love with her husband William, who didn't know he wasn't the father to their unborn child. He saw her that night, following her vehicle to the home of a child she taught at school. The child's father was a singleton and had asked Mrs Parker to tutor his daughter on several occasions. *Of course, she would oblige, the little whore couldn't be loyal to her husband for long. She deserves to be punished. Not caring about anyone else but herself,* he thought, working on the supposition she was always unfaithful.

He had to do his own homework on the two of them, with paragraphs of details, which would make his strikes flawless. He knew his abilities to live out his own values, to overcome obstacles made him top of his game, especially when it came to methods for investigating the concept of his focal points, evaluating his impact on his victims and concluding his success. His intelligence had gradually matured, and his capabilities became stronger day-by-day. He didn't need a teacher to help him, especially one that would abandon him at a critical time by falling pregnant, totally ignoring his existence and spending all of her time raising a bastard child.

He carried on with his work in the late afternoon, then hurriedly headed home. His place was his castle, which he had lived in all his life. He inherited the property and kept it in pristine condition. His favourite room was in the basement, his hidden gem, his sanctuary he had built by himself. It took years of organising and perfecting. It comprised of a secret entrance. The floorboards creaked as he strolled over to the kitchen sink, placing his empty lunch pack from the day's hard graft, into it to get washed. He didn't possess a dishwasher; they were useless pieces of machinery, which would continually break down, costing a fortune to get fixed. Problems he didn't want or need with his busy schedule. The cupboards were meticulously organised, he began to make himself some supper. He wasn't overly hungry this evening, as his stomach churned with excitement and a little apprehension. The vegetable soup boiled on the stove, he poured it into his handcrafted bowl and sat at his wooden table like a king. He knew what he had to do tonight and played the scenes over and over again in his head, until he was satisfied with the outcome.

Evening was turning into early nighttime, his car pulled out onto the county road 24, then turned left onto Hendricks Avenue. The West Pushmataha Street was visible, he knew it was a short drive to reach Timberlane Rd, which led him to his destination of Hickory Circle. He had forgotten how many times he had driven this route to be near Eleanor. He loved to watch her when she was in the kitchen, staring out the window to the lake, situated at the bottom of her yard. What a beautiful lake, with its smells and sounds stimulating his senses every time he visited.

He had watched during some of the days, snapping turtles in the shallow waters, which enjoyed basking in the sunshine on rocks to the edge of the lake. On the rare occasion he managed to sight an American alligator, which would be big enough to cause significant damage to any prey.

Beautiful sounds echoed on the days he strolled around the lake, walking the bird trails, watching the diversity of habitants, like the American robin with its reddish-orange breast, picking the red berries from the Yaupon holly tree. Singing its beautiful, sweet tune to the passers-by, who stood still listening, mesmerised and taken to a different realm of tranquility. How he loved its aura. Its beauty captured him in a way nowhere else could. He stepped out of his car in the dark, listening to the noises of his nocturnal friends. It was a sign everything was perfect; the night was going to be a success.

He knew William was out this evening and Eleanor was home alone. He was off teaching softball to those energetic young ones, something he was never good at himself, never getting picked when they had to team up. He was always the last to be chosen. His blood started to boil at the memories of his youth, he knew he had to control his feelings, his emotions. This was not the time to bring them to the surface. He walked slowly up to the window situated to the side of her kitchen. She was beautiful, standing at the sink washing her husband's dirty dishes. He smiled and made his way around to the backyard. His next opponent was about to be knocked off the board.

A loud humming noise stopped him in his tracks. *What the hell is that noise?* he contemplated. Lights shone through the leaf-fallen trees and vegetation, flickering as the vehicle drove slowly along the road, adjacent to Eleanor's home. It pulled into her driveway; the engine turned off. 'No! This can't be happening, why is he back?' said the man who was surreptitiously hiding in the shadows and becoming irate at the sight of her husband's return. *My plans can't be fractured at the second number thrown with my dice. This wasn't the plan on how my moves were to be. He has played a move I wasn't expecting, but think, I'm a brilliant game player, what are my options? I could take them both or I could be patient and let them make the wrong move. He will be going out again tomorrow night. I'll wait and take my turn then,* he mused.

Chapter Six

Outside was bitterly cold and dark. Clara and Adam had been allocated a room in the Sheriff's department. It wasn't a large workspace, but they both agreed it was more efficient than working from a motel room. They were giving access to all the office equipment, internet and one laptop, which they kindly turned down. They were thankful they had their bureau issued ones. These were regularly updated with the latest software and of this era. A large whiteboard was gifted, covering a good portion of the room and a coffee machine. 'This will have to do,' Agent Perez stated.

'I took photos of the hunting traps when Dr Cameron left, they both have the same markings. They're hard to make out as parts have been worn away. To me it indicates they aren't newly bought and someone's going to be two short next time they go hunting!' Clara began. 'I also took photos of the industrial chain and thought these items would be a great place to start.'

'I agree, we can't visit warehouses or stores now, they will all be closed. We'll visit them first thing tomorrow, there can't be that many stores selling these items to companies and the general public, surely?' Adam wrote Evan's name, age and time of death on the board. 'We need a map of Butler and its neighbouring towns. The arrow shaped on the ground, Dr Cameron never mentioned it, which direction did you say it was pointing?'

Clara pulled out her pad, 'Erm... northwest. Is that where you think his next victim will be? But that could be anywhere,' her frustrations were starting to show, they hadn't even begun to investigate. God, she needed something to eat and more to the point, she needed a drink. She hated being back here, being where it all went wrong.

'So, what do we know so far? The unsub has to be in quite good shape to be able to lift a dead weight. The kill was premeditated, he or she has clearly thought this out, what with the traps and the chains already set in place,' Agent Perez continued to scribble notes down onto the whiteboard. 'It looks personal, he or she didn't gouge out the eyeballs to kill Evan, he did it postmortem, so why? What was so significant about the eyes?'

Clara was listening to everything being said and totally understood why Special Agent in Charge Adam Perez was here. He thought quickly on his feet, didn't prolong the information that needed to be processed. Her first impression of him was one of a pretentious, studious guy that had procured an easy life and literally had everything handed to him. Now she wasn't so sure. She had seen a caring side to his demeanour, taking time to listen to people and stay very calm.

The art of thinking outside the box seemed to come naturally, whereas Clara wasn't so quick to perform, yet got the job done. Adam turned from the whiteboard to see what the commotion was. 'Here, a map, its old but nothing has changed around these parts so it'll give us the basics, plus we can use google maps on our cells for any queries,' Clara explained. She pinned it to the wall next to the whiteboard, circling in red the crime scene of where Evan Thomas was found. She worked out northwest from this point, dotted a line as far as the map would allow and faced Agent Perez.

She could tell he was feeling some respect towards her, contributing the backup work and implementing the right tools for the harsh case ahead. Clara needed to keep on his good side if she wanted him to put in a great report to her boss, Miller. This case had to be cracked, put to bed without any more deaths. *I will work with him and not against him. I need this.*

'Our plan of action tomorrow morning will be to visit suppliers and to retrace Evan Thomas's steps. Where was he prior to his death, who was in his company, did anything unusual happen within his evening's events? I think we need to pay a visit to his wife. I know the local police have been, but we may get some useful information out of her regarding her husband's lifestyle. Get your coat, you can drive,' Agent Perez said without hesitation.

The SUV pulled up outside the imposing gates of the large stately home, which the Thomas family inhabited. Ground lighting shone up, radiating the facade of the house. 'Wow I'm definitely in the wrong line of business. Did Sheriff Harris say he owned a bar? Must be a popular hangout place for the locals, to be able to afford this little beauty,' Clara voiced out. 'Does his wife know the full extent of his injuries?'

'I don't think that's relevant at this time, we don't want to shut her down before we can question her. Her name is Charlotte, they have twin daughters aged 10 years, Ellie and Harper, so we have to tread carefully, show compassion. I'll do the questioning.'

Clara glanced over to Adam, saying nothing as she drove up the long driveway, parking right outside the front steps. They rang the bell and waited a few minutes and the door opened; an elderly lady appeared. 'Yes,' her voice came sharply.

'Hi, I'm Special Agent in Charge Perez and this is Special Agent Strong. We are from the FBI and have been assigned to investigate the case of Mr Evan Thomas, may we come in? We won't take up too much of your time as we understand the family needs space to grieve.' They flashed their badges.

Clara knew this wasn't the wife, she was too old in the face. The door opened, the elderly resident walked away, assuming the two agents would follow. A large wooden doorway was open in front of them, they entered into a kitchen, a beautiful portrait of the family hung on the dining room wall. that was the size of Clara's whole apartment back in Durant. The lights were dim, the sound of sobbing came from a couch that was situated to the rear of the room, facing out towards glass windows, that seemed to never end in height.

'Charlotte darling, there are two FBI agents here, they need to talk to you,' said the elderly lady in a quiet manner. The woman on the couch looked up and blew her nose with a handful of tissues.

'Okay mom,' a sombre voice was heard, the agents prepared themselves.

'Mrs Thomas, thank you for letting us talk to you. We can't even imagine what you must be feeling, but we are here to ask you a few informal questions about your late husband.' Agent Perez knew it was a mistake to use the word "late" as soon as he heard her sobs increase to an uncontrollable noise. Her mother sat down beside her and patted her right arm, as though that would stop the crying. It worked.

'Sorry, it's just so raw. I feel like I'm in someone else's nightmare. My daughters don't really understand what's happening. How do you tell 10-year-olds their papa has been murdered?' Sobbed Charlotte.

'We won't take up too much of your time, we just wanted to ask if you or your husband noticed anything different leading up to last night's events. Have you seen anyone hanging around the house or did he mention any trouble in the bar from previous nights?' Perez asked in a calmly manner.

'No. He was always at that bloody bar, every night without fail. It consumed him, but he said he was doing it for our girls. He socialised to bring in new customers, to show off his bar and what he had built from scratch. He never told me what went on, to be honest I didn't want to know. He started to drink most of the profits. Look where it's got him,' her voice cracked, tears fell once again.

'You said he was at the bar every night? Did he always take the same route home?' Clara interrupted, but thought it was a question needing answering.

'Yes, he falls through the front door religiously at 11.15pm, smelling of booze and women. Last night I had a headache and went to bed early, so I didn't realise he hadn't made it home,' Charlotte experienced a concoction of emotion's when she relaid her husband's repeated movements.

'He doesn't lock up then, at the bar?' Agent Perez continued the questioning.

'No, he pays Joe to manage things, Christ what's going to happen to our business, how am I going to run things? I wouldn't know where to start.'

The two agents could see Charlotte Thomas's mindset wasn't in a place where they could carry on asking questions. Agent Perez stood up; Clara followed. 'We appreciate your time Mrs Thomas; we will see ourselves out. We will be in touch soon I'm afraid, as we need you or someone in your family to officially identify Mr Thomas.'

She nodded. Emotions and tiredness had engulfed her like a dark cloud. Staring into oblivion her mother took her by the arm and lead this newly widowed, single mother of two, upstairs to her to bed.

Clara started the SUV and asked Agent Perez what he wanted to do next. He rested his head against the vehicle window, explaining there was nothing else they could do tonight and suggested getting something to eat. Clara was relieved as she had been ravenous all day. 'You're the local girl I hear, where do you recommend?'

Her heart sunk at that moment; mixed thoughts of her life came flooding back. Her mood changed quickly; she knew it was because she was back here. She wasn't a local. She wasn't about to explain her past to this stranger, who she only met in the early hours of this morning, plus it wasn't anyone else's business. Her brother's disappearance had been the dawning of her own tribulation, and all her life she pushed her thoughts to the side, keeping herself busy. As she matured, her thinking capacity grew, making it increasingly difficult to grasp and control her thoughts. That's when she found comfort in the bottle. Jack Daniel's was her only real friend. Well JD and Frank. Inner strength was always there in her head, but it was weakening, laying deep, yet never moving. If it did disappear, she knew that would mean trouble. There would be no turning back from the bottle.

'What did you think about Charlotte's mother?' Adam perked up and asked.

'What?' Clara wasn't listening as her mind was in a dark place.

'Charlotte's mother, she was very stern, didn't seem to be upset about her son in law's death. Just an observation. You okay Agent Strong?'

'Yeah, I'm good. I just need food and my bed. This diner has easygoing food for us, if that suits?' She replied in a monotone voice. 'We're booked into the motel across the road from it.'

'Great, Special Agent Strong,' said Agent Perez.

'Clara, my name is Clara. Surely, we can be on first name terms when we aren't in the company of others?' she snapped, remembering Agent Perez was her boss on this case and had to control her attitude. *Get something to eat and get some sleep. You don't need your friend tonight, you had enough of him two nights ago.* The image of amber liquid in a whiskey glass, swirling round a large ice cube was making her heart flutter.

She pulled over and parked up. The cold night air wrapped around them both as they disembarked from the vehicle. There was a hushed stillness, the moon casted shadows on the ground, whilst the stars were clearly visible. To city residents, this wasn't an experience they ever captured. Lights from high rise buildings polluted the night skies, the orange hue was all they would ever see. Adam Perez embraced the chill against his skin, feeling alive and ready for something to eat.

Adam opened the door for Clara like a real gentleman, even after she had snapped at him earlier. The waitress showed them to their table, provided them both with a simple menu. Food was consumed, there was little conversation between the two agents. Adam asked for the tab, reaching for his billfold to pay. The waitress came back to their table and Clara noticed her staring down at her. 'Hi honey, I hope you don't mind me asking, but aren't you the sister of the little boy that went missing all those years ago?'

'No, I think you have the wrong person,' Clara retaliated.

'Carol, no wait Clara, that's it, Clara Strong. It's me Betsy, I went to school with you and your little brother. Well, I never. Didn't think I would ever see you back after everything that happened. How's your Mama doing? Last time I saw her she wasn't looking good?'

The wooden chair that was warmed by Clara's backside whilst devouring her meal, flew backwards, hitting the person sitting behind her. She grabbed her coat, knocking the salt and ketchup from their table and ran outside. She inhaled the crisp air and unquestionably needed a drink. Adam Perez followed her outside, buttoning up his coat, not uttering a word. They took their bags from the vehicle, booked themselves into the 3-star motel, which sat uninviting opposite the diner. It was old and grubby. Clara didn't care. She said her good nights to Adam, whose room was allocated down the dingy hall from hers. He gave her a smile that looked reassuring, she closed her door with too much force.

Her heart was racing, she was becoming agitated. *He must be asleep by now;* she hoped, opening her creaky motel door. At a slow pace, she closed it behind her, creeping past Adam's room, noticing his lights were still on. She didn't take the elevator because it would make too much noise. Clara had a date with her amber friend. The craving of those dry spices, with the hint of nuts and that smooth smoky palate made her smile and warmed her heart.

Chapter Seven

The knock on her motel door was loud, making her head pulsate. The beating sensation that manifested last night, intensified even more. 'What?!'

'Special Agent Strong, it's time to get going,' Perez shouted, annoying the hell out of her. She rolled over, reached for her cell, which was balancing precariously on the side table. Bright lights of the numbers indicated it was 7.30am. It was too early to rise, she pulled the covers over her head to hide. Alcohol was still swishing around in her system, she needed pain killers, fast. The knock came again. 'You in there, Agent Strong?'

'Yes!! Give me a second, I'm just getting changed,' her aching body shuddered from head to toe. Slamming her feet onto the red wiry worn-out carpet in a mood, she pulled herself up and made her way to the shower.

'I'll meet you in the foyer in a couple of minutes!' Agent Perez shouted once more, with a tone of annoyance.

'Yeah, yeah,' she muttered under her stale breath, 'Fuck where's my clothes?'

Clara made her way to the foyer, wet hair tide back. Her clothes Adam noticed, were from the previous day. Being from the BAU made his observations sharp. The rims of her eyes were red and sunken. It looked like she had no sleep. She didn't look like a professional FBI agent, she knew this. Pulling her suit jacket tight so it would take the creases out, wasn't working. Clara had thrown herself together, Agent Perez shook his head in disgust. He wasn't happy, she could tell.

'I'll drive, as I see you aren't in any fit state to be behind the wheel, Special Agent Strong!' He emphasised her name, snatching the keys from her hand. They got into their vehicle, she waited for him to start the engine. He threw the keys on the dashboard and turned to face her. 'I am not prepared to compromise this case because my so-called partner is inebriated, can't even dress herself in a respectable manner to meet the public and when investigating a seriously complex case. Do you want to explain?' he demanded.

Clara hadn't seen this side of Adam. She sat up straight in the seat, as though that would be the answer. 'No, I'm fine, I have nothing to explain,' she blurted out.

'It was a rhetorical question Special Agent Strong. You are apparently very close to being thrown out of the FBI as I understand, this morning's events would sort that out nicely. You are a disgrace to the bureau and as your senior I should report this to your assistant director back in Durant.' Agent Perez's face was reddening with anger, waiting for Agent Strong to give him some bullshit story about how she only had one drink from the motel mini bar. He continued and what he said next, hit home. 'Get out of the vehicle, get some clean clothes on, straighten yourself up. This is your only warning. Don't push me Agent Strong. You obviously have personal issues, but while we are here, you will give me one hundred percent of your time and professionalism. You understand?'

Clara didn't react and exited the vehicle in silence. She was up to her neck in deep water. The waves crashing hard against her weak body, every time she had one of her episodes. *No more cockups. Jesus Clara, pull yourself together and concentrate on this case!* Her mind echoed as she went back inside to change, not just her clothes, but her attitude.

She returned within minutes, feeling smarter, a little fresher and in addition, more professional. Her head still throbbed, but she would ignore that fact. Agent Perez threw papers onto her lap, containing a store that could have sold the items found at the crime scene and a few potential businesses, which may use those specific alloy chains.

'I want to apologise for my conduct. It won't happen again. This case is important to me, I'm totally focused to get this son of a bitch,' Clara blurted out before Perez could explain where they were heading. She scrunched through the few sheets of paper, recognising the hardware store in Butler town centre. 'I know this place, follow the road and take the second left.'

Butler Specialised Parts and Parts sat back from the main street. It's rusty, red neon sign trying desperately to stay lit. They made their way inside and glanced around, looking for some assistance with their inquiries. A stout lady in her 50's stood behind a wooden counter, which could only be described as historic, she was chewing the top of her pen, which had started to leak. The assistant wore an orange and black dress, a lime green apron and had hair that would in-habitat a thousand bees. She had a touch of blue ink to the left of her mouth, which the agents chose to ignore.

'Why hello there folks, how can I be of help?' the colourful assistant asked playfully.

'We are with the FBI, I'm Special Agent Adam Perez, this is my partner, Special Agent Clara Strong. We were wondering if you could help us with some items that may have been purchased at your store?'

'Why honey, of course. I would love to be of some assistance to you, but the FBI. Is it to do with that god awful murder in those woods?'

Clara felt nauseous, not from last night's alcohol, but from the body language the flirtatious woman behind the counter was expressing to her partner.

'We're just following up on a few lines of inquiry, that maybe…,' Agent Perez took a quick glance at the woman's name badge, '…helpful to our investigation, Mary Louise.'

'Then what y'all want me to take a look at?' she asked in a less coquettish tone.

Clara got out her cell phone, reminding the woman she was also present in the conversation. 'These hunting traps for starters, would they be something you sell?'

'Gosh let me see,' lifting her thick rimmed glasses that were hanging around her neck, sitting high up on her large chest. 'Why yes siree, they would be our foothold, double spring steel bear traps. The trap has a chain with a swivel snap at one end and a ring at the other; the spikes on its jaws point inwards. These horrible things have a pressure plate between two metal jaws and teeth as sharp as my granny's dog! Horrible devices. We sell very little of these, anti-fur campaigners protested outside in our yard for months,' she explained.

The two agents were surprised at the woman's knowledge. 'Would you know if any of these have been sold, say in the last year?' asked Clara.

'I need to get our logbook. Customers can pay any which way they want, but our boss always wants the customer's details written down, with every damn purchase. He says it helps build up relations or some other.' She bent down behind the counter then plonked a large logbook onto the dusty old countertop. 'Let me take a look.'

As the woman was sieving through the large disposition of customer's names and details, Clara slid away, unnoticed, into the back of the store. Tins of vanish, wooden poles, hammers, netting, brush handles were all strewn across the floor in a dysfunctional manner. She could see an enormous rack filled with reels of chains. 'Bingo!' She opened her cell, scrolling down to the photo of the chains, which she took back at Dr Cameron's morgue. The sizes were hard to distinguish, until she noticed at the very end of the rail, right at the bottom of the rack, her grade 80 alloy chain. She took a photo and walked back to Agent Perez, who was blushing with embarrassment at the obviousness of the woman's demeanour around him.

'Two purchases of the traps in the last 18 months. Aww wait, one customer returned his. Do you want me to write the other name down for you honey?' the assistant asked Agent Perez.

He nodded and turned to face Clara. She lifted her cell. 'Out the back.'

'Mary Louise, would you happen to know if you have any details in that logbook of purchasers who bought the grade 80 alloy chain, again in the last year?' Agent Strong asked.

Mary Louise made it obvious she only wanted the handsome FBI Agent to call her by her name. But she answered Clara anyway.

'Darling, I can tell you that without looking. Jackson's Lumberyard, Oak to Interior, off East Pushmataha Street on the Dansby Road. They have a credit account with us, as Zachariah Jackson the owner, buys that chain on a quarterly basis for his transportation trucks. Nobody else buys the stuff.' She was deliberating whether she had satisfied the two agents with her assistance. Writing the necessary details down, she handed it to Agent Perez with a wink.

'Thank you for your time, we appreciate your cooperation,' Perez stammered, as he hurriedly made his way to the main doors.

Clara navigated; the SUV GPS was too temperamental in the midst of Alabama. They turned off East Pushmataha Street, heading towards Jackson's lumberyard. The dirty diesel trucks with their heavy loads were stopping for no one. The drivers oblivious to the fact the roads were two way. Agent Perez steered carefully up Dansby Road, avoiding the 80,000-pound loads hurtling past. The roads were overcrowded, the truck's engines deafening to the smaller users.

Jackson's Lumberyard, Oak to Interior, gave the impression speed was the key to their success with loading trucks racing around the yard, kicking up dust and debris everywhere. He parked in front of the large imposing wooden building. The smell of oak, with its smoky spicy leaf fallen bouquet, rustled around Clara's senses when she exited the vehicle. For the first time since arriving in Alabama, she felt alive and invigorated. The smells brought her back to her childhood, the better days of her past, not those that were questionable.

Through the foyer, the two agents noticed large statues carved from wood. Below these sat children's wooden toys, some left natural, some painted with vibrant primary colours. The craftsmanship was impressive, stopping the two agents in their tracks. Entering through another set of doors, brought them to the main offices. It had one occupant who sat on the edge of a large black painted desk, screaming down the phone.

'I told you, if anyone asks where it came from, tell them your cousin flipped you some over. I don't care, y' listening to me? I've gotta go,' he slammed the receiver down, throwing the two agents a look of annoyance. 'What y'all want?' He muttered.

'We're with the FBI, we're looking for Zachariah Jackson!' Clara exclaimed.

'He ain't here, just little ole me. What you want and see him for anyways?' The thin lanky man mumbled.

'And you are?' Agent Perez inquired.

'Didn't tell ya my name, and I don't about to either.'

'I wonder if you could help us. We are inquiring about the chains used to transport your lumber,' said Perez calmly.

'Jesus, you're late with that one, ain't ya? That was reported stolen 8 or 9 months ago. The boss reported it to the Sheriff's office, he heard nothing back. So, they send the feds for some stolen links do they, well ain't that mighty,' he guffawed in the agents faces.

His tone and attitude riled Clara. The door slammed shut behind them, hearing an almighty bellow. Clara's hand quickly hovered over her Glock.

'Johnson! What the heck are you doing sitting on my desk. Get your arse over to the yard and load up. You're supposed to be in Pennington later this afternoon,' the man finished shouting, realising he had visitors. The thin man slipped from the desk, vacating the room.

'Sorry about that. If you don't keep on top of their movements, they'd cheat you out of every minute. My name's Zachariah Jackson, I'm the owner of this establishment. How can I help you folks?'

'I'm Special Agent Perez, this is Special Agent Strong. We were asking about your chains used for transportation. But I hear you had some stolen. When was that?' Asked Perez.

'Back in March, what's that about 8 months ago. Nothing was done, so I accepted my losses and now keep an eye on the staff. A lot of them aren't with me full time. Some are drifters with their truckers' licence. They aren't the easiest people to please, but they're bloody hard workers. What's this about? I'm sure the FBI aren't here to investigate stolen chains,' Zachariah Jackson asked, curiosity visible on his face.

'We're investigating a murder and the type of chains you use have been found at the crime scene. Do you have surveillance cameras and footage from when you think the goods were taken?' Agent Perez asked politely.

'God have mercy on their souls, what's wrong with folk, sickening. We've gone over the footage more times than I wanted, there's nothing to see. Bloody security lights for nighttime are temperamental, only work when they can be bothered,' Zachariah explained.

'Could we get a copy, also a list of staff, permanent and temporary?' Agent Strong interrupted.

Zachariah downloaded a copy of the surveillance and printed off all information containing the staff. Perez was amazed technology was used here and not good old-fashioned systems.

Perez and Strong's next stop was Evan Thomas's bar. They walked to their SUV, Clara faced the sun's rays, which radiated her energy levels again. God, she needed all the help she could to get through the day. 'What's his place called?' She asked, squinting her eyes, looking down to get her bearings. She hadn't read the reports last night back at the motel, instead she was studying the bottom of her whiskey glass.

'Alabama South Avenue Bar & Grill. We passed it last night on the way to our digs.'

Clara knew it. She was served some good Irish Bushmills whiskey at that bar just last night. Her memories were vague, however she remembered sitting in a quiet corner by herself. That's all she could recall. Her head started to ache, developing a heaviness due to anxiety. Worries of returning, smelling the alcohol, fighting temptation was not what she wanted to do on a sunny, autumnal afternoon. *Fuck!*

Agent Perez found his way back, without Clara's help. She was particularly quiet, Perez knew why. He was a behavioural analyst; it was his job to know. Parking up outside the bar, the agents noticed it was extremely crowded. They walked up the steps and entered. The place was full to capacity, a young girl handed them a menu and apologised for the wait. She told them it's never been so busy.

Most of the town had no doubt came to eat in the murder victim's bar. Clara and Adam had seen this happen many times. Gatherings like these made gossip ripe, then the Chinese whispers would start. Everyone wanted a piece of the action. The committee of vultures were out, soon to be feeding on the dead bar owner's carcass.

'We aren't here to eat, we're FBI, I need to speak to Joe, Joe the bartender and manager!' Perez shouted above the hum of loud noise. 'You stay here Agent Strong; I don't want you wandering off!'

'Fuck you, treating me like a child….I'll do...' She was stopped by someone tapping annoyingly on her shoulder. She knew Perez hadn't heard over the madding crowd of gossipers. Turning around to see who wanted her attention, she gasped in astonishment. 'George? George Edwards is that you?'

'Little Clara!' His blue sapphire-coloured eyes, shone through his soft wrinkled skin and welled up with soft tears. 'Is it really you?'

Clara's heart was in turmoil. This man who stood before her was the only positive human being she had in her life as a child. She had her brother Grayson, but that was cut short, splitting Clara's heart open every time she thought about him. George was the father she longed for, not the drunken child beater she was biologically born to. Dark memories came rushing back of seeing her brother being beaten, his small body turning black and blue, while their so-called mama, stood and watched. Clara at 10 years old could take the pain from his hands, she learnt to think about the enchanted forest and her fairytale friends. They all had names; they told her stories during one of her beatings. Her brother was too young to cope, not just physically, but mentally. The two children use to sneak out their back bedroom window and visit George. He would teach them life skills, like how to skin a swamp rabbit, gather sticks and debris to build small safe fires in the forests, raise and care for livestock. He was their rock. They felt safe, even if it was for a couple of hours. Sure, they knew when they returned home their punishment would be severe, but that was their life.

Until Grayson disappeared. He was 8 years old, playing down by the lake with Clara, catching crappies, bluegills and other species of fish, a skill George helped them develop. The summer day was perfect with the sun splitting the trees, the warm air softly blowing against their little soft faces. They laughed, swam in the cool waters, smoked their winnings on the small fire, slept by the side of the lake with a belly full of supper. That's when he vanished. Grayson wasn't lying next to Clara when she woke, he had disappeared.

Life for Clara would never be the same. She grappled with the guilt of not protecting him, not keeping an eye on him. The palpable sense of loss overwhelmed her heart, it would never feel full again. Her parents blamed her. They punished her severely, neglecting and disowning her as their daughter.

'Have you seen your mama, Clara? She isn't doing too well, and Doctors don't reckon her body will see through to the spring next year. I know she would love to see ya Clara, you know, to say her piece,' George Edwards said in a soft tone, sounding sincere, waking Clara from her memories.

'George, I'm in Alabama to work, my time is limited, the case we are working on is complicated and complex,' she replied.

'Work? Case, What Case? You with the police department?' His questions bombarded Clara, she felt claustrophobic and confused.

'I'm not sure if I can visit this time around, you know, with what we went through. I can't just forgive and forget. So why are you taking her side after all this time?' She expressed her feelings, with nothing but sadness.

'Clara, she can't change the past. Your mama was protecting you both. She was told if she interfered, your beatings would be countless. She was helpless Clara.'

'Is that what she tells you George, and you believe her? Well, I'm sorry for disappointing you, but she doesn't deserve my time. I wasn't their child after that day. Anyway, it's been great to see you again George, you take care of yourself,' said Clara, cutting him off far too quickly. She had to, otherwise she would fall apart in the middle of Alabama South Avenue Bar & Grill.

'Agent Strong! I've spoken to Joe and...' Perez stopped in his tracks. 'Sorry, have I interrupted you?'

'No, George and I were just saying our goodbyes,' tears welling up in her eyes.

With that George walked out the doors with his takeout, looking back and giving Clara one of his reassuring smiles. It broke her heart to see him go. She loved that man, worshipped the ground he walked on. Sadness raced through her; she knew she had to be careful not to let Agent Perez see her personal life get in the way of her bureau work.

'You ok?' Perez asked, sounding pretty concerned.

'Yes, did you get any information from Joe?' Quickly changing the subject.

'We need to retrace Evan's steps the night he was murdered. We can piece together everything back at base,' he stated.

When the agents proceeded out of the bar doors, the weather had changed. Thick dense fog blanketed the surface of the road, with visibility virtually impossible. The freezing fog had replaced Clara's therapeutic sunshine. It was The Fall, which was renowned for being the foggiest season of the year. As summer fades to winter, colder air blows in and right now in Butler, it was extreme. Clara and Adam zipped up their parkas, walking along E. Smith street. Straining their eyes, they noticed a few houses set back off the sidewalk. Perez opened his cell, rang Sheriff Harris, asking if he would send a police officer over to talk to the occupants of these houses. They continued walking, looking to see if any surveillance cameras were present. It was a waste of time; the fog had come in fast; the pair could see nothing. The forest was still taped up, a patrol car sat guarding the entrance.

They decided to head back to the Sheriff's office. The work carried out in the foyer of the courthouse had developed quickly. Clara's head still pulsating, the paint fumes adding to her self-inflictions. She noticed an additional worker. The two painters turned to see who was coming in. Michael, who helped them when they first arrived at the courthouse, waved and carried on painting. The other painter wasn't so friendly. He kept on with his brush strokes, watching the FBI agents head towards the rear of the building.

'What's up with you today Eli, you seem agitated?' Michael asked his working partner.

'Just had a late night, a bit too much caffeine. That's all. Now can we get this finished and get home?' Asked Eli Davis, with zero patience.

'Okay, was just asking!' Replied Michael, with a sense of displeasure.

Back in their small cramped makeshift office at the back of the courthouse, Perez asked Strong to check out the surveillance footage from Jackson's Lumberyard, while he looked over their employees, checking the purchaser of the hunting traps.

They sat in silence drinking their café noir's, Perez took a large bite of his grilled cheese sandwich, complements of Joe at the Bar & Grill. The ticking of the wall clock was loud, the only noise audible in the room for a good half an hour. 'Eureka! I've got something,' Perez said excitedly.

Clara got out of her chair, accompanying her boss. 'What have you found?'

'The guy who bought the traps, is also an employee of the lumberyard,' he divulged. 'He's definitely a person of interest.'

'Jesus, who is it?'

'Benjamin Johnson. He has worked at the company for 7 years.' Perez lifted his cell again and rang Zachariah Jackson, hoping he would still be in his office. After the third ring, he picked up.

'Hello, Jacksons Lumberyard,' said the voice on the other end.

'Hi, It's Special Agent Perez from the FBI. We spoke today. I was wondering if one of your employees would be available to come over to the police department to answer a few questions. Nothing to worry about, he may be able to help us with our inquiries. It's Benjamin Johnson?'

'I'm afraid he's on the road, won't be back until tomorrow now. Damn fog has slowed down logistics. I have to put him up in a motel. Bloody weather. He should be back tomorrow morning, then back into work again for 5pm. I'll let him know,' Jackson responded, curiosity still emanating from his voice.

'Thanks Mr Jackson, we'll be in touch again,' returned Agent Perez.

'We'll visit him the first opportunity we get tomorrow.' Perez elucidated his point to Clara, who was still glued to her laptop screen, trying to catch a thief. 'Any luck with the surveillance footage?'

'No, the camera shows very little. Employees clocking in and out, but nothing of interest to report. What about Dr Cameron with forensics? The counter and note, they could be potential clues if fingerprints are found, we still don't know if Evan

Thomas wasn't struck before he was chained up, for definite. Dr Cameron said he wanted to dig deeper.'

Just as she said that the door opened, Sheriff Harris showed his face. He handed Perez a piece of paper. 'Results from Dr Cameron's toxicology and forensic tests.'

Perez read:

DR CAMERON [BUTLER COUNTY CHOCTAW]

ANALYSIS OF HOMICIDE VICTIM TOXICOLOGY/FORENSIC

REPORT

Mr Evan Thomas. *Working paper 1.1   12.10.23*

'Postmortem toxicology testing results conclude: Quantifying and interpreting drugs and or other toxicants in the blood, show no recent drugs on the deceased at the time of death.

Liver tissue results conclude: no toxicants present.

Stomach contents results conclude: investigative examination for acute poisoning, high concentrations of drugs or toxins- not detected. However, Blood alcohol concentration [BAC]tests determine named victim, shows 0.40%, could cause difficulty in walking, speaking, confusion, nausea and drowsiness.

Hair and Nails testing results conclude: amphetamines, cocaine, marijuana [THC]and heroin: not detected. Scrapings below named victim nails conclude: no other skin cells detected.

Enucleation: removal of entire eye globe, with separation of all connections from the orbit, including optic nerve transection. Smooth edged knife. Professionally surgically removed.

No skull depression. Neck trauma detected postmortem.

Cause of death: Exsanguination-blood loss/bleeding out from ankle joint of tibia, fibula and talus bone connection. Cartilage, ligaments, muscles, nerves and blood vessels damaged.

Victim's clothing comparison to questionable fibres indicated if applicable -negative.

Conclusions of Paper – no fingerprints detected.

Conclusion on counter- to follow.

'We have nothing so far, apart from the type of knife edge used and our unsub is meticulous with his techniques. This is definitely premeditated,' Perez sighed, frustration in his eyes. 'The victim had copious amounts of alcohol in his system. Maybe that's why our killer chose him. Easy target! But we need to find out why he removed the victim's eyes postmortem. It indicates a personal attack. Who had a vendetta against Evan Thomas, or was it someone who resembled him?'
'Sick son of a bitch, whatever possess someone to act out such a heinous crime?' Sheriff Harris asked, with pure hatred for the unsub.
'You'll be surprised what people are capable of. Take Charles Frederick Albright, also known as the Eyeball killer. An

American murderer and suspected serial killer from Texas who was convicted of killing one woman and suspected of killing another two back in the early 1990's.'

'Christ do I really want to hear this?' Harris interjected.

'He was adopted by Delle and Fred Albright. His adopted mother was extremely strict, accelerating his education, putting immense pressure on him to enrol in med school as a surgeon. He ended up surgically removing all his victims' eyes, taking them as trophies,' Perez explained. 'The human brain is a complex organ, it controls emotion, thought, your motor skills, vision, breathing, the list is endless. If someone has experienced trauma, for instance in their life, then their prefrontal cortex will begin to function less effectively. That could be dangerous.'

'D'you think our unsub could be doing the same thing? Killing for a personal reason?' Clara asked.

'At this stage we won't rule anything out. He stated, he has only just begun! The arrow means something, direction of his next victim? But where? Who's he going to target? Fuck, we are going to have a long night ahead Agent Strong, I suggest we get some food sent in.

'No surveillance cameras in operation in the area of E.Smith Street. Folk haven't had to use them in such a small community. Occupiers of the houses facing the sidewalk where our victim walked saw nothing! Another dead end I'm afraid, but we are looking at the bar and grill surveillance camera to see if we can find any leads that end. So far nobody left the same time as Evan,' Sheriff Harris contributed.

'That's what Joe the bar manager told me too, he left on his own. We'll just have to keep digging,' Agent Perez concluded.

The Sheriff left; Perez followed him. 'I'll be back in five minutes Agent Strong.'

Wondering where her boss was going, she turned back to her small desk and took a deep breath. Clara had an urge, a gut feeling she needed, wanted even, to talk to Frank. Her vulnerability was maybe the cause. Frank was her confidant; he knew all her secrets, except one. Her past. The strange feeling of separation struck Clara, she felt confused. Why was she thinking about Frank of all people? She picked up her phone and dialled his number.

Chapter Eight

The freezing dense fog filtered through the whole town. It was nearly time for him to finish his daily job. He enjoyed his work. It gave him time to reflect on his life and how it was moving nicely forward. He had God as his advisor, putting all his faith into him. His heart warmed, understanding his actions were correct, knowing at the end of his game, when he won, he will be redeemed by his saviour.

He needed the time during the day to evaluate his work that he carried out at night. *Eleanor Parker would have said her final goodbyes to her sweet little children at her school this afternoon. Darling little children, all playing together in the school yard, sharing candy and singing nursery rhymes as they leap over their skipping ropes.* He quickly cut off his thoughts. He never experienced that as a child. He sat alone at recess. Being taunted by the other children. It was a sign of weakness he wasn't about to accommodate. Not today.

He was delighted with the bleak surroundings outside, such a perfect scene setting before his eyes. *This was meant to be,* he thought. *Eleanor's husband William would be at the elementary school this evening, giving the parents a lecture on mathematics and how to teach them at home in fun ways.* The perp laughed at the thought of all those pathetic people, sitting and pretending to be the best parents at the school.

Heading home, he carried out his routinely duties, being meticulous not to leave anything out, like washing the plates after dinner. Looking around his favourite room in the basement, checking he had everything to play his game, he felt satisfied. *How silly I am! Nearly forgot the dice.* He looked down at it, admiring the craftsmanship. The four sides with numbers 1-4 were beautifully carved out, the two sides that were vacant of digits had petite ornate carved out words, My Saviour and New

Life. He squeezed the dice tight in his palm, breathed in the air of his games room, the smells of earth and wood stimulating his senses to kill, then left.

He got into his vehicle; he was pleased the mechanic took it this morning and fixed the fuel gauge. It made things so much sweeter. Driving to Eleanor's wasn't difficult in the dense fog, he had driven the route countless times. Even in his sleep he knew every pothole, every obstacle on the back roads to his destination. The soft grey coloured air was still, engulfing his car. He drove slowly along Hickory Circle, trying not to rev the engine and make too much noise. He abandoned his vehicle in a small hiding, off the gravelled road, ensuring it went undetected by Eleanor's nosy neighbours. The man opened the trunk, reaching in for his rucksack. He had to bring the items that were essential for the work ahead, they were crucial. He gripped the shabby looking rucksack tight against his chest. The grey shaded fog now encircled his body, making him hidden from view. The stillness of the night hung to him like a forever companion. He walked slowly around the front of the house, noticing that William's car wasn't there. He breathed in the cold air and exhaled steadily as he crunched quietly on the gravel path to the rear of the building.

Her beauty captivated him, but she had to die. Watching her closely he felt imperious. His body straightened in desperation to begin his game. He had longed for this night; he had planned every little detail down to the last nail. The number of times he visited her beforehand, getting to know her better, being a friendly face whenever she wanted company were countless. And then there were the times he visited Eleanor without her knowing or even being aware he was in the same vicinity.

He loved Dogwood Lake, with its spectacular wildlife and different types of fish, which he loved to catch. Being a fisherman gave him opportunities to sit and watch the world go by. How he loved his life. Tonight, though he wasn't catching his usual spotted bass or perch, he had bigger things to reel in. And his catch was magnificent, beautiful to watch. He knew, without a doubt that Eleanor would take the bait. Dogwood lake was invisible tonight, there wasn't a single sound from the nocturnal creatures residing near Eleanor's jetty. The old wooden structure sat in silence, about a foot above the lakes surface. Eight gleaming white metal circular posts, stood tall along the edges, supplying the jetty with support. Placing his rucksack down halfway along, he reached in and brought out his flashlight. The beam from it was powerful. He faced the house and started to wave it frantically around, hoping and praying the light reached Eleanor's kitchen patio doors.

Eleanor sipped on her black coffee, reaching over for another ginger biscuit. The start of pregnancy wasn't treating her well. Her vomiting had subsided, but the feelings were always present. Dunking her biscuit into her beverage, she was distracted by light coming from her yard. She looked down at her coffee, the biscuit dived to the bottom of her mug. 'Crap!' She made her way to the sink, pouring her ruined drink down the drain, catching sight of the beam of light.

'What is that?' She didn't know if it was something reflecting off the water, *but it couldn't be, it's too foggy,* she surmised. Eleanor couldn't make out how close the light was. She walked over to her coat stand, slipping on her thick blue parka, along with her hat and gloves. It was freezing outside, and she didn't want her unborn baby to get cold. She had to keep them both warm. Her parenting skills were already kicking in.

He heard the sound of the patio doors sliding along their rims. The pleasure within him rose. He knew what he had to do. Her footsteps were getting closer to him. He could almost smell her, touch her. But he must be patient, the plans have been made and he must adhere to them.

'Hello! Hello! Is there anyone there? Hello, do you need assistance with your boat?' She shouted. Her instincts told her someone was on the lake and the fog had caught them off guard. *Were they looking for a place to dock their boat? She thought.* 'Hi! Can you hear me?' It wasn't the first time a user of the lake docked at her jetty, normally in an emergency, like water seeping in or engine trouble. She didn't mind, it came with buying the house. Eleanor loved to watch boats cruise by, or fishermen cast their lines in the deep waters to catch their supper. She followed the illumination and heard someone shouting.

'I was fishing on my boat, I needed to use your jetty, but I didn't secure the damn thing up properly and it came untied, its drifted back onto the lake! It's no good trying to find it tonight, the weather is still coming in thick and fast,' the man called out. He knew the fog was an added bonus, giving him a better excuse why he needed to dock and standing helpless on her jetty.

'Okay, if you need to phone someone to come and pick you up, you can wait up at the house,' Eleanor shouted back in a friendly demeanour.

'Thank you! I can't actually see which direction I need to go, this damn fog,' he retorted in a confused manner.

'Your voice sounds familiar, keep talking, I'll make my way down to get you,'

'Thanks Eleanor, yes, we definitely know each other, I'm so embarrassed about this. I'm sorry to drag you out on such a cold night.' He stood grinning to himself, waiting for that unforgettable moment when they met. His heart raced, his body still. They were only a few inches apart. 'I'm just here Eleanor.' He lifted the flashlight to his face and smiled.

'Oh my, I thought it was you. I didn't know you had a boat and fished? Come on up to the house and get warmed up. You must be freezing standing there? We'll put the kettle on while you wait,' she said with a concerning expression.

'I wouldn't want to put you out. I can wait out in your front yard for my lift. You've done enough for me tonight already,' he said with intention.

'Nonsense, I won't hear of it,'.

'I just need to find my rucksack; I placed it down on the jetty when I was attempting to tie my boat, but the fog has come in quick, now I can't see it.'

'I'll give you a hand, then we can get a coffee.' Eleanor walked along the jetty; she knew exactly where she was by every wooden plank. The scores indented at the edge of a rackety old piece informed her she was halfway along. The man kindly shone his light. 'Found it. It's quite heavy, would you mind carrying it, it's just that I'm..'

'Pregnant!' The change in his voice made Eleanor turn around.

'What did you say?' She asked. Her body froze, her eyes couldn't find him amidst the darkness and fog. Eleanor didn't know if she misheard him, hoping and praying she did.

'You're a whore, sleeping with all the guys and falling pregnant. Does William know it's not his. You were like that when we were younger. We had the best time in the yard, we played games, and you taught me how to ride my green bike. Then you had that bastard baby and treated me with contempt. I was a nobody to you and you left me alone. You're nothing but a…..'

'Stop! What are you talking about? You have me confused with someone else. I've only known you 6 or 7 years. Why are you saying all these things? I need to go,' Eleanor's voice shook with fear. She had to get her unborn baby back to the house, she had to be its protector, find a safe place, away from this man. She needed to get past him on the jetty. Legs feeling weak, she started to walk back in his direction, heart racing with every step. Her breathing was becoming shallower, her body shaking from fear.

'It's such a shame, your life could've turned out so differently. You could've enjoyed the time with your husband, but you had to sleep with that parent. I saw you. Racing over to his house, pretending to help the little one with work. You're a liar, a cheating whore.' His voice was scaring her, she no longer recognised him. He wasn't the man she befriended all those years ago.

'I need to go. My husband will be home any minute. I would like you off my property.' She knew and he certainly did, William wasn't home for hours. The flashlight turned off, making her passage through even more dangerous. The only way out of this for her was to pass him on the wooden structure, otherwise she was cornered, and he had arranged that in his scheming plans. Breathing in deeply she moved forward, trying to reassure herself everything would be alright. He came into view, he stood only a few feet away, but she carried on, shutting him out of her vision. She was past. He had let her go. Quickening up her pace with all the strength she could muster, wasn't going to be enough. That coffee she promised him, wouldn't get made.

His hand raised up high, flashlight still in his grip. With an almighty blow to the back of her skull, her world went dark. *She needs to know what she did was a sin. She should be ashamed and asking God for forgiveness.* His anger gradually settled, he needed to concentrate on completing his moves.

Eleanor's still body lay helplessly on her wooden jetty. He removed her parka, hat and gloves, folding them up tightly, placing them in his rucksack. Then Lifting her arms, he dragged her down onto the private little inlet that sat to the left-hand side. He had his flashlight clutched under one arm, his knife sticking out of his top pocket. He knew the cold water was always going to be the hard part, the move he dreaded the most. It took his breath away and he had to relax his own body to keep going. His chest was now deep in freezing lake water, Eleanor was half floating, half sinking. He pulled her towards him and shone the light along the underside of the structure. 'There!' He found the two ropes he had tied to the white poles. It had been over two weeks since he had executed this part of his plan, and he was relieved to see they were still in good condition. Tying one of her wrists to the wet ropes successfully, he stretched over to reach for the other. Eleanor's face bobbing in and out of the lake, the cold waking her; coughing and choking on the water he was stirring up. She started muttering nonsense about her baby. Her other wrist now tightly wrapped.

'Please, my baby, please,' her words incoherent. Her head kept sinking under the water, soaking her face and bringing her awareness back. Eleanor's lips were a shade of blue like a darken sky before a rainstorm. She tried with all the strength she had left, to cry out for help, but it was no use. Her body was shutting down. Her emerald eyes now red with horror. Their sparkle had disappeared, and they would be lost forever. She kept slipping in and out of consciousness. Until she had no more strength to fight. 'Please…'

He stood watching for a few moments, her limp body, floating in the cold waters of Dogwood Lake. The lake she would have shared adventures on with her child, teaching them how to fish and swim. He tilted his head smiling. 'It's not just you Eleanor that needs to be sacrificed. Your bastard child ruined my life, you ignored me after you gave birth to that baby. God, help us to sacrificially, generously, cheerfully, willingly give to the work that you've given us to do as your people here,' he preached.

Feeling for his top pocket with his numb hands, undoing the button, he pulled out his knife. His body started to shiver uncontrollably, he couldn't afford to become hyperthermic, he hadn't finished. The man stood close to his victim, finding her belly under the freezing water, rubbing his left hand over it. He whispered her name softly, 'Eleanor,' while his right hand entered the water.

Blood emerged and surfaced to the top. The lake had turned red. He knew he needed to get out of the bloody water. The Alligators could be nearby, and he didn't want to be a victim himself tonight. He struggled to get onto the small area of shingle, his wet clothes weighing him down. The feeling of numbness in his feet and legs were intense. He fell onto the ground, reaching for his rucksack, which sat on the jetty. The fog was dense and still present, he knew he still had time to get home before it lifted. Tonight, had been a success.

With shivering hands, he reached inside his sack, picking out the leather pouch containing his dice and counters. He turned the flashlight back on, moving some shingles to create a smooth area. He rolled his dice and looked down, the number 3. *I was hoping he would be next. He will be sorry; he won't be able to use me as a punchbag anymore. I'll show him, I'll have the upper hand. He never protected me from all those bullies, he slaughtered me as a child and now i'll be the one in the ring who will win, bigger and better.*

Picking the dice off the ground, he cleaned it off, placing it back in the leather pouch, lifting out the counter with 1 carefully crafted in the centre. It was very similar to Evan Thomas's counter, but instead of a deep red 4, he thought he would make it a pretty colour, for a pretty lady. The carved 1 was a striking yellow, vibrant and joyous to look at. He was quite sad to leave it behind with the whore. She didn't deserve such gems. Lifting out the piece of paper, which were small little clues to help along the fortunate, privileged detectives, solve the mystery, similar to one of his board games, he wrapped the counter inside. Placing it on the jetty, scattering a few shingles around to decorate his drama, he smiled.

The last move was to shape an arrow in the ground. Feeling cold and a little disoriented, he nearly forgot. He chortled to himself. *Nearly finished, then home to my own coffee.* Gathering larger waterworn stones, he carefully placed them facing a south easterly direction on the tiny inlet beach. Kicking away any footprints, he lifted his rucksack, shone his flashlight to check nothing was left and whispered a sweet non endearing, goodbye to Eleanor.

He stopped, remembering to see if any of her clothes had snagged when he dragged her body to the water's edge. Satisfied his game had been excellently executed, he took a moment to reflect. Killing her in the cold waters would eradicate any evidence that he was even there, which pleased him even more. How he loved to play, loved to win his moves against his useless opponents. *They aren't the true players, I am the only dexterous game player here,* he reflected, looking down at his bluish hands, restricting blood causing them some discomfort.

Walking back on tiptoe, to ensure no footprints were made, he noticed Eleanor had left her patio doors open. *Silly girl, it costs a lot of money to heat a home these days, what was she thinking?* And he kindly closed them back up, using one of his elbows. He found his vehicle amidst the darkness and freezing fog, jumped in and started the engine. The heat blasted through the vents and through his frozen veins. His body was shaking from the cold water and pure adrenaline. He had struck another opponent from the board. *I think it's time to celebrate,* he mused. He slowly drove home to put the kettle on the stove, whilst he changed into warm comfortable clothes.

Chapter Nine

His car pulled up outside his house, the fog still lingered. He was exhausted and happy to get home. The mathematical lecture went extremely well, he was complemented by all the parents afterwards, which kept him behind that little bit longer. William was ready for a beer and to sit down on his favourite armchair.

He unlocked the front door; it was a mutual agreement between the couple the front door should be locked at all times. Entering the large foyer, he shouted out. 'Eleanor, I'm home. Bloody parents kept me chatting afterwards and I couldn't get away. God, am I glad to be home! Eleanor, are you there?' As he walked towards the hub of the home where he always found her sitting, marking homework or reading a good novel, he continued, 'I was saying I would have been home earlier but.... Eleanor honey?' He sat a carton of milk on the breakfast bar.

He checked all the rooms downstairs then headed up the long winding stairs to the bedrooms. 'Eleanor, are you in the bath? Eleanor honey, can you answer me?' Silence filled the house. William's chest tightened with dreaded fear of something just wasn't right. 'Shit! Where the hell is she?' He mumbled to himself. As he chased through the house, being unsuccessful in every room, his anxiety levels increased. *Surely, she wouldn't be putting trash in the bins outside in this ungodly weather.*

But he slid the patio doors open to check, shouting out her name, 'Eleanor, come on, this isn't funny anymore, come back in otherwise you and the little one will catch your death, it's freezing out there. Eleanor!' The eerily quietness of the moment sent William into a panic.

He ran to the bottom cupboard in their laundry room, grabbing a flashlight. He switched it on, 'Work you damn thing!' It didn't comply. With his hands trembling, he pulled out some new batteries from the drawer, which spilt over the floor, he fumbled to pick them up. *Calm down William, she is probably outside getting some fresh air?* He replaced the batteries, chucking the old ones to the floor.

'Honey, are you out here? Eleanor, would you answer me. I didn't mean to start an argument before I left this evening, I was just tired and……Eleanor, please answer me. I'm sorry okay, I love you!' It wasn't even an argument; it was a heated discussion about if he could bring milk home on his way back from his lecture. She didn't want to drive to the store in the dense fog. William always put Eleanor first, but this evening he was cold, tired and didn't want to lecture parents. He left her on bad terms, now here he was trying to find his pregnant wife who he adored, on one of the foggiest nights he had known.

He shone the light in all directions. His sight was restricted, he could only see a few feet in front of him. He called her name continuously, making his way down to the lake and their jetty. 'Eleanor! I'm sorry!'

Dogwood Lake was still, not a ripple or sound came from its direction. Underneath she floated, lifeless and hidden. Her dead body swamped in blood. William stepped onto the wooden structure; its creaks were audible as he slowly stepped forwards. His foot kicked something, so he bent down to get a better look. In amongst a pile of small stones, was a piece of paper wrapped up like a ball. *No Eleanor, please no!* His fears escalated. He knew during her first weeks of pregnancy she wasn't coping. Her hormones were scattered, and she had bouts of depression. She was delighted to be pregnant, but some days her head told her something different.

'No! Eleanor, tell me you are okay!' Unravelling the note, a small counter dropped into his palm. He was too afraid to read it, too afraid to come to terms with what he might see. Hands shaking, he read, 'Gaining another victory over my opponents.' His knees dropped to the floor. *What is this? Where's my wife? What's happened to her?* He looked at the counter, throwing it down on the deck. He had to move, he needed to find her. Shining the flashlight on the water; he couldn't make out what he was seeing. The water was murky, it looked like sediment suspended on the surface. William jumped down onto the inlet, right next to the display of stones beneath his feet. 'Eleanor!'

He looked up and peered under the jetty, the beam of light searching frantically. The density of the fog was thinner here, he could see further. That was a mistake. He saw her. Her head tilted to the side, softly moving with the tiny natural pulse of the lake's water. Her wrists tied to the posts either side. Her lifeless body, pale and limp. William froze. He couldn't move. His brain unable to process the scene. Staring at the blood encompassing her corpse awakened him from his terror. Diving forward, he reached his wife, 'Eleanor!' He screamed.

***

Finishing off the last mouthful of her takeout, thanks to Agent Perez, Sheriff Harris burst into the room. The two agents knew something was wrong by the look on his face, 'We have another body.'

Arriving at Eleanor and William Parkers home, the two feds, followed by Sheriff Harris, walked down to Dogwood Lake. The area was somewhat chaotic. Two officers were already present, along with Dr Cameron, his team and William. Blankets huddled the husband, whilst the coroner's assistants propped up lighting and deployed a lightweight shelter tent over the victim.

'Can one of you tape up the front of the house. Keep outsiders the other side of it?' Shouted Sheriff Harris. The younger of the two officers quickly responded, leaving the other officer standing, staring into the tent. 'Deputy Dubois, this is Special Agent Perez and Special Agent Strong from the FBI. What can you tell us?'

The fog was slowly lifting, but traces of it still noticeable in the night sky. Deputy Sheriff took a step towards the two agents, his face changed. 'Special Agent Strong, you look familiar. Do I know you?' He asked, ignoring the events unfolding around them.

Clara shook her head, 'So Deputy, can you bring us speedily up to date?'

'The victim's name is Mrs Eleanor Parker, resides at this address with her husband William. He was lecturing at Butler Elementary school this evening, came home to find his wife under the jetty, dead,' his words spilling out, matter-of-factly. 'He tried to untie her wrists that were bound to the posts. The knots were tied in a professional way, which made it impossible. He ran back up to their house and called us. He thought she might still be alive, but when he saw the amount of blood…' Deputy Dubois paused, 'That's not the worst. The coroner and his team have managed to get her to land, we'll it's not pretty. The husband informed me she was pregnant with their first child.'

'Get the medic to take Mr Parker back up to his house, get the poor man some dry clothes for God's sake and make sure someone sits with him. We don't want him doing something stupid. He's just lost his wife; God knows what state his mind is in right now,' Harris said, wanting to begin the investigation quickly, so they could catch this monster.

Deputy Jeremiah Dubois got straight on it. Leaving Perez, Strong and Harris to start. 'We'll give the husband time to change, then we'll go and speak to him,' said Perez.

'So, he comes home, finds his pregnant wife in the water. Is this even the same unsub? Are we looking at two unconnected murders?' Asked Harris, 'Christ the Mayor of Butler will have a coronary! He relies on tourism to keep us all afloat.'

'We'll have to talk to Dr Cameron, see if he'll allow us to suit up and take a closer look,' suggested Clara, 'I'm certain they could do with a few extra pair of hands.'

'I'll let you two carry on. I'm going up to check the front of the house and see if Mr Parker is okay. I still have a duty of care with the community, especially under such shitty circumstances,' with that he walked up the garden slope, disappearing out of sight.

Dr Cameron handed the agents full suits, gave them a little lecture about how to process the scene. It was part of their job description, they had probably covered more area in one case, than he had all his working career. Climbing under the tape, they decided to walk down the jetty together. It had yet to be processed thoroughly. There was a marker flagged beside blood spatter found, which Dr Cameron had commented on before the agents started their search. Maglites on, walking slowly and steadily inching forward, planks creaking one at a time as their weight slowly shifted the boards in a downwards motion, Clara told Perez to stop. She bent down, noticing something in between the wooden planks. It was lodged in tightly, 'Can you pass me an evidence bag?'

'What have you got?'

'I'm not sure, it could be nothing,' said Clara. Gripping tight around the item, so it wouldn't fall into the lake through the planks, she pulled it out, inspecting it. 'It's one of those counters, identical shape to the one found in Evan's pocket. Gotcha!' Placing it in the evidence bag, she handed it over to Perez. 'There's our first connection.'

'Good find Clara,' Special Agent Perez commented. She was taken back by hearing her name, but this wasn't the time to dwell on it. They continued to the end and turned. Leaving the jetty, they moved beside the tent, where the dead woman's body lay, her corpse surrounded by examiners. The night sky was becoming more noticeable, with the fog slowly diminishing and the moon's rays endeavouring to illuminate the lake's surface once again. Special Agent Strong noticed the remnants of Eleanor's blood drifting out onto the lake. *What a beautiful night this could have been for the couple,* she thought.

'Agent Perez, sir, come and have a look at this,' she said quietly, not disturbing the coroner with his medical examinations. The stone shaped arrow, facing out to the lake made Clara disquieted by the prospect of another possible victim being out there. 'He's messing with us; he's playing some kind of sick game.'

'Can you take a photo? We'll get the team to take some, but for now we'll just use your cell,' Agent Perez assured her.

Clara snapped a few pictures. Using her compass app, she could see it was pointing southeastwards, 'Fuck what's his M.O?'

Modus operandi, every killer had his or her own special way. They now had to dig deep to see what this killer's was, which emanated Clara's determination.

Google maps located them northwest of the first crime scene. She showed Perez her cell, 'But it could have been any of these houses he committed his crime, why here? Why Eleanor Parker?' She said running her finger over the screen of her phone.

'Keep looking Clara, we can gather up all the info, then head back to the Sheriff's department,' Special Agent Perez proposed in a friendly tone. His voice sounded like he wanted this temporary partnership to work. He was her boss, yet he wasn't coming across with authoritative tones, like earlier this morning. 'Stop! Just beneath your left foot.'

She froze, not knowing what she was about to stand on. Shining her flashlight at her feet she noticed a small piece of paper. Using some tweezers, she lifted it up, shaking it gently to see if there was anything written on it. It was crumpled, but she could just make out the marks, 'Gaining...another victory...over my....op...opponents,' she read out, bagging and sealing the evidence, 'This is one sadistic piece of shit. It looks like a corner of an invoice. I can just make out a few numbers.'

Dr Cameron appeared from the tent. Exhaustion evident in his eyes. He ripped off his gloves and removed his face mask. Standing up straight, he drew in a breath. He looked stunned, drawing in another deep breath and resting his hands on his hips. 'That's the worst case I've had to deal with. I need some air,' he said, looking at the two agents.

'We've found some physical evidence, hopefully we can connect them, begin to break down our suspect's defences. We'll send them to get forensically analysed at your office. There was another counter and note, so we're dealing with the same unknown subject. Can you give us any information about our victim?' Asked Perez.

'The subsequent blow to the back of her head caused her to have a seizure, concussion. She would have experienced blurred vision, been slow to respond, difficulty with her speech and total confusion. We found forward impact blood spatters on the jetty. Looking by the droplets, I guess it was a medium velocity attack, say with a blunt object. She was dragged to the inlet, as slight drag marks were found in the area. They tried to cover up their tracks,' Dr Cameron explained, tired and struggling to comprehend who would've done such a thing. 'Both wrists tied to the poles with blue rope, underside of the walkway, decomposition changes and proceeds slower in the water, primarily due to the cold temperatures. Now we've removed her body from the lake, putrefaction has accelerated. It hinders the accurate interpretation of postmortem. When we placed her on land, well, it was harrowing. We found multiple stab wounds penetrating the uterus area. Direct traumatic injuries seem to have been in my opinion, intended and premeditated. Looks to be a smooth edged and not serrated edged knife. Similar to that used at our first crime scene. Can't tell you about the length at this stage, but I'll be able to shortly. Her unborn, as small as it was, had no chance of survival,' he looked up into the sky and shook his head, 'I think you have your work cut out agents and I will do my damnedest to help!'

The pair stood in total silence. Dr Patrick Cameron showed passion and empathy for the first time, since this investigation began, back in Butler Forest. The thought of what this woman endured at the hands of the unsub, was incomprehensible. The three stood together, with a silent bond of determination that they would catch this Killer, now a potential serial killer.

'I will take her back to the morgue, my team will continue processing the scene, I will send them up to the residents after they have finished down here and I will contact you as soon as I find out more, you have my word,' said Patrick.

Parting ways, Clara and Perez walked up to the house. Thinking about everything that had happened in the last 48hrs, sent Clara into deep thought. 'You good Agent Strong? We need to try and talk to Mr Parker, hopefully he will be willing to speak with us, we will have to treat his house as a crime scene,' said Adam.

'Yeah, I'm just wondering what kind of person we're dealing with here. The two victims are poles apart, different genders, age, methodology of his killings are diverse,' she answered.

They entered the house, seeing William Parker sitting in his armchair beside the breakfast bar in the kitchen. Deputy Dubois positioned himself against a barstool. Eleanor's empty coffee mug still sitting upside down on the draining board. William Parker's clean clothes looked to give his weak body a sympathetic hug. Special Agent Perez coughed and asked if they could come in.

'Sure,' William said, looking down at his feet.

The two FBI agents stood leaning against the clean kitchen island. Deputy Jeremiah Dubois nodded in recognition and said nothing. Agent Perez started, 'Mr Parker we're extremely sorry for your loss, we are Special Agent Perez and Special Agent Strong from the FBI. We would really appreciate your cooperation in piecing together the events of this evening and understanding your wife's background, family, friends.'

'Okay, whatever you think,' said William, paying very little attention.

Adam Perez looked at Clara and flicked his head to the side. 'Is it okay if my partner takes a look around?' Perez asked William.

'What?' He looked up, his face pale and his eyes bloodshot.

'Is it okay if Special Agent Strong takes a look around. We will have to cordon off the house too, get the forensic team up here. We hope you understand?'

'It didn't happen in here, why aren't you out there looking for this sick bastard who…who.' Emotions overwhelmed him, he took his anger and frustrations out on the people in the room.

'We have to gather up as much information as we can, to get a better understanding of who had a grudge against your wife,' Agent Strong commented.

'Do what you want, you'll not find anything!' William shouted in annoyance. His face saddened by his wife's sudden death.

Clara left Agent Perez, William Parker and Deputy Dubois in the kitchen. She always hated this part of the job. She felt like she was treading harder on an already broken heart and crushing it into oblivion. Clara also knew that uxoricide was more common than not. It was something they could never rule out. She understood men who killed their partners, experienced both an unconscious dependence on their wife and a resentment of her. William, in Clara's eyes, didn't seem to be that kind of husband. She also knew people aren't always who you think they are.

Putting on latex gloves, she slid her hand up the wooden handrail, taking her upstairs to the bedrooms and washrooms. The first room she entered was a luxurious bedroom. Decorated in decoupage, floral pink and green wallpaper, with a bed that was bigger than her pokey little kitchen area back home. She always compared other people's homesteads to her own. Behind the headboard on the wall hung a beautiful hand painted picture of the couple. Their faces clearly radiating happiness with the fact they were getting their portraits painted. She remembered seeing a portrait in the Thomas's home, painted in the same style. Lifting the sheets off the bed and piles of freshly ironed clothes from a chair that were neatly folded, she found nothing. The en-suite was as tidy and clean as the rest of the house. Bleach smells hit her sinuses, kick starting her throbbing head symptoms she had been experiencing since that morning. Finding nothing of significance upstairs, apart from the cleanliness, she headed to the rooms on the ground floor. There was a door to her right, next to the bottom of the stairs, a room you would have missed if you weren't snooping around. She put the light on, realising it was a home office. Files lined the shelves, books on mathematics dominating the walls. Only a handful of art books were noticeable, and baby books sat next to decorating nursery room magazines. The wallpaper was very masculine in style, feeling separate from the rest of the house.

Clara rubbed her hand softly over the top of the desk, lifting unmarked maths papers and yellow sticker reminders for the week. A striped blue and white A4 jotter sat centre of the desk, which Clara flicked through, slowly. Her eyes caught sight of something, she turned the pages back. Her heart pounded; she couldn't believe what she was seeing. There in the corner of a page, was a gap which had been ripped out. The shape was identical to the piece of paper found in Evan Thomas's pocket. Lifting the jotter and finishing off her search, she headed back to the kitchen.

Agent Perez was being sympathetic to William, who was an emotional wreck. The Deputy Sheriff was making coffee for the victim's husband. Knowing what she did, Clara walked around the kitchen area, entering a small room which was connected. She saw cooking utensils and electrical goods on the counter. Her suspicions came to light. Sitting on the left work top was a block of kitchen knives. 5 strikingly expensive looking knives, one was missing.

Chapter Ten

The room was quite cool, lighting turned up to the max. Agent Perez sat one side of the table, sieving through notes and photographs, which Clara blue toothed to the photocopier and printed off from her cell. William Parker sat opposite, shaking. His body wouldn't settle, he was in a state of shock. His good looks diminished and in their place sat a pale colourless face, a dishevelled man who looked old, lost and confused.

'Mr Parker, you aren't under arrest. You willingly agreed to come down to the Sheriff's department to answer some questions and give us a formal statement,' Agent Perez commenced. 'Can you explain to us how the piece of paper found at our first victim's body, matches that, of your personal jotter found in your home?' Perez moved the evidence bag, towards William.

'I don't know what you are talking about. What first victim? Are you telling me my wife isn't the first? Can someone explain to me what the hell is going on? I thought I was down here to talk you through things and sign my statement.' He glanced down at the table, 'That's Eleanor's jotter, she bought that a while back, to write down ideas on how she wanted to decorate the nursery,' his body slumped over as he sat on the chair. Hands grasped together, his face looked towards the brown worn out carpet, he shook his head in disbelief. The man was crumbling before the agent's eyes.

'Could you tell us then William, about the missing knife in the kitchen? Do you have any recollection of what happened to it?' Continued Perez. His interview tactics came across with very soft tones, friendlier than Clara would have been. 'We just need to get to the bottom of all this William. We can't afford anyone else to fall foul of this person's actions. Do you know anything William that will help us? Did you and Eleanor argue, and things just got out of control?'

'No! No! Stop saying those things. I love my wife, I have always loved my wife, she is my world, my life. Why are you asking me all this? I don't know anything about a knife. I never use them; Eleanor does all the cooking! She knows I can't cook,' William Parker started to cry, his tears falling hard, stopping for no one. Perez handed him tissues from the box.

'We know you had an argument, Deputy Dubois informs us you had a difference of opinion with your wife, before you left this evening to lecture. Is that correct?' Asked Agent Perez.

'We…we never argue. Recently she has been up and down with her moods and I….I just became tired of not being able to do the right thing by her. I was exhausted, I shouldn't have taken it out on her and now…….' William still had plenty of tears to shed and Perez, being a behavioural analyst, knew he should stop and that the man who sat in front of him, wasn't their guy.

'Okay William, sit still for a couple of minutes, I will be back.'

Perez left the room, asking an officer to stand in with him until he returned. Clara was waiting outside in anticipation. 'Well did he confess?'

'It's not him. I've conducted enough interviews in my time to know when I am being lied to. And I believe that man in there, is telling the truth. He talks about his wife as though she's still alive. The guilty normally talk about the victim in a past tense from the get-go. We'll keep an eye on him, but for now we have no strong forensic evidence to arrest him. It's all circumstantial. Okay the paper is a match; we have no fingerprints connecting him though, to say he was responsible. The jotter is newly bought so they haven't been using it for us to get any sort of trace. As for the missing knife, anyone could have taken it from their premises, plus it hasn't been located. We will get the sheriff to rota out a wellness check on him, keep him close to the case.'

Frustrated with the result, Clara headed back into their small office, where they were trying to fit the pieces of the puzzle together. Picking up a non-permanent black pen, she started scribbling down the few leads they had. Agent Perez walked in, throwing the file of evidence they had accumulated so far, down on the desk.

'Look it's 2.30am, we both need to get some sleep, first thing tomorrow with fresh eyes and head, we can examine the case so far,' suggested Special Agent in Charge Adam Perez.

'Sounds like a really good plan,' Agent Strong retorted.

***

Sleep for Clara last night, was a nightmare. She tossed and turned, seeing her brother's body lying face down in the lake near their home in Lisman, just 7 miles from Butler town. Blood swirled around his lifeless body, and she couldn't get to him quick enough. He floated away peacefully into the centre of Lake Rainer, slowly disappearing into the deep waters with his frail limbs sinking a bit at a time. His face tipped up at an angle and his eyes opened, as his body descended to the bottom. Clara must have been awake more than she slept. Bags under her eyes were noticeable, she lowered her head as she met Agent Perez in the foyer of the motel the next morning.

'Change of plan, Zachariah Jackson rang me first thing this morning telling me Benjamin Johnson arrived back early and headed straight home. I think we should pay him a visit, don't you?' Said Adam Perez in a determined voice.

'Is he local?' She asked, trying to suppress a yawn. She didn't want her boss to get the wrong impression, thinking she was hitting the bottle again.

'He lives at Martin Avenue, about 7 miles from here. It's in the next smaller town of Lisman, Do you know it?'

This couldn't be happening, first the nightmares and now the realisation of seeing it in the flesh. She hadn't been back to her hometown since she left all those years ago. Martin Avenue was located right next to Rainer Lake. Her home was along the road opposite, Edwards Avenue. George's home sat right next door to her mamas. Trees would have lost most of their leaves, knowing the lake would be visible from Johnson's location.

'Agent Strong! Are you with me this morning? We need to tread carefully with him. We can't spook him. He is just a person of interest at this point, we have no real evidence to connect him, apart from the hunting traps, but we need to hear his side of the story why they ended up at a crime scene. We'll have to be careful too, he could be armed and not appreciate company.'

Her head nodded in agreement, as she opened her window to get the fresh cold air of the Fall. If she ever needed a drink, it was now. Her thoughts jumped to her mother, *what if she was sitting outside on the porch, watching people passing? How would I cope if I saw her? God, I feel like I'm going to vomit.* She felt the space in the SUV close in around her. She took in an enormous amount of fresh air and held her breath for 5 seconds, then exhaled, slowly and quietly.

'I'm a good listener you know. It's part of our training at the BAU. I can see being back here is having a negative impact on you. I was very harsh yesterday morning, but I thought you needed a little rebuke, just to get you back on track and to get you away from where your head is all the time,' Adam Perez said, out of the blue.

'What? I'm fine! I don't want to talk about it, I can't, I never have….. I don't want to sound rude Sir, but I have problems processing it in my own head. It's….I just can't. I'm sorry.'

'I joined the FBI when I was just 23 years old. My family background was so emotionally dysfunctional that I had to get away. My mother's idea of parenting was that of a disciplinarian who took to the bottle. My father got fed up, deciding to leave us when we needed him the most. It's only this last four years that my father and I have reconnected. I have a sister that doesn't communicate with anyone and a brother in Leavenworth Disciplinary maximum-security prison in Kansas. He joined the military to start a new life, but trouble followed him into adulthood, he just took the wrong path. Me, I stuck my fingers up to all of them and joined the bureau.'

Clara stared at her boss; he kept his eyes on the road as he drove. She didn't know how to respond. 'I thought when I first saw you, that… that you came from money, had a good life. I really had no idea, I'm so sorry.'

'No need to apologise. I've done alright for myself, thanks to pure determination that I wouldn't follow in my mother's footsteps and hit the bottle at every opportune moment. I think most of the bureau guys have some sort of history, which made them join up. Not lecturing you by the way,' Adam Perez said softly.

'I appreciate your honesty. I'm just not ready to off load, but if I am, I know where to find you. Thanks Agent Perez,' said Clara.

'We're nearly there; can you direct me from here?'.

'Sure, it's a through road, then avenues veer off from it. Martin Avenue is the first dirt road as you enter Lisman town on your left.'

They drove into Lisman, crossing over a bridge with Bogue Chitto River below them. Largemouth bass, crappie, bluegill and catfish swimming desperately to escape the hungry mouths of the Ringed-saw turtles. Clara remembered the fishing days she had in Rainer Lake, which sat northeast of this river. Her heart rose up, then inevitably sank. She remembered Grayson's last words to her before they fell asleep, "Love you sissy, we caught some goodens today." She had to smile at that memory, his little face was a delightful sight as he drifted off to sleep at the water's edge. Clara's stomach knotted as the lake was in full sight to the left of her. The body of water was surrounded by trees, some losing their leaves to the Fall, green turning orange, turning red. Floating quietly one by one to the ground. She was mesmerised by the lake's beauty, the colour of the surface changing with the skies above. But she knew it was also ugly; it consumed people and never brought them back.

Agent Perez drove down the dirt track, arriving at Benjamin Johnson's home. They noticed a white pick up parked out front. The yard was scattered with trash. Two old trucks abandoned and left to rust, filling the space. Empty fuel barrels stacked up precariously against a wooden outbuilding. A dog was heard barking to the rear of the property. The shabby house was rundown, with shutters hanging on just a few hinges. The two Agents parked up and proceeded towards the front porch. The rails to the side were full of rot in the section buried in the ground. The whole place was a walking hazard.

'We only want to speak to him, understand his moves over the last three or four days,' whispered Agent Perez to Clara. She nodded her head, standing to the side of her colleague as he knocked on the door, hoping it wouldn't collapse with his efforts. A minute later the door opened, a woman in her thirties stood eyeballing them, cigarette hanging from her mouth. Still in her pyjamas, and not looking pleased she had been disturbed.

'Hello ma'am, I'm Special Agent Perez, and this is my colleague Special Agent Strong. We were hoping to catch a word with Benjamin Johnson. Is he here?'

'Na, he ain't home from work. You'll have to come back later,' she said, trying to shut the door, but Perez planted his foot in the doorway quicker.

'We were told he had already returned home, by his boss Mr Jackson, so would you mind fetching him so we can have a chat, then we will be out of your way.'

Her eyebrows lowered, the margins of her scabbed lips rolled in and tightened. She was seething the feds had called her out. Clara noticed that the dog out the back stopped barking and a creaking noise of an old door echoed round the side of the house. 'He's making a run for it!' Clara shouted.

The two agents, hands poised on their glocks, hightailed it down the porch steps and round the side of the house. They drew their weapons, Perez signalling to Strong to go right, while he headed left. They were both quick on their feet. Clara could hear someone in the distance, running and gasping to catch their breath. He was headed for the forest at the back of his yard, twigs snapping and birds fleeing from the noisy intruder. *Shit! He's heading for the lake, damn you Johnson!* Her own body dodging obstacles as she carried on chasing him. 'Johnson! Stop! It's the FBI!' She noticed her health and speed were deteriorating, she blamed Jack Daniels. Determined to catch her perpetrator to keep her job, she pushed deep, shortening the distance between them. The trees started thinning out and the view opened up to Rainer Lake. *Perp Clara, where's the fucking perp? This isn't the time, concentrate!*

The snapping of branches reverberated to the left of her. 'Stop! FBI!' The smell of the water, the trees, grabbed her senses, pulling at her heartstrings, tying them in knots. Controlling her emotions she hurdled over branches that had fallen prey to previous storms. She could hear the sound of the light winds, whispering through the trees as though they were calling out to her. Her thoughts lightened and she listened unintentionally as theirs whispering songs started to sooth her sentiments. She didn't want to be here, yet somehow, she felt some sense of peace and calmness. It didn't feel right, where was the guilt, the unjustly cruel stabbing sensations, which had attacked her all of her life. If only circumstances were different right now, she could take a moment and not be chasing a potential suspect on Lake Rainer, but she was and she had to get her head back in the job.

She heard someone yell and noises of foliage being thrown together, breaking in the process. Her head pounding, legs aching, she looked passed a thicket of dense bushes near the water's edge. To her surprise she saw her runner lying on the ground holding his ankle in pain. Running over to him, she looked down, recognising his lanky stature. Getting her cellphone out, she rang Perez.

'Why the hell did you run for Johnson? We just wanted to talk. Do you have any weapons on you?'

Johnson shook his head. Grabbing under his left arm, she pulled him to his feet, he wailed in agony. 'Shut up, you're not dead are you!' She escorted him back through the forest, turning her head to see the lake, just as it was disappearing from view. *I will be back Grayson.*

Sitting Benjamin Johnson down on one of his wooden benches around the kitchen table, they asked his wife to get some ice for his injury. The obnoxious guy who they encountered yesterday at Jackson's lumberyard, wined like a schoolboy who had fallen in the school yard. 'Why did you run Benjamin?' Asked Perez.

103

'Run? I wasn't running! I had an errand to do, and this bitch chased me down. I know my rights, I'm gonna 'av your badge!' He groaned.

'We know that's not the truth, so we'll ask you again. Why were you running?' Clara said, with her heartbeat trying to get back to a normal rate.

'Fuck you bitch! You've cost me a week's worth of work. Can't be driving now, and you'll pay!' Benjamin spat saliva as he moaned and complained in Clara's face.

'So, you won't mind if we take a look around then?'

'You can't do that; you don't have a search warrant. You can get off my property. I know my rights under the fourth amendment, so get off my land.'

'Then I'm afraid we will have to arrest you with murder. Stand up, put your hands behind your back.' Special Agent Perez looked straight at him, to let him know he was being deadly serious.

'Murder? Are you crazy, I haven't murdered anyone! What y'all talking about? Look, wait, I was running coz I had a stash of…of pot stored in my shed out back. You gotta believe me!' His eyes were full of fear at the mention of murder, his big attitude shrunk in front of the agents.

The noise of his wife Sarah, slapping down a bag of weed on the table, made their heads turn. 'There, now you can get out of my house, or I'll call the cops and say us poor defenceless folk are being mistreated.'

Adam Perez ignored Johnson's wife and started to read Benjamin his Miranda rights.

'Stop, wait I'll show you around. Just let me get up on my feet.' The desperation in his voice informed the agents their actions had got the better of him.

'We've information, you bought hunting traps from Butler Specialised Parts & Parts. We need to see them,' said Clara.
'They're out in the shed. Sarah shut that dog up!' His voice back to being authoritarian towards his wife, letting the feds know he was still in charge of his crib. He lifted a key from the sideboard and limped outside, like a wounded puppy. The rotten shed was held together by planks nailed in all directions to add stability. Benjamin Johnson's hand shook placing the key in the lock, opening it up he told them where they could find the traps. 'I have a hunting licence and all.'
Under the shelf where the hunting traps should have been, an empty container sat. His voice echoed pure fear as he tried to explain they should be there. Adam Perez nodded to Clara. She reached for her handcuffs in her back pocket.
'Benjamin Johnson, I am arresting you. You have the right to remain silent. Anything you say can and will be used against you in a court of law....' He fought against her, trying to push her down. 'You have the right to an attorney. If you cannot afford an attorney, one will be appointed for you. Do you understand Benjamin?' Handcuffed and shouting expletives at the agents, they put him in the back of their SUV. They were confident they had reasonable grounds to arrest this man.
'We need to get a court order issued, so we can search his premises,' explained Perez. Clara phoned Sheriff Harris to see if he could get a search warrant for Martin Avenue, Lisman. 'We're going to find something; I have a strange feeling he's hiding something else in that god forsaken place,' he said.

Chapter Eleven

Kicking his feet under the table in the interrogation room, Benjamin Johnson was also foaming at the mouth. His rage was heard down the corridors of the Courthouse. His wrists breaking out in sores as he was shaking them furiously, they were handcuffed to the desk, and he was being persistent trying to escape from them. The two agents sat opposite him not saying a word. They stared at him with a nonchalant expression, sitting back in their chairs, looking at their watches. The exhaustion was starting to wash over Benjamin's face. Perez told him he was entitled to have an attorney present, but he wasn't allowing anyone to tell him what to do and say. 'I don't need some hotshot to tell me what to be at, I'm innocent and you can both go to hell. God will punish you both, you pieces of trash!'
'Okay, Mr Johnson, as you are aware we have evidence to connect you to the death of Mr Evan Thomas. We need to know your whereabouts on the evening of the 12th of October, between 22hrs and the early hours 01.00 hrs of the 13th of October?' Began Agent Strong.
'You don't have anything on me, y'all think I'm crazy?' Benjamin responded in a sarcastic tone.
'Mr Johnson, please just answer the question,' continued Clara.
'Why don't you do your detective work and find out for yourselves! Useless idiots. You think you are something!'
'Mr Johnson, I don't think you understand why you're here. Do you understand the extremity of your arrest today? This isn't some kind of crime you get a slap on the wrist and return home. We are talking about murder, taking someone's life.'
They had nothing to connect him to Eleanor Parker's death, but they were hoping to break him down so he would confess to both. A knock on the door interrupted the interview. Deputy

Dubois stood at the entrance. 'Can I have a quick word Agent Strong?'

Clara exited the room. 'What's the problem Deputy?'

'We found something up at old Johnson's home. We know he is a skilled hunter, we found snares, guns, camouflage clothing, night goggles and get this, hunting knives, all with straight edges, sharp enough to skin a deer in one fine swoop. God damn, its all below in his basement. He also lied to you; he doesn't have a licence,' he finished his sentence and gave a wide grin. 'Think we've got the son of a bitch agent!'

'Send the knives to Dr Cameron, ask him if he can match any of them to either crime scenes. Tell him we are holding a suspect, but we need more solid evidence to detain him for longer or to charge him with murder. Thanks Jeremiah.' Clara knew exactly who Deputy Dubois was, as soon as she met him last night at Eleanor Parker's house.

Returning to the interrogation room, she lent over to Perez to convey the message. He didn't react. 'So, Mr Johnson, can you confirm to us your whereabouts?'

'I was at home, smoking my tobacco and drinking my beer, Sarah can tell you. I was in. So, can I go now?' When he gave them his alibi, he thought he was off the hook. 'Can one of you transport me home, my ankle is swollen like a brown bears backside.' He rattled the handcuffs for the Agents to unlock them.

'Mr Johnson, you won't be going home today or for the next 48 hours. You just sit tight, we'll get an officer to make you comfortable in one of the cells,' Agent Strong announced.

'You son of a bitch! You can't keep me here; I know my rights. You'll be sorry. God owes his mercy to positively no one, you hear?' His voice sounding weaker as the two agents made there way back to the make-shift office.

Pouring two cups of coffee from the machine, Clara handed Adam his and sat down. 'Do you think he is capable of two murders? He doesn't seem to have the mental capacity to be a killer or was that just all show?'

'We need to build a better profile for our unsub. Let's start from the beginning. Evan Thomas, aged 39yrs old, successful businessman, liked his booze and women. Eleanor Parker, 32yrs old, Elementary school teacher, married, recently found out she was pregnant. Both lived in substantial size houses, so they weren't short of a few dollars.' Perez spoke as Clara stood back up, detailing evidence onto the whiteboard. Two counters found. Red 4 and a Yellow 1. What the hell is he playing? Why are two different people, with completely different lives, targeted? Is it just random people or has he a connection to them. Ask Hannah on the desk to run background checks on both our victims. There has to be a connection.'

'Hannah? Don't you think she'll be out of her depth with such a task?' Asked Clara.

'We all have to start somewhere. Ask another officer to help. We need everyone working on this case before he kills again. The arrow pointing south eastwards, we need to contact all residents who fall along that line of sight.'

Clara dotted the line as straight as her eyes would allow her to on the map pinned to the wall. She opened the map app on her cell and zoomed in on the location. 'There's a cluster of houses in this area, a few shops, a garage or car dealership in Butler, then after that it goes into woodland.'

'We'll see if Sheriff Harris can make a start on informing those residents. Tell them to be vigilant, not to venture off on their own. He won't want to scare them, but at this stage we have no choice.' Clara could hear the urgency in her boss's voice. 'What's the significance of the notes? Is he playing with us and wants us to catch him? The counters are the things that are puzzling me the most. What do the numbers signify?' He looked up on the board, his mind full of concentration, trying to connect any dots. 'Fuck! Think Adam. We know what the first note means, but only just begun, how many more kills? Was the 4 on the counter his 4th victim? Why was the second body we found, counter 1? Is he going to kill two more people, 2 and 3?' He took a sharp breath in; Clara could hear the clogs turning in his head. He was a profiler expert after all.

'What are you thinking boss?'

'The second note said…what was it? Gaining another victory over my opponents! It's one big game to him. He's killing people that have done him wrong. We don't know if that's recent or a while back. The killings are personal as he is attacking different bodily parts. What did Eleanor and Evan do to our unsub, that his only revenge was to kill? We need to dig deep with the two victim's background checks. Did they have crossed words with the same person? Is there anyone along this southeast line that has also had a run in with the same person?' He hit the map with the side of his fist. 'It's a long shot, but we need to get out there and make inquiries.'

'I'll go see Sheriff Harris and Hannah,' Clara left the room with some urgency. Adam nodded, still staring at the whiteboard. She knocked on Harris's door and entered. 'Sheriff Harris, we need to talk to the residents that live or work in these buildings.' She retrieved her phone and swiped the map down in the southeasterly direction. Sheriff Harris put his glasses on and looked over her shoulder at the cell. 'We believe one of these residents will be his next victim. We need all the help we can get. Sally Lane, Evans Drive, Maureen Lane and around this area. Here in Butler there's a cafe, gas station on South Hamburg Avenue and look, the courthouse runs in line too. Shit! There's a clothing store, then a garage or car dealership. Could you organise your troops to do door-to-door, tell them to be careful. Inform the locals not to go anywhere alone. Keep their eyes open for possible danger. We need Hannah to gather up as much information on the two victims. Did they have grief with the same person over anything, even if it sounds insignificant. We don't know who we are dealing with. We are unsure of his thoughts and behaviours.'

'Shit Agent Strong, we'll have a full-scale panic on our hands if we say that to the residents,' he said, with a sense of foreboding. 'My team is small; we will have to split them up, otherwise it will take forever to cover those areas.'

'If we don't, we will have another death on our hands!' Clara told him straight.

Harris went into the room where three of his officers were sitting at their desks working away. 'Carter, fetch Hannah from reception.' The officer did as he was asked. He went into the reception area, noticing she was standing next to Eli Davis, one of the painters, laughing and getting friendly.

'Hannah! The boss needs you in, now!' Carter shouted. Jealousy spilling over his face.

When she entered the room, Sheriff Harris relayed all the relevant information to his team. 'We won't be going home folks until we have informed everyone on the list. Let's try and keep safe please. Hannah, we need you on another job. You'll have to step up and do some real detective work, do you think you can handle that?'

Hannah looked nervous. She nodded to Harris and Agent Strong, following her over to an empty desk. Clara showed her the quick process to obtain information, relating to background checks. Her fingers clicked away on the keys and Clara left her to it.

Returning back to Perez, her phone rang. She looked at the caller ID. It was her boss from Durant, Assistant Director Miller. She was reluctant to answer. They had two people dead and no real leads. *Fuck!* 'Special Agent Strong speaking.'

'Agent Strong, what's the latest? How's the investigation going? Have you found the perp?' Miller rhymed off, not taking a breath.

Why does he have to phone me? Where's Thompson? Thompson was Clara's SAIC at Durant. She answered straight to him, but she had the impression Miller was putting pressure on her from a higher level. 'We are following leads and have someone detained as we speak. We are gathering up evidence. The Sheriff's office isn't exactly swamped with police officers, so things in that department are pretty much stretched.'

'Special Agent Strong, before I forget....' There was a pause. 'The young teenager you managed to find, Emily, well she wants to talk to you. Something about, saying thanks. Her and the family want to thank you in person, but I don't....'

'Sir, sir I have to go, Agent Perez is shouting for me. I will keep you posted,' her thumb switched her cellphone off, cutting the conversation short. She walked back to Perez. It was just a small, white lie. If there was ever a time she needed a drink again, it was now. Looking down at her hands she noticed they were shaking. Her pulse began to race, her stomach twisted in a knot. She knew her body was experiencing withdrawal symptoms and she had to push through it, her job was on the line.

'Have the officer's been dispatched?' Perez asked.

'Yep, and Hannah is covering the background checks,' Clara replied, as calmly as her body would allow.

Perez's phone rang, he put it on speaker. It was Dr Cameron. 'I have some information on those counters. They are handcrafted from Longleaf Pine, characteristics of which are hard, dense and possess an excellent strength-to-weight ratio. A lot of people use longleaf pine in a treated board and post form for decks, fences or as dimension lumber for building construction. The paint within the two counters is acrylic, non- toxic, washable and baby safe. Great choice for children's toys. The colours have a protective sealer on the surface, we've narrowed it down to a transparent acrylic spray. They've been done with precision. Our man is meticulous to detail, he has precise fine motor skills for sure. Also, nothing was found in the Parker's home. Clean as a whistle.'

'Thank you, Dr Cameron, we really appreciate the call. We'll be in touch.' Perez faced Clara, 'I think we need to visit Jackson's lumberyard again and take a better look this time!'

Clara wanted to drive. She had to keep busy and take her mind off the amber liquid that always consumed her life. The weather had deteriorated, with the air fresh and a cool breeze. The lightly falling rain looked misty and vaguely covered the windscreen as Clara drove. Trucks pelted by, giving up little space for other users. Reaching their destination, the agents entered the building, stopping at the children's wooden toys. 'We need to bring one of these back to Patrick Cameron so he can take fragments and compare to the counters,' Clara suggested.

'Can I help you folks? You interested in buying one of our toys? Is it for your child?' Said a small smiley woman.

'No, sorry, we aren't together and……we are FBI. These toys which have been crafted. Can you give us a list of the people who have made them? That includes the painting process too. Thanks,' said Strong.

'Is there something wrong with the toys?' The woman inquired, with an expression of confusion. 'You know, all our workers details are confidential, and I can't just hand them out to strangers!'

'This is a double murder investigation. We can come back with a search warrant and cause disruption, which I know Mr Jackson wouldn't be so happy about. We also need to take this toy truck, we will happily sign for it, but we can't promise it will be untouched,' explained Perez. 'You wouldn't happen to know what wood is used to carve out these toys?' Lifting the little truck up, he inspected it closer. Red, yellow and blue vibrant colours shone under the lights above. Heading inside, the woman nonchalantly answered with, Longleaf Pine. Printing off the list and handing it over, she gave them a look of contempt, then sat back down behind her desk.

Adam and Clara put the toy truck in the back seat of their vehicle and jumped in. Scrolling down the list, Clara caught sight of Benjamin Johnsons name. 'Our Mr Johnson seems to be in the forefront of our investigation. His name just keeps appearing at every turn.'

'Do the makers also decorate their handy work?' Asked Perez.

Tapping her fingers on the list, she stopped. 'Nope! Looks like we have ourselves a local artist here in Butler who has that pleasure.' Agent Perez started the engine and Clara navigated. 'His name is Joseph Martin, he lives on Desoto Rd. Go to the centre of town, take a right onto North Mulberry Avenue, then it's a slip road off to the right.'

'It's amazing you still remember the area like it was yesterday,' said Perez with a full smile on his face. Clara's face wasn't so bright. Her thoughts returned to Rainer Lake and how her whole body had experienced a sense of calmness. Her battle with the bottle was due to the constant flashbacks of that day, which sent her head spiralling into despair. Were the memories overpowering her mind? Why was she constantly blaming herself, worsening the pain. She had tried therapy sessions in her late teens, they just made matters worse. Bringing the subject to the surface gave her nightmares and she went through a period of night sweats. *Seeing the lake again, might, might help me.*

Chapter Twelve

The house stood tall and elegant. It was very unique, turn of the century French design with balconies overlooking the moderate size grounds. Trees highlighted the path leading up to the front porch. Joseph definitely had an artistic eye for design. His home looked out of place. Distinguished in its architecture, compared to the other houses on Desoto Road. They were wooden, worn out and dated. The curving brick walls either side of the steps had been newly constructed with the contrasting block's appearance noticeable. 'He must be a very successful artist, owning this type of property,' commented Clara, thinking about her little apartment back in Durant. *God, I miss my own comforts and Frank!* Clara and Adam hoped he answered quickly so they could get out of the drizzling rain. Perez knocked hard on the door. A very tall, well-dressed man answered promptly. He was middle aged, but his personal grooming regime made him look younger. 'Can I help you?'

'Yes, we were wondering if we could speak to Mr Joseph Martin. We're from the FBI. We were hoping to gather up some information from him, which could be relevant to our investigation,' said Agent Perez, in a soothingly calming voice.

'I am he! What investigation?' The man replied, accentuating his syllables.

'We are looking into the murder of two local people. We were wondering if we could come in for a few minutes?' Continued Perez.

'I've nothing to do with any murders, I can assure you. Please, leave me be, I have paintings to finish, so if you don't mind!' Joseph Martin shrugged his shoulders in a dismissive manner.

'Well, actually we would love to see your work. People speak highly of your talents and said nobody else comes close to what you can accomplish,' Clara responded, thinking quickly on her feet. She guessed this man enjoyed the highlife, the praise, the compliments and recognition. She was right. He hesitated for a moment, then nodded.

'You can come in for a moment, but then I must insist you leave me to my work.' He stood tall, proud and produced a small grin. Adam glanced over to Clara. His expression was priceless. The home had gleaming hardwood floor throughout, with classic tiles covering the bottom half of the hallway walls. There was an exquisite dining room to the right and a beautiful well organised kitchen to the rear of the house. The floorboard's creaked as they walked through the kitchen doors. Clara noticed most of his furniture was bespoke, hand made with a lot of care. The bowls in his glass cabinets looked to be hand painted in a floral design. Everywhere you looked, the items told a story of how they were made.

'You have a beautiful home Mr Martin. Do you design and make all this yourself?' Clara questioned. Trying to boost his ego once more.

'I design the items, then I employ men from Oak to Interiors to build them. It works well. They are so skilled at Jackson's lumberyard, quite handsome too,' he giggled under his breath.

'We were impressed with the wooden statues in their foyer, especially the eagle sitting on a tree stump,' Clara had this, she continued. 'The craftsmanship is outstanding. We noticed the children's toys too. We heard Mr Jackson donates to children's charities in the local area.' Her eyes caught his and she was praying he wouldn't catch on she was being nice for a reason, to get some answers, real important answers. 'The lovely secretary informed us that you were the artist who decorated the pieces. Your talents are endless Mr Martin. May we have a look at some of your work?'

His dark brown eyes bore into Clara. He held his stare longer than she wanted. She could see he was considering her request. 'If I do then, I would appreciate it if you kept your hands to yourselves and touch nothing.' He left the kitchen, taking the pair up the stairs to the second floor. Paintings adorned his walls, their vibrant colours grabbing both the agent's attention. Clara noticed they were all paintings of people. No landscapes or abstracts, just portraits of people of all ages. Some were smiling, some had tears, others had expressionless looks upon their faces. 'What medium do you use Mr Martin? On your portraits?' Inquired Clara, before they entered into his workspace.

'Acrylics, always acrylics. Watercolours are too muted and dull. Acrylics enhance people's features. It gives them more depth as though you are looking into their souls. Take this chap for instance. He's, or should I say was, a dear friend of mine. I wanted to paint him for years, but he kept refusing. Then he became ill, so I took a photograph of him, he was still fit and healthy enough and transferred that onto canvass. Unfortunately, he didn't live to see the end result. Look at his face, beautiful man. His eyes just light up every time I pass him. He hangs right here, next to my studio.'

The two agents were listening carefully to him. Suspicions raised. He entered his studio. The ambience was bright and airy, the room itself filled with painting easels, paint brushes, palettes, stainless steel palette knives, stacked paper up on a desk to the rear, and flash head lighting in front of a chair at an angle, illuminating one section of the area. Huge reflectors stood behind, ready to bounce off the light and find the subject. It was impressive. There was a blue screen behind the stack of paper.

'What's behind there?' Agent Perez queried.

'Just portraits I've finished and need collecting by their owners. You see, after my dear beloved friend passed away, I thought it would be better for me to carry on taking photographs of my clients and paint my subjects from that. I like to take my time you see. I can't be rushed and some of these people have no patience. I give them a call when their portrait is completed. I insist on my services to find the correct place to hang the painting in their house. Can't have a masterpiece stuck in the spare bedroom for no one to see it. By the way I haven't got any toys in here from the lumberyard, they only send them over when needs be.'

As Joseph Martin was explaining his working life, Perez noticed a small desk with a new pack of tubes, which where acrylic paints. The cellophane was ripped slightly, they sat neatly in a container. There was two of each colour. They were composed in a proper sequence, starting with blacks, then all through the colour spectrum, reaching the pinks and whites at the end. His heart skipped a beat. Along the line of colour, he noticed a gap amongst the reds, the yellows, purples and greens. Four tubes were missing or misplaced. Was he over thinking? Was it a coincidence the two colours they were investigating weren't there. And two other colours gone. Making four. Perez's head was spinning. 'I notice you use the best acrylics. You seem to have misplaced some,' he said.

'What? I can't have. They were all there before I went away to…' he stopped. He didn't want to say anything else. 'I would like to get on now, if you don't mind. I have work to do,' his persona sat uneasily with his guests.

He hurriedly walked over to the door; the two agents followed. Clara quickly reached for her phone, snapping a photo of the container full of paints. 'Sorry, I was just admiring your set up here. Thank you for your time, Mr Martin. Maybe you will allow us back again so we can ask those questions?'

Back in their vehicle, heading to Dr Cameron's office, the two agents sat quietly thinking about the case and the suspects that have cropped up. Clara looked at Adam, who was driving, 'Do you feel like everyone we have spoken to, has some kind of connection to the two murders?'

'Yeah, William's missing knife, piece of paper, Benjamin with the traps, stolen chains and hunting knives in his basement. Joseph connected to the lumberyard and his colourful paints. You could almost think they're in it together or are keeping some big secret,' answered Perez. 'We'll drop this toy truck off to get tested, see if Patrick Cameron has anything new to report.'

Entering the morgue, Perez reminded Clara to mask up. Dr Cameron looked up from his work. 'I'm glad you're here! I have some information on the size of the knife used for Eleanor Parker's wounds. The thing is you have to remember, the wound from a stabbing motion is deeper than the knife is long. The straight line extending from the tip of the blade to the forward-most aspect of the handle is approximately eight inches. The wounds extend slightly beyond, but not reaching nine inches. I've manipulated the wounds, approximating its edges to define potential blade width. We have one and a half inches. It sounds like a standard kitchen knife. The set of hunting knives retrieved from your suspect living in Lisman, are too large. No fingerprints on the paper or counter found on the jetty I'm afraid, but the first piece of paper fits perfectly to the jotter found at the Parker's home,' he continued working as he spoke, not looking up to acknowledge them. The agents appreciated the extent of his workload. 'It was from a new jotter so that particular part wasn't handled by anyone. Oh, and I nearly forgot, Mr Parker's home so far is clean. Not a shred of disturbance indicated.'

Clara glanced at Adam. Her head shook in disbelief. 'We brought a wooden Longleaf pine truck decorated in acrylics,' she said, trying to move the case on and get answers.

'Leave it over there,' pointing to the metal table, pushed against the wall. 'I will let you know agents.'

Clara's phone buzzed in her pocket. It was Hannah. 'Hi, what's up?'

'Special Agent Strong, surveillance from the bar has brought up something you may find helpful. Sheriff Harris told me to contact you right away!' Hannah's voice was shaky, nerves still engulfing her confidence.

'Okay Hannah, what is it?'

'Eleanor Parker was seen leaving Evan Thomas's bar with friends, twenty minutes before he did. The same night he died.'

'That's brilliant Hannah. How's your background checks going?'

'I'm still on it, I'll call you as soon as I find something,' Hannah blurted out.

Clara turned to Adam, 'We need to bring William Parker back in for a chat!'

***

Bringing William back into the interrogation room so soon after taking him home, didn't sit well with the agents. The man was trying to grieve. But now they had to question his marriage. He sat opposite them. His tired dark eyes, stared straight through Perez. His attorney sitting by his side. William had no fight in him, he didn't want to incriminate himself. If he said something that didn't sit right with the feds, he knew they would take it out of context and use it against him. The agents were hoping William wouldn't remain silent. They needed to start getting answers. The case was not moving forward quick enough, and they knew there would be other potential victims. 'Mr Parker, thank you for coming in. We appreciate you are still grieving. We need to ask you a few questions to clear up matters. How was your marriage with Eleanor?' Perez began.

William looked at his attorney, who shook his head, 'No comment.'

'We know that the two of you had an argument yesterday evening. Did it get out of hand William? Was it an accident and you panicked?' Agent Perez continued.

'No comment.'

'We have forensics combing through your house as we speak. The bathroom upstairs has a strong smell of bleach. Is that where it happened? Did you find out that your wife was seeing someone else and flipped? She frequented Evan Thomas's bar on more than one occasion, didn't she Mr Parker?'

'What? Who's he? No, she didn't. She didn't drink, she was pregnant. She wouldn't have gone to the bar!' William shouted. The attorney, sitting stern faced beside him, advised him not to say anything.

'Evan Thomas was found in the forest, note in his pocket, written from your jotter. Mr Parker, you wrote that note, didn't you? You got angry with him, big businessman taking what he wants. Then you got angry with your wife. She cheated on you, and you found out!' The questions firing at William, confused him.

'No! We were in love. We loved being with each other.'

'But we have surveillance footage of her leaving Alabama South Avenue Bar & Grill on the evening of the 12th of October. Where were you Mr Parker, between 22hrs and 0100hrs? Mr Parker, answer the question please!' Agent Perez insisted.

'Do you have any real evidence connecting my client to either of the crimes? Or is it all circumstantial? No? Then we are done here. When you connect Mr Parker to either victim, feel free to call me. Come on William, I'll give you a lift home,' his attorney said smugly.

They both stood, William turned to Clara and Adam as he was leaving, 'I didn't do it.'

The interrogation door closed; the pair sat staring at the desk, covered in notes that pointed the finger straight at William. 'He's right, we haven't got a shred of evidence connecting him or Benjamin Johnson. We'll have to charge Johnson for not holding a hunting licence and possession of cannabis, but we haven't anything to hold him here for the murders. The unsub has gone out of his way to make our job impossible. He's clever, I'll give him that. What aren't we seeing?' Perez gathered up the papers and left the room.

Clara took out her cell. Texting Frank might help her calm down. She was at a low point, and it crept up on her so quickly. She asked him how things were going back in Durant. The memory of her attack came to the surface. That's the first time she had thought about it. Her jaw clenched tight, and she noticed her shoulders were full of tension. Not getting any solid leads with this case was making her irritable. The concoction of anxieties put Clara on edge. *I need some fresh air and a strong coffee.*

Chapter Thirteen

Outside the courthouse Clara sipped her extra strong coffee. Her mind wandered. She was thinking and analysing everything that was happening. Her brother, her drinking habits, the sick mother she hadn't seen since a teen. The case, it should be forefront of her own personal problems, but it was nowhere near. She couldn't stop thinking. If only things had been different for her growing up. They weren't. She was unlucky. The unspeakable abuse her brother Grayson suffered, made her hackles rise. *He was only eight years old for christ sake! Why were we punished? We were so young; innocent and they didn't care. They didn't deserve us. We didn't deserve that life.*

A voice from behind interrupted her thoughts. She turned to see who was there. Carter, one of the police officers had been looking for her. 'Special Agent Strong, I've been told to let you know we have just about finished informing the residents of the situation at hand. I've been assigned to talk to the occupants of this building. I can tell you, a lot of them aren't happy. They want to know why we haven't arrested anyone yet,' his face looked nervous as he conveyed the message.

'Thanks……. Carter isn't it?' She asked.

'Yes Ma'am. The secretarial staff of the courthouse, on the first floor are panicking and requesting we double up security on the doors until this is all over. I tried to explain that we can only afford one officer as our manpower is stretched.'

'You did right. Do you know if there were any residents not in, when the officers did the rounds?'

'We put letters through their postboxes informing them of what was happening. We told them to contact us if they felt unsafe or concerned,' he said.

'We need to catch him, before we have another death on our hands,' Clara raised her concerns out loud.

Just then, Michael and Eli stepped outside, walking up to Clara and Carter with worried expressions. 'We're finished for the day and are heading home. Is there anything we can do to help? We know you're stretched, we overheard them talking inside. He needs catching,' said Michael.

'Yeah, we're all working hard to make sure this monster is caught and put away for good. Thanks, will keep you posted. Stay in this evening. Don't venture out until we get this son of a bitch,' said Clara.

The two workers walked swiftly over to their vehicles. Eli threw his ladders into the back of his pickup and sped off. 'The town folk are nervous, everyone is on tender hooks,' whispered Carter. Clara knew she had to organise her life. People's lives depended on it. The job was her life, she didn't know anything else. A new sense of responsibility washed over her; she wouldn't let him take another life. She gulped down the last of her coffee, turned to Carter and told him they had to catch a killer, and fast.

Inside the foyer of the courthouse, people were gathering. They were looking at each other with suspicion. These people have lived alongside each other for years, but now there was a killer amongst them. The mayor of Butler and the town council made an executive decision to allow the staff to leave early today. It was nearly clocking off time, but Mayor Taylor thought he was being considerate, understanding the urgency. They filed out the door, not looking back. Jumping into their vehicles, they made a quick dash home. The scene was eerily quiet, no one spoke. It was like an apocalypse. Darkness was about to descend; it was as though the end of the world was approaching.

Officer Carter locked the main front doors after the last man exited. The officers were here for the long haul. Clara wanted to see Perez. She had an uncomfortable feeling in her stomach about Joseph Martin, the artist. She wanted to run a background check on him. Agent Strong found her boss in their little makeshift office, staring at the whiteboard. His tie was off, and his sleeves rolled up.

'Sir, I'm going to look into Mr Martin. I can't put my finger on it, but something isn't sitting right with me. Is that good with you? Sir?' She tried to get his attention several times, but all his attention was focused on one thing. The whiteboard.

'No fingerprints, no trace of him. What is his game?' He murmured to himself.

The door opened. Hannah stood flapping a sheet of paper in the air. 'I've found a connection. The two victims attended the same school here in Butler. I know there's a seven-year age difference. Eleanor was in middle school when Evan was at the high. I found her maiden name on your systems, it was Garcia. Also, their families attended the same Pentecostal church when they were younger. The Christian congregation serving the Butler community was known for strict religious practices. Some of which were questionable. I don't know if it's relevant, but I thought I would let you know.'

'Hannah, great work. What's the name of the church?' Asked Perez.

'Norton Pentecostal in Butler. It's just off South Mulberry Avenue, Norton Street. I'll keep looking. We're sending out for food, would you like some?' Hannah asked.

'Yes thanks,' Clara replied. She got out her laptop, entering Mr Joseph Martin's name into the FBI's informational systems and waited. It took a few seconds for his face and details to surface.

'Holy shit!'

Perez gave her a look of confusion. 'What's up?'

'Looks like our Mr Martin has done time for abuse of position of trust: causing a child to watch sexual activity, assault with intent to resist arrest and get this, taking and having indecent photographs of children, what's wrong with these sick bastards?'
'How long did he serve?'
'He got the statutory five years. It says here they couldn't prove the images were being distributed on the web. So, he's served his time, getting out only 6 months ago,' Clara felt sick to the core. *Why are children always the target of fully grown adults, especially the males.* 'Do you think we need to pay him another visit?'
'Yeah. Tell Sheriff Harris to hold our food, we're heading out. Two visits in one day. Mr Martin is gonna be incensed.'
The daylight was disappearing, the dampness of the misty rain in the air had cleared. Moonlight had already descended onto the ground, serving as a flashlight for the agents as they proceeded towards Joseph Martin's front door. 'How are we going to play this?' Clara queried.
'We'll let him know we're aware of his background, persuade him to let us in to look around. You know, tell him let us in or we can stir up trouble, bring everything to light again. Your neighbours don't need to know, and your reputation will be untarnished if you decide to comply, or words of that effect,' explained Perez. He noticed there were no lights on. Looking up at the studio window, it was in complete darkness. Knocking hard on the door, they stood waiting. Shouting his name, the two agents manoeuvred around the side of the house. They needed their maglites to watch their stepping.
Clara rattled the side door to see if it was unlocked. No luck. Walking carefully around to the rear of the building, they peered through the kitchen window. A lamp was on and sat on a dresser in the corner. They couldn't detect any movement or hear anyone shuffling around inside. 'Look! There is a door open over

to the right. I thought it was a cupboard, but there seems to be steps.' Shining her maglite through the window made the light reflect back, it was difficult to get a proper clear view. 'He doesn't seem to be in sir,' she announced.

'I'm going to see if Sheriff Harris can do his magic again, get a search warrant. Where the hell are you, Joseph Martin?' Asked Agent Perez. He dialled Harris's number at the police department. The phone rang once.

'Sheriff Harris.'

'It's Agent Perez. Joseph Martin isn't in, and we've probable cause to ask for a search warrant for his premises. He has a studio on the top floor, we can make out a basement too. We need to search his whole house. His connection is too strong to be ignored. I know I'm putting you on the spot Sheriff…yes, I know…..but we have a killer on the loose which makes it an exceptional circumstance. I appreciate that….yes, thanks.'

Clara gave him a look of concern. 'What?'

'He doesn't think Judge Trueman will consent to it. He's going to ring him now, explain the severity of being able to access his property. Right, it's no use hanging around, I think we should go and talk to Joe the bartender again. He's located in the heart of the town; he may know more about the victim's and our potential suspect's backgrounds. It's amazing what bartenders hear after a few drinks from their customers.'

Shit! Come on Clara. You're doing okay so far. Ask for a soda and ice at the bar. That way you'll be distracted, your hands will have something to do.

Driving back to Alabama South Avenue Bar & Grill, Clara fidgeted in her seat.

'I can go in on my own if you aren't up to it,' said Perez, out of the blue.

'I'm fine. I want to see if he has anything new to tell us…..Thanks anyway.'

'We can grab something to eat if the crowds have got fed up with gossip.'

'Yeah,' her hands still noticeably shaking. Perez wasn't oblivious to Clara's battles. He knew the signs of someone who drank and so desperately wanted to turn their back on the liquid. His mother fell victim to the bottle most of her adult life. Her rage inflamed, especially on the days she struggled to keep herself sober. She lost her battles, deciding to embrace it as her only friend and companion. Adam Perez didn't know to this day if his mother was still alive. He had no feelings towards her. He was so relieved to have left home when he had. Empathy for Clara was there, he just didn't know how to help her.

A pretty black-haired girl showed them to a booth. The atmosphere was very different from their previous visit. This evening was calmer with tables still full of couples and families enjoying their wings and burgers. At the bar area sat what looked to be the local single guys with the company of their preferred beverage. Clara tore her eyes away, concentrating on the menu. It shook in her hands, so she laid it on the table, grasping her clammy hands together on her lap. She sat with her feet on tiptoes, her legs jerking up and down, so she lowered her feet flat to the floor. *Choose your food Clara, you haven't eaten for a while, or had a drink! Nope, soda and ice, soda and some ice. Butler Burger and fries.*

After food, Joe joined them in their booth. Clara hadn't met him before; she was surprised at his strikingly handsome good looks. His fair curly locks fell to his shoulders, framing his strong looking face, while his green eyes were mesmerising. Her mind was definitely preoccupied. She didn't give Jack Daniel's a second thought. She realised she was staring, so she shifted her gaze over to her boss. 'Thanks Joe, we can see you're busy.'

'It's all about calmed down now. No more food to dish out, Harley has the bar. How can I help you?'

'We can't divulge too many details about our case, but we're hoping you may know our two victims and these three men.' He took a small slip of paper out of his top pocket, handing it to Joe. 'Do you know any of them?'

'Erm….well Evan, he was a good boss. He treated me like the son he never had. He loved his twin gals, but he always craved for a son. We never had a cross word. He let me have total control of the bar. It was, is, thriving. Customers came and went, he sat up at the bar, drinking most nights and watching….. the ladies.'

'What about Eleanor Parker?' Asked Perez.

'I've seen her in the bar before. Her looks were striking, you couldn't but look. She only ate with friends, never a partner. She was quiet, almost sad looking. Couldn't put my finger on it, but she just didn't seem happy. Evan tried it on with her, the night he was, well, you know. But she left before he did with her friends.'

'What about these three men. Do you know any of them?' Asked Clara.

'Damn right I do. These two were barred from here about 5 months ago. This guy, I've never heard of,' Joe admitted.

'Barred for what?'

'Joseph Martin had just come out of prison, we know why. Sick bastard. Evan gave him the benefit of the doubt, let him drink at the bar. He was always trying it on with the locals. This particular evening he tried it on with the wrong person, Benjamin Johnson. Can't remember who threw the first punch. Joseph definitely wasn't a fighter. It was like a girl scrap, no offence Miss.' Clara raised her eyebrows, pursing her lips closed to let him know the female race wasn't all the same. 'There was damage done, broken tables, glasses, but when they were thrown out they shook hands and slung their arms round each others' shoulders. Best of buddies.'

'And William Parker? Has he ever been in here?' Clara inquired. Her feet and legs still bouncing under the table.

'Can't say I've ever heard of him. Is he related to Eleanor?' Asked Joe.

'Yeah, her husband!'

'Maybe ask him why she was always looking so sad,' he said, not meaning to sound like he was telling them how to do their job.

'Trust me, we have,' Agent Perez said with frustration. 'Excuse me.' His cell rang, he got up from his seat to take the call. Clara and Joe held a momentary glance.

'Do you fancy a drink; sorry I never caught your name?' Joe broke the silence between them.

'No, I'm good thanks. I don't touch the stuff,' lies poured from her mouth. She drank more than she should, years had been taken from her every time she entered Frank's bar. She needed to leave, step outside, feel the air on her face and breathe deeply to help her body calm down. 'Thanks for your help, Mr…?'

'Joe, call me Joe.'

Clara slid out of the booth to find her boss. He stood in the doorway, still on his cell. His face was red, his eyes full of frustration. The call finished, he turned to his work partner. 'Good news, we have a search warrant. Bad news, the judge is only allowing us two and one police officer to enter. We've only got a warrant for his studio. The rest of the house is out of bounds.'

'Bloody Judge, doesn't he know what we're up against?' Clara said, pent up anger racing through her veins.

'He'll issue it first thing in the morning as he is apparently out to dinner this evening, doesn't want to come away from his fine dining!' Perez ranted.

They headed back to the sheriff's department. Looking into the office and the adjoining room, the two agents noticed all the police officers were running around, working their fingers to the bone, trying to keep their community safe and to find out as much information as possible to assist the FBI. 'Bloody Judge Trueman, sitting on his fat arse and sipping champagne!' Berated Perez. Clara had to look at him. *Did he really just say that?*

'Back to the drawing board?' She asked.

'Yeah, this case has so many different directions. Maybe we need to look at it from a different angle. Stop concentrating on the potential suspects and concentrate on our perp's mind set and M.O. It may bring us closer to understanding what type of person they are,' he picked up the pen and stared at the board.

Chapter Fourteen

He knew the feds were closing in on him, sniffing around and on his trail. He had seen them. His excessive confidence came across as arrogant, but he was delighted with that. He was the one that kept throwing the dice, controlling the game. When the feds took their turn, they always fell on a move that sent them back, only a few paces, but enough to keep him ahead. The holy grail was just around two more corners. It would provide closure for his old life and resurrect a new one.

The next move of his game was to eradicate another opponent, which enabled him to step forward. They had to die. There was no room for error now. Once this move was completed, then it was just one more opponent, the last of his game. This would make way to a straight run to the finish, the end, the glory. His pre-marked board would be clean. Everyone wiped out with only him standing. Victorious in his abilities to have won, to have outsmarted the others. The mechanics of the game with the rules and interactions would be his biggest triumph. Standing on the winning podium, his saviour would reward him with eternal life. Give him everything back he craved as a child. He had to complete the game, there was no question about it. His plan would fail otherwise, he had come too far to allow that to happen. Finishing was paramount and he had to keep playing like a pawn piece, keep low key and under the radar.

His life was like a game of chess which was one of his favourite board games that sat on his shelf, taking centre stage. Taking down one opponent at a time, the pawn nobody pays attention to. Everyone is focused on the bigger pieces, the queen, the king, with their wealth and status, not the weakest piece standing on the board. Nobody concentrates their energy on a piece of minor importance. Why would they, when the others are far more superior to him. But that's exactly how he wanted it. Not to be seen or stand out from the crowd. Small and insignificant, until he achieves his final kill. Historically, the pawn represented a soldier or part of an infantry. He could relate to that part. He was brave and loyal to God.

In amongst his collection of book's sat an etymology and word usage book. He would scroll down the pages, night after night, learning about the history of his components. The term *pawn* is derived from the old French word *paon,* which comes from the Medieval Latin term for "foot soldier." Outside of the game of chess, "pawn" is often taken to mean "one who is manipulated to serve another's purpose." He was serving God's purpose. Being instructed to carry out the duties of a brilliant player and executioner. It was all piecing together with precision.

He sat in his basement studying the collection of books and games he had accumulated as a child, right up to the present day. What an extraordinary collection. Every board game had its place on the beautifully crafted live edged shelves. Their original pristine boxes stacked in order of manufacturing date. The illustrations on the boxes still vibrant in colour. They had been cared for by his own working hands, kept in immaculate condition. They were his lifelong friends as he played each one, over and over. They filled his heart with companionship, and he told them stories of his day when he moved the different components around the board. They all held a piece of him, inside their boxes.

Two of the boxes positioned on the shelves, predominant to all the others, Chess and Boggle. He repaired them incessantly as a young boy. The connection was too strong, he couldn't cope without them. Secretly playing these games in his parent's front yard as a small child, gave him comfort. He yearned for companionship, and they provided him with enough to see him through to the next day, month, decade. He hid out of sight, not to be seen by his family, who had abandoned him, cut off all ties, disowned him.

He got up from his seat and ran his fingers along the side of the boxes. The two which held a light to his heart, gave him the vision that he would find his way in life. Everyone needs a safe haven, and he was in his, the basement of his home. He felt safe and loved here, appreciating it even more as he grew, learning more about himself. His home was always in his heart, he carried it with him everywhere he went. He knew God was tucked up inside there too. Smiling at the sight before him, he took in a deep breath. 'I know you will be beside me as I play my next move.'

The kettle on his stove could be heard whistling. He ascended the stairs, made himself a strong coffee and decided to put together a toasted bagel with cheese and tomato toppings. Cutting the tomatoes up for his freshly toasted supper, he looked down and chortled at the sight. 'I knew this knife would be of some use again.' He retrieved the block of cheese from his perfectly organised refrigerator and cut the slices slowly. Each one, the same thickness and all with precise straight edges. His hand control was undeniably impressive, he stood tall and breathed in the air, which was smoky from the grill.

Finishing off his culinary skills in the kitchen, he took his food back down to his favourite place. The smell of fresh food in amongst his treasures made him feel ebullient. He was king of his castle. His life was turning out perfectly, everything he wanted, yearned for, even desired, was happening. He knew it was down to his own skills and the guidance he received from God. The two of them worked alongside each other in harmony.

He placed his plate on the desk, retrieving his very first game he was given, from the lower shelf. His parents never bought it for him, they didn't even know he existed. There was a family that lived next door and used to wave to him every time they passed by. He was normally sitting in the front yard on his own, playing with little mounds of dirt and an old truck that only had two wheels. It was the Dubois family. They were forever trying to coax him round to their house, to play with their son. He was four years younger. Jeremiah Dubois repeatedly asked him over to play with his new toys, his brand-new bicycle, but unfortunately the killer's strict Christian parents wouldn't allow him to associate with other children. They were afraid he would embarrass them, reduce their status in the community.

He always remembered one particular Sunday, the Dubois family were heading out and Jeremiah ran up to him with a present. He had never been given anything new in his life before, so this day was special. It was the dawning of his love for games. He unwrapped the blue paper and just stared. He was unable to read the box, so Jeremiah explained how to play. He could play on his own and learn how to spell. The game Boggle introduced him to the dice. He was infatuated by the numbers and used it for everyday things. He numbered places in his home and threw the dice to see where he would go. There was never anything waiting for him in these places, he didn't care. It was the fact a small dice could decide your day. He laughed at the memories. The dice was still dictating his moves.

The Dubois family secretly handed him a new board game when they could afford it. He remembered he had to hide these from his parents and siblings. The game of chess he played on his own, learning the skilful tactics on how to move and revenge your opponents. If they ever found out, he would have been accused of stealing and sent to hell for his sins. Searching round the house he knew nobody went down into the basement. It was dark and creepy, making others scared of its existence. His little collection started to mount up, his knowledge of solving puzzles, problems and dilemmas became ever more powerful. He wouldn't show off his new abilities to his family, they would just take it away. It was his secret and his to keep. Now that basement was his kingdom.

The books belonged to one of his sisters. She was an avid reader, especially of the bible. He stole them, one at a time, all through her school years. He was inconspicuous, hiding them alongside his games. If he was unable to make off with one of her books, he would tear the pages out, the ones which looked like they would help him with his learning. When he heard someone coming, he rushed, only managing to tear off a corner. But it would do. There was always something written down he could use. There were loose panels in the basement at the time and he carefully placed everything he got behind them.

He inherited the large house by chance, he wasn't sure why, but he knew he deserved it. He transformed every room to his own liking. Planning and detailing every space, right down to the last screw. He was always conscious of his favourite room. He never wanted his games room to be noticed, it had to stay hidden. If anyone saw it or entered it, everything would be taken from him, it would be lost forever, and he wasn't about to give up his life's work for anyone. He felt nauseous at the thought, sweating slightly on his forehead.

'Right, my next opponent was number three on the dice,' his mind started to gather momentum on how he had planned the next kill. David Torres was the target, the playing piece that had to be removed. *He isn't going to be easy, but I know what needs to be done to succeed.* He willed himself on with gritted determination. *He thinks he can use his fists on me again, then he is sadly mistaken. God has directed me towards the light, and I will follow his instructions and make him proud.*

David Torres owns a car dealership and connecting garage, just on the outskirts of Butler town. Aged thirty-eight years old, he is married with one son, Hudson Torres. His wife Amelia is the same age and runs a small fitness club from their home, over in the next smaller town of Lavaca. Their substantial property has been converted and modernised at every opportunity. The Torres's lifestyle is fast and opulent, Alabama style. Past Cotahome Creek, Northeast of Butler, along the meadowlark rd is Lotts Ferry Road. It was here he parked up and observed. No one took any notice of his vehicle; he could have been out hunting for all the neighbours knew. He soon acknowledged all different kinds of deceptions were connected to their home.

The perpetrator saw Amelia wasn't faithful. He didn't blame her; she was married to a monster who used his fists. *He won't be able to hurt me or his family anymore. He is made from the devil himself. God will punish him, and he won't be allowed into heaven. Only trustworthy people like me are allowed to enter. I am a saviour to the wife and son, and they will thank me afterwards. Those hands will never be able to hurt anyone again.*

He watched their house in Lavaca, for over a year. He used to sit, watch and observe, just like the others. When David went to work early morning, his wife would start her exercise and dance classes. They had the money to convert the double garage into a studio, which sat underneath the main part of the house. Amelia entertained two classes, three times a week. The last class of the week was when one of her participants stayed behind. Noah Cooper, a fitness fanatic and a truck driver who worked for Zachariah Jackson. He was a large stack of muscle and six foot tall. The watcher was envious of Cooper's strength and physique, but he didn't dwell on it, he had other important things to think about. He had to focus on the game.

The kill was originally planned to happen in the Torres's home, but too many folks visited. Like women in their tight designer leotards, practicing their vertices pulls, horizontal pushes and rotational twirls before they entered class. The males oscillating their toned bodies, trying to impress onlookers. No doubt they would be oblivious to anything happening around them, due to the fact they were all self absorbed.

But the best option was to carry out the move at his place of work. The car dealership and garage. He knew all the employees. Which days they worked, their clocking in and out times and when the boss stayed behind on his own, to count his precious money. Tomorrow night was that night. The perpetrator would be ready.

He ran his eyes around the room, seeing if everything he needed tomorrow was sitting out. The objects gleamed and shone like precious jewels. The cupboard to his left was open. It was beautifully crafted out of wood and painted a deep green. He had left it open on purpose. One shelf occupied, one shelf waiting to be filled. He wanted Evan Thomas to see him, to watch him from the top shelf, as he orchestrated the rest of his success.

One of the books taught him all he needed to know about the human body. Page 34 of his biology textbook informed him the human eyeball is slightly denser than the water in the jar. This meant Evan's eyeballs had a greater amount of mass per unit of volume, than the water did. This creates a slight imbalance of weight between the eyeball and water, which causes his eyeball to float in his old, pickled vegetable jar. He sat back in his gaming chair feeling intellectual. All his wealth of knowledge sat upon the shelves in his room. Eleanor's blue parker, hat and gloves were folded neatly next to the jar. The bottom shelf would be utilised tomorrow evening. He was ready to play. He smiled knowing his complex ideas were artful and full of depth.

Yawning and stretching, he decided to have an early night. Switching off the light, he headed upstairs. *Work tomorrow daytime, then another shift at the car dealership in the evening. God, I am really busy.*

Chapter Fifteen

Waking up in the early hours of the following morning, Clara showered, dressed and knocked on Perez's door. She was feeling agitated coming off the booze. She slept very little. Walking around in her motel room was driving her crazy. 'Boss, are you up?'
The door opened. Adam stood in front of her, towel wrapped around his midsection. Her eyes struggled to look elsewhere. A full blush surfaced her cheeks, she swivelled on her feet and strolled down the corridor. 'I'll wait for you downstairs!'
'Give me ten!' His voice echoed behind her.
Slipping into the driver's seat, Clara waited for her boss. Her cell rang. 'Frank! You're up early, everything okay?'
'Yeah, just wanted to see how things were going down there.'
'We are going round in circles. Few leads but…..'
'I meant with you,' he said softly.
There were a few seconds of silence. 'I'…. I'm doing alright. Miss you're chats.'
'Yeah, its great to hear your voice. Your bar stool is missing you too. How's the Jack Daniel's separation going? Proud of you by the way. Just wanted you to know that.'
'Separation anxiety is definitely a thing. But if I can't do it when I'm here, I'll never beat it. Missing that stool too. Get the soda and ice ready for my return. Frank, I have to go….. thanks for calling,' she whispered as Perez jumped into the vehicle.
'Hurry on back Agent Strong,' Frank's last words radiated warmth through her heart.
'All good?' Perez asked.
'Just couldn't settle knowing he's still out there. You?'

'Up at 2am, pacing the floors,' Adam replied. 'Right, ready? Sheriff's office to pick up the search warrant, we'll see if Joseph Martin answers this morning!'

Police officer Carter let the two agents through the main doors of the courthouse. Security was still paramount. As they entered, they overheard raised voices between Michael and Eli.

'Another day off! We'll never get these jobs finished and I need paid!' Michael exclaimed.

'I can't do it today, something important has cropped up. You can manage!'

'Jesus Eli! What's going on with you lately?'

'I told you; I need away today,' he stomped off, leaving Michael to hold the fort.

'You, okay?' Clara asked.

'Yeah, can't seem to keep him at work for more than a couple of hours a day. Don't know what's going on? Anyway, you have enough to do, what with all the happenings going on,' Michael said with total sincerity. 'I better get back to work before I get fired. Hope you have better luck today catching him.'

'Yeah, need to wrap this up quickly.'

Meeting Sheriff Harris in his office, he passed them the search warrant. 'Sorry folks. I tried speaking to Judge Trueman again this morning, but he's sticking to his guns. Mr Martin's studio and that's the lot. I'll send over Deputy Dubois to stand firm with your guy. Apart from that, my hands are tied,' he said with a dejected demeanour.

'It's better than nothing. Thanks Sheriff,' Agent Perez said.

'Charles, my name is Charles. If there is anything I can do in the meantime?'

'You could do more background digging on our three people of interest. William Parker, Benjamin Johnson and Joseph Martin. Is there anything we aren't seeing. There must be a connection.

Also, if any of your officers can contact Dr Cameron and see if he has any updates for us.'

'Right on it.'

Driving along Desoto Road, Clara Strong got a text from Deputy Dubois, saying he was on his way over. They pulled up outside, exiting the SUV. The sound of the Deputy Sheriff's vehicle minutes later, gave Perez the go ahead to knock. Waiting patiently, the door opened, and Joseph Martin stood in the doorway rolling his eyes. 'Not today thank you, I'm too busy to accommodate the feds.'

'Mr Joseph Martin, we have a search warrant, allowing us to search your art studio,' Agent Perez said, holding up the form. State of Alabama written in bold lettering across the top. 'Officer Dubois will accompany you to your kitchen, keep you company until we have finished.'

'Are you crazy? You can't traipse in and look through my private things,' Joseph raged at the intrusion.

The deputy and two agents pushed their way through. Jeremiah Dubois escorted Mr Martin to the rear of the house, Adam and Clara headed upstairs. The room was cluttered with artistic pieces. 'We need to find some solid evidence to prove he's connected to this case,' Adam said.

Putting on their latex gloves, they turned over sheets of paper, canvases and other materials. The slight scent of acrylics filled the room. A pungent citrus-like smell gave Clara a heavy head. Walking towards the back, she wanted to know what was behind that screen. Clambering over an open box, she noticed spray tins. Pulling one of the blue tins out, she read, 'Acrylic lacquer, premium automotive formulation designed to give a lustrous durable finish. Dries quickly, has superior adhesion to metal, and dries to a high gloss sheen. Once dry, it can be machine or hand buffed for an even glossier appearance,' she placed the spray in an evidence bag. *If that matches the counters, then he has a lot of explaining to do!*

Leaving the spray on the box to collect later, she reached the screen. The room extended further around the corner. Boxes piled high, different labelling stuck on the sides. Her eyes captured a small black and white sticker, standing out from all the rest. To Clara's professional eye, it looked handmade. Pulling off the top boxes, she reached in and grabbed it.

The label read, "High Quality Material."

Slicing the top using the side of a palette knife, she surveyed the contents inside. They didn't bear any resemblance to any artists instruments or materials she recognised. Studying the items as she pulled out a plastic bag and unwrapped the contents, her heart rate fastened. There was a photograph of Eleanor and William Parker. She had seen this picture before, but where? Studying it, her memory came flooding back like a torrent of water. It was the portrait hanging up behind the Parker's bed. *Okay, this doesn't mean he is our unsub. He explained he took photographs to copy onto canvass,* her thoughts rapidly swirling around.

Then she gasped. Under this photograph sat one of Evan Thomas, his wife Charlotte and their twin daughters, Ellie and Harper. *This can't be. Out of Butler and surrounding towns the two victims happen to be Joseph Martin's clients. What's the chances of that happening?* Clara lifted and bagged them. Another 12 photographs were in the pile, which she also seized.

Looking to see if there were any more, she noticed a solid wooden case sitting on the bottom. Lifting it out she unclipped the metal plate. Opening it up and reaching in, she held a plethora of photographs in her hand. Her stomach convulsed, collapsing her body to the floor with overwhelming pain.

'Clara? Are you okay?' Perez shouted. He rushed over. She was kneeling, trying to calm her breathing. Surrounding her body on the floor, lay photograph after photograph of children. Unclothed and vulnerable. 'Holy shit!'

Downstairs, Deputy Dubois stood against the kitchen sink watching Joseph Martin. He was sitting at his table irritated, bouncing with annoyance. 'How long are they going to be? I don't know what you think I've done, but you will be extremely disappointed.'

Jeremiah stood in silence. Making the atmosphere frosty and uncomfortable on purpose.

'Can I at least get some water?' Whimpered Joseph. 'You can't keep me sat here like this. I have rights.'

Again, Deputy Dubois remained silent.

'God damn it!' He went to stand up, Dubois put his hand out.

'I can't let you do that Mr Martin. Please sit down.'

'I need something to drink.'

'I'll certainly get you some water. Glasses?' Jeremiah asked.

'Behind you, top left-hand cupboard.'

The deputy swung around, looking back at the table. Joseph still sitting, staring at the officer. Dubois opened the cupboard door, so Joseph stole an opportunity to move. His chair slid back, falling backwards with the force. Dubois swung around, dropping the glass to the floor. Hurtling over the fallen chair, his left foot caught one of its legs. His face smashed against the ground, disorientating him. He rose, hand to head, blood seeping from the gash he created.

'Agents!' He screamed.

Clara, bent over, raised her head. 'Did you hear that?'

'Shit, it came from downstairs,' Perez shouted.

She scrambled to her feet, ignoring the constant pain in her stomach. Jumping down two steps at a time, they entered the kitchen. The back door was wide open, blood on the floor.

'Fuck!'

Bolting to the door, they separated outside. The rain clouds decided to open up. Glock at arms length, Clara ran down the left side of the house, towards the front yard. 'Shit! Where the fuck are you?' Looking both directions, she proceeded down the path to the road. The tall trees blew in the wind, pelting rain hitting the leaves to the ground. *Which way? Come on Clara, you know this place. Where would he go?*

She wiped the rain from her face with her sleeve. Hair dripping wet, falling into her eyes, she made an executive decision to head up the North Mulberry Avenue. She remembered a woodland area up on the left. Lifting her radio from her belt, she called it in. 'Suspect fleeing from Desoto Road, one officer on pursuit. Not sure which direction he is headed. I'm heading towards Gibbons Boulevard Forest. Possibility of an officer injured. Need back up!'

Her voice washed over by the torrential downpour, as she screamed Dubois's name. Pumpkins lay squashed from the rain in the neighbours' yards. Halloween decorations blew around in the wind, starting to untie from their locations. A storm was brewing, and Clara could feel the palpable sense of tension forming in her pursuit. A blue truck hurled past, soaking her to the bone. 'Shit!' Rain was bouncing off the road, making visibility difficult. She ran up a side bank which skirted the woodland. 'FBI, come out with your hands up! Mr Martin, you are surrounded by officers. Come out into the clearing!' Clara could hardly hear her own words.

She moved deeper into the woods. The canopies of the tall trees extinguishing the noise of the rain, swaying firmly with the approaching winds. Her vision moving in all directions. Weapon poised. The quietness started to engulf her body the deeper she went. The murmur from the trees sounding ever distant. She could hear the uneven sounds of rain falling. 'Jeremiah, it's Clara.

Can you hear me? Are you okay? Are you hurt?' *Come on, answer me, damn it!*

She felt her whole body working hard to find both Jeremiah and Joseph. Her leg muscles running warm, the cold air of The Fall entering her lungs. She could feel her calves burning as she manoeuvred over fallen branches. She stopped in her tracks. A distant groaning sound echoed through the forest. 'Jeremiah?'

Her feet took her in the direction of the noise, she used each tree for protection. The smell of damp wood made Clara breathe in deeply, leaves crunching underfoot. She noticed a figure slouched up against a large rock. 'FBI, hands in the air where I can see them!' She swung around, weapon pointed straight at the person sitting on the ground.

'I'm okay. He's double backed and heading in the direction of Hamburg Avenue,' Deputy Dubois said, blood now streaming down his face.

'I need medical assistance at Gibbons Boulevard Forest, off North Mulberry Avenue. Officer injured.'

Jeremiah told Clara to go, after she finished her radio call. He would wait on the medics.

She knew he was right. She couldn't let this killer get away. Clara ripped off part of her blouse and tide it round Dubois's head. Placing a hand on his shoulder, she left.

Heading out onto the road, she raced down the sidewalk to Hamburg Avenue. She was breathless, exhausted, taking a quick second to recover. Hands on hips, she stood up tall and there he was, running across the parking lot of a store. 'Stop!' her voice wouldn't come. She knew where he was heading and how to get there quicker. Her legs, numb and cold from the rain were slowing her down, but she dug deep, determined to catch him.

The wind swirled around the trash in the alleyway. Garbage bags strewed across the entrance. She remembered the other night back home in Durant. The alleyway. Her attackers. She put the thoughts to the back of her mind, pushing forward. Negotiating her way through moving hurdles. Glass bottles rolled in front of her, newspapers and trash from the nearby stores flying into the side panels. The end of the alleyway was in sight. She ran out onto the adjoining path, looking both ways. Her eyes caught his rear end heading around the corner. The wail of police sirens in the distance, gave Clara hope. She turned the corner, noticing Sheriff Harris had stopped down wind of the perpetrator in his police vehicle. He exited and ran straight at Joseph Martin, who turned on his heels and headed towards a tall wooden fence.

He took a leap of faith to get himself over, clinging onto the top with every muscle he possessed, his finger's grappling with the pain. Clara and Sheriff were right on his tail. Grabbing a leg each, they pulled him off, scraping his face down the old wooden panels. Groans were perceived by the two pursuers. Martin's face was red and scuffed. Anger radiated through his eyes. 'Joseph Martin. You are under arrest.'

Chapter Sixteen

The chair to the side of his bed was uncomfortable, especially because her wet clothes clung to her cold body. The nurses attended to the side of his face, sewing the long gash with care. Jeremiah Dubois sipped some water, throwing back pain killers. Butler hospital was quiet, so Clara asked one of the nurses for a towel. Drying her hair and face, she said, 'You feel better?'
'Yeah. I'm embarrassed. Wasn't even a punch to the head. Bloody chair!' He managed to give out a little laugh. 'You got him then! He was as quick as a swamp rabbit. I should've known.'
'He's an opportunist. But he's in custody, I'm heading down shortly to interview him. We're just letting him calm down for a while. Dr Cameron has sent a few of his team to his house as we speak. Judge Trueman had no problem extending the warrant to the whole property as soon as he heard what we uncovered,' Clara's stomach knotted at the thought of the photographs she found.
'Why are you here? I mean it's nice of you to see if I'm okay but....,' his voice weakening.
'I...I was concerned. Nasty gash. You looked like you lost a lot of blood. Plus, I need my shirt back!' She said, looking down at the torn material, still covered in blood. 'I think it needs a dry clean first.'
'Yeah, I reckon you're right. I'm all good,' said Dubois.
Silence engulfed the room. She wanted to ask him, but she didn't know where to start. Her cell rang. Unknown number. She let it ring out. 'Probably my landlady back home,' she said, breaking the quietness. Dubois attempted to laugh again; his head was too sore. The stitches felt tight and uncomfortable.

'You were best friends with Grayson. I remember the two of you used to sneak off to the lake, your handmade fishing rods, metal pails just in case you caught a bluegill or two,' Clara managed to say.

'Yeah. I was wondering if you recognised my name. I'm sorry about Grayson, he was my best buddy. I missed him everyday after he…. disappeared,' his words sounding sincere.

'I've never spoken about it; I struggle with it every day. Everything was such a mess back then; we were kids in a screwed-up home. I remember the two of you at elementary school, always the jokers. He loved being there, he felt safe, and it took away all the pain and anxiety he endured day in, day out,' her body started shaking. 'Sorry Jeremiah, I need to go,' she stood up, touched him softly on his arm and left. Tears streaming down her cheeks.

She got in her vehicle and cried, bashing her palms against the steering wheel over and over, trying to release her pent-up emotions she had been suppressing for eighteen years. She inhaled the dampness of the SUV, closed her eyes for a while before she felt ready to head back to the motel.

Taking a long hot shower, she put on some pressed dry clothes. She wanted to be on top form to interrogate Joseph Martin. She couldn't think about the disappearance of her brother now. There was a murderer and paedophile to put behind bars.

The courthouse was still secured for the workers, every visitor searched. Clara made her way to the sheriff's department.

Perez and Harris were in discussions with the officers, who were still searching for connections. She entered the room, and officer Carter acknowledged her presence. 'Any updates?' She asked.

'Not yet ma'am. We're working around the clock. We're totally baffled by the whole thing,' Carter responded. 'How's Deputy Dubois doing?'

'He's good. Stitched and sore, but probably eager to get back at it,' she responded.

Agent Perez asked Hannah to keep hassling Dr Cameron about the acrylics and the lacquer spray. Now they had full access to Joseph's possessions and a free hand to search, he was hoping the matches would comeback straightaway. It would save them trying to match up the small wooden truck from Oak and Interiors, against the pigments of the counters.

Perez looked at Clara, 'Are you set?'

She shook her head, following him to the interrogation room.

Joseph Martin sat slouched in his seat. The agents entered and Joseph ignored their presence. The young police officer who was standing guard left the room. His attorney, a young female in her late twenties, sat beside him.

Sitting opposite, they began.

'Mr Joseph Martin, we have arrested you today under the Sex Crimes Against Children Prevention Act of 1995. Finding photographic evidence of child pornography within your home. As we speak forensics are searching through your property. You have also been arrested for the suspicion of two murders of Mr Evan Thomas and Mrs Eleanor Parker. Do you understand?' Agent Perez asked.

'Murders, now hang on there. Are you feds trying to frame me? This is all wrong. I have nothing to do with any murders!' He protested.

'We have reason to believe you are responsible for both murders on the grounds that, items found at your residents connect you straight to items found at both murder scenes.' Perez knew that they hadn't yet got a match from Dr Cameron and was hoping he would come up trumps during the interrogation. He glanced at his watch.

'My client is remaining silent throughout this interview. I have advised him to stay quiet until we have gathered up our own evidence and information, which disassociates him from the allegations you pose against him,' Miss Myers explained.

'Mr Martin, we found these photographs in your studio, at your home in Desoto Road. Can you explain why they were found there?'

'I've never seen them before. You put them there. I know your game. Let's frame the homosexual gay, he is definitely the type to murder folk!' Joseph Martin said, raising his voice.

'Mr Martin, please. Keep quiet and let me do the talking,' Miss Myers insisted.

'We are talking about these photos. Our tech guy is going through your laptop as we speak Mr Martin. I hope for your sake he doesn't find anything. Did you know the Children's prevention act, directed the Congressional directives commission to increase the base offence level for child pornography possession offences, by at least two levels and to add a two-level enhancement for the use of a computer in such cases. Mr Martin, it's not looking good for you. I suggest you start talking.'

'No comment.'

Perez was getting frustrated. Clara studied Joseph's posture and demeanour. His body language was hard to read. She knew Perez coming from the B.A.U, would be cognisant to his actions the other side of the desk. Joseph was fidgeting in his seat, scratching his arms, rocking back and forth. Clara knew this was an indication her boss was getting the upper hand.

Perez asked him another question. Joseph's eyes looked towards the door.

'Mr Martin, why are these in your possession?'

Joseph Martin stared at Agent Perez, pausing before he finally answered. 'Some one put them there. Could have been one of my clients when I did a photoshoot with them.'

'Please Mr Martin. I'm advising you not to utter another word. You will only incriminate yourself,' Miss Myers was becoming agitated and uncomfortable in her seat.

'Okay, let's move on. Evan Thomas. We know you drank in his bar. Did he not like you because of your past history? Were you interfering with his customers at the bar, causing them to leave? Did he get mad with you? I see you're on the Sex offender's register. Serving five years jail time,' Agent Perez kept the questions coming. 'Eleanor Parker was at the bar too. Did she not like how you conducted yourself and confronted you? Did she get wind of your past too? Being an elementary school teacher, she would have been pissed at you. Both are dead Mr Martin, and you are the connection.'

Perez didn't mention the paint, the counters. He was waiting for Patrick Cameron.

Why hasn't he asked what items of his were found at the scenes? Does he know he has been found out? Thought Clara.

Agent Perez was considering a break in the interview, when the door opened. Officer Carter wanted a word. *Let's pray its what we need,* he thought.

Perez left the room. Joseph Martin looked at his attorney with grave concern. 'What's happening?'

'I'm not sure. Sit firm, don't worry about anything,' Myers said.

Perez sat back down, looked at Clara and smiled. She knew then, they had him. They had caught the son of a bitch that killed those poor innocent people. Their families would get closure. Justice would be served, and she could go home to see Frank.

'Mr Joseph Martin, at your property we have discovered pornographic images of children. Upon your laptop we have found stored information which provides a means for other users at other locations to send and receive files. Bulletin boards. Graphic files of child pornography have been sent and received from your laptop. We see you have set up a paid membership for your customers, ranging from $10-$40 a month. Our tech officer has beaten your systems. What do you say Mr Martin?' Perez was determined to carry on until the end.

'No comment,' he mumbled.

'Mr Joseph Martin, at your property we retrieved acrylic paints and a transparent lacquer spray finish. The pigments, binders and vehicle of these paints are a match to those found at both crime scenes. The lacquer contains the same cellulose acetate butyrate and acrylic resin, also found at both scenes. A total match. We also know you befriended Benjamin Johnson at the Alabama South Avenue Bar & Grill. We believe while you were at his home, during this new friendship period, you took hunting traps from his shed. Was he out cold with alcohol and you saw an opportunity? Or did you sexually pay him? Did he get the chains from his work for you?' Special Agent in Charge Adam Perez felt he had Joseph Martin cornered. 'Your paintings were also found at both of the victim's homes. You had the opportunity to plan and execute your own work while delivering these portraits. Taking paper from William Parker's office, also the kitchen knife. It's all stacking up against you Mr Martin.'

'This all sounds circumstantial Agent,' Miss Myers piped up.

'I believe we have enough evidence to hold up in court, for both accounts of murder and the indecent acts against children's rights and the distribution of pornographic materials. Do you have anything to say?' Perez finished off with.

His eyes filled with tears. 'I'm innocent, I didn't kill anyone. You have to believe me. Someone has set me up.' Joseph Martin's words weren't even heard by the two agents as they left the room.

Officer Carter escorted Joseph Martin to his cell. The two agents stepped into the sheriff's office and saw the officers tidying up their paperwork and finishing off reports. Smiles across their faces, happy to see this case being put to bed.

'Thank you, folks. You truly came through. He will be going away for a while. A round of drinks on us at the Bar & Grill,' Adam Perez announced.

Clara was in two minds whether to go or not. She managed last night. Drank soda with ice. She didn't want everyone to know about her drinking problem. *If I feel the urge, I'll leave.*

The Sheriff's department closed up for the day. Courthouse staff had already left. All personnel of the building had gone home or made their way to the bar. Officer Carter was still on duty. Life carried on, residents needed help with day-to-day problem, which felt easy in comparison to what they had just experienced. Carter joined them at the bar, he was drinking water. 'Cheers everyone, well done. It's great to work with you all. We make a good team.'

They clinked glasses and Clara drank her orange juice. It was refreshing after the day she had. Fries and spicy chicken wings placed in the centre of the table for a meal of grab and share. Sheriff Harris came in slightly after the others, Deputy Dubois in hand. Everyone clapped as he sat beside Clara.

'Agents, we appreciate your work here in Butler. Our residents can sleep well at night thanks to you,' Sheriff Harris lifted his glass of water in the air. 'Cheers.'

'You not having a beer with your guy's Sheriff?' Clara asked.

'Nope! Don't touch the stuff. To be honest this is the first time I've been in here since….since my last proper drink, many years ago. But I'm over it. I don't even crave for one anymore.

Remembering what it used to do to me, makes me even more determined to keep off it,' he replied. 'That's why I didn't know Evan Thomas. Never came in.'

'Can I ask how you turned your back on it? Was it hard?' She was digging for answers.

'Took me a long time. Kept looking at my wife and kids thinking, what if I wasn't here, who would be there for them. They deserved better than an old drunk falling through the door at the end of a shift. I noticed you are on the juice.'

'Er yeah. Long story.'

'If I was giving someone advice, it would be to focus on something important in their life. And use the 20-minute rule for drinking less. Take a 20-minute break before you drink your next one. It reduces cravings and keeps you from going overboard. It helped me, until one day I just stopped. Apparently, there are apps on your phone now to help. You should look it up,' Charles Harris smiled at Clara, letting her know, her secret would stay with him.

Her cell rang, interrupting their conversation. That unknown number again. 'Sorry, I need to take this,' she stepped outside where there was less noise. 'Hi, Agent Strong speaking.'

'Clara, it's George, George Edwards. I tried to phone you earlier. Listen, don't hang up. It's your mama Clara. She has been admitted to Butler hospital. It's not looking good.'

Chapter Seventeen

Evening finally arrived. It was time to play his next move. 'Always ahead of the feds. How stupid are they? Arresting the wrong man,' he smiled, looking at himself in the bathroom mirror. 'Tonight, will be another victory to me. I will play my game and enjoy Gods blessings afterwards.'

After brushing his teeth and combing his hair back, he went into his bedroom, questioning whether to wear his black or blue jumper. 'I feel like it's a blue night,' guffawing at his own words.

Descending his stairs, heading to his favourite room, he glanced over to the kitchen draining board. He tutted to himself, rolling his eyes and sniggered. 'How can I forget you?' He picked up the knife he had just cleaned after his supper of meat and vegetables. His games room sat spotless with everything in its place. Evan Thomas had been shut away for the night, tucked up next to Eleanor's clothes. He noticed a little bit of the green paint from the cupboard had peeled off. His brows furrowed slightly at the imperfection. *I'll sort that out when I get back later.*

He picked up his dice, he knew he didn't need it. There was only one number left with his game, but he wanted to see if he could throw it first time, keep the momentum going. The counters were safely tucked away with the dice in his leather pouch. He placed them in the top pocket of his coat, the knife took its normal position in the other. He tapped it twice with his hand. 'Are we good to go?'

The night's sky was clear. The moon shone brightly, and it reminded him of Evan Thomas's kill. 'Looks like I'm centre stage again. This will be a fine performance,' he started his vehicle and drove away, whistling a merry tune to himself.

He couldn't park at David Torres car dealership, he had planned to park in the store next door, along Hendricks Avenue. It was open until 1am, so he knew his vehicle wouldn't be sitting alone in the parking lot. Opening his trunk, pulling out his rucksack, he nonchalantly walked past the front of the car dealership showroom on Patton Street, looking around as though he was out for a stroll. He saw there was a light on. *Good, he's in.*

There was a side alley beside David's dealership, trees rimmed the edge of the pathway. He turned into the entrance of the alley, proceeding to the back of the huge substantial building, cladded with silver corrugated tin sheets. The garage was incorporated in the same building. This was perfect, it made his plan flow much more smoothly and efficiently.

He knew the small back door would be locked. This wasn't a problem; he had a key. He was careful when he visited at first as a potential buyer not to get caught. And he succeeded. Then there were other occasions he visited David; each time was purely work related. The shiny gold key glistened in the moonlight as he turned it, unlocking his first hurdle. He knew the layout of the business; he had done his homework thoroughly.

David Torres was sitting at his large office desk, calculating the takings for the week. He always did on a Thursday evening. Sheets of paper stacked up high to the left of him on his desk, from all the garage maintenance work carried out for the general public's motors. To the right of him sat the car sales, along with the finance deals he offered, to get people's attention and custom.

The unknown intruder moved down the corridor leading to the main office. He saw his opponent sitting in his leather chair, counting his money like Ebenezer Scrooge from the Dickens novel. That book was on his shelf. It was one of three fictional books he owned. He preferred factual information. He knew the characters and how it all turned out nicely in the end. *Not for this cruel man it won't. He will die tonight, and all his money will go to his wife and son. It will be the last time he sits on his mighty throne.*

He turned on his heels and headed to the garage area, the connecting door's key was hidden above on the ledge, to the left of the door. *He must be more careful with his security. Anyone could pose a threat to his business.*

He turned on his small flashlight to look around the room. The place was always tided after the day had finished. An ice cap, white Toyota GR Corolla sat centre of the room, ready for a service in the morning. *Perfect!*

Vibrant red toolboxes sat around the side. A grey universal socket tool, with its drill adapter attachment, sitting neatly on the bench. His eyes scoured the room until he found the tool he needed. This one needed some serious planning. Timing was everything.

He took a deep breath, deciding he was ready to play.

Placing the jack next to the Corolla, he plugged in the air compressor, turning it on to the max. The noise was almost deafening, there were no other sounds. He knew David Torres would be able to hear it from his office. He slipped his rucksack under the nearest work bench and waited for his opponent to move.

'What the hell!' Torres said to himself. He got up to investigate. 'Hello, who's there? Jimmy is that you?' Nobody answered. 'Come on, stop messing around. I haven't got time for this. Jimmy, seriously!'

He saw the connecting garage door was open. Switching on the corridor light, he walked towards the opening. Poking his head through to the confines of the garage area, his fingers flicked the light switch on.

'Jesus! What the hell are you doing sneaking around? How did you even get in?' Torres said with a shaky voice.

'The front door was open, I saw you were busy at your desk, so I snuck past, not to disturb you,' he grimaced.

'What are you looking for? Can't it wait until the morning? I've got loads to do,' David asserted his voice with more clarity to the familiar figure standing in front of him. 'Why's that compressor on?'

'I accidentally pressed against it. I didn't want to put the main light on. I was here the other day getting my car serviced. When I parked up and jumped out of my vehicle, I started talking to one of the mechanics and put my rucksack down. I must have walked off without it. I can't find it anywhere. It's got my spare vehicle key in it. Can you give me a couple of minutes to check?'

'Well hurry up. I can't stand here watching you fumble around, looking for your things!' Torres blurted out. His anger was starting to buildup and the perpetrator could see David's fists clenching.

'Any chance you could quickly help me, then I'll be out of your way in no time?'

'For God's sake!' Replied Torres.

Precisely, the killer thought.

David Torres turned the air compressor off. He moved flex sockets, set of chisels, a couple of impact drivers, trying to find this man's rucksack, and get him out of the way. The killer stood behind him, slipping on his latex gloves quietly. Not looking for his rucksack. Not hunting under tools. Just observing his prey.

He was a stout man, too fat for the killer's liking. But that was helpful, it made his plan even better. Picking up a torque wrench from the work bench, he smiled, *what a useful tool to have.* His hand clutching around the long arm of the wrench lifted up into the air, then came crashing down.

David Torres head split with the full force of the impact, splattering blood in all directions. He grappled with the tools seated on the work bench to hold himself up, to stop himself falling. Collapsing to the ground, his head sounded like a billiard ball bouncing off the side of the game table.

'Oops. Are you okay? Did you fall and hurt yourself?' He chortled.

Blood oozed from the back of his head. His hair soaked with the red liquid elevated the killer's emotions to a higher level. The concrete floor patterning with droplets from his broken frontal skull bone. The feeling of self adulation hit him once again, and he stood tall amongst the bloody surface his victim had created.

He took off his shoes, he couldn't afford to leave his bloody footprints on show and walked over to jack up the Toyota Corolla. 'Think that's high enough,' he said. All pleased with his trappings so far.

His body clenched with shock at the distant sound of a phone ringing in David's office, swaying his concentration. *Inconsiderate people. Don't they have a life? Don't they know my hands are tied and I can't answer?* He stood completely still until it rang off. Walking back to the unconscious man sprawled across the floor, he lifted both of his arms, dragging him over to the car, turning back admiring the blood pattern he had created on the floor.

Switching the main light in the garage off, he didn't want to create a scene or an audience, not yet anyway, he put his little flashlight back on.

Rolling David's large figure under the car, leaving his arms stretched out to be on show, he started to lower the jack. He heard groaning and stopped. Incoherent sounds were coming from below the vehicle. 'Stop, what's happening? Why……please.' The sound of the victim vomiting made the perps stomach convulse.

The killer lowered onto his knees, shone his light and peered at the sorrowful sight before him, under the Toyota. The ice cap white paint work, now faintly covered from the distant spray of blood. Lying on his front, head tilted to the side, he saw a disgusting pool of David's last supper. 'Now David, where's your manners? We are trying to play here. What was that, David? You want to beat me up again? I think you aren't in a position to be demanding anything. You not feeling too good? That's a shame. I felt like that every time you used to physically abuse me, with those dirty fists of yours. You remember? Every time our loving parents decided to abandon us, you took it out on me. I was frustrated too you know. But never mind all that now. It's my turn. My turn to do you some harm. God has granted me permission David. He will reward me with eternal life. But first you must die.'

The phone in the office rang again. 'Shit! Can't you give me peace!' He growled.

He slowly cranked down the jack until the car could lower no more. Agonising sounds reverberated across the garage floor. He slid the jack away from under the vehicle, rolling it in the blood to its rightful place, along the side of the garage walls.

Now for my favourite part.

He grabbed David's hands and pulled them straight, his fat body crushed with the weight of the Toyota Corolla's engine. *Perfect.* Reaching up to his top pocket, he found the knife. He didn't want to rush things, not this part. He had waited years for this moment, he wasn't going to let a ringing phone rush him. He also knew he couldn't stall and soak in the enjoyment too long. He had to move. A game had to be won.

Caressing David's hands, he noticed they were still moving, his fingers slightly twitching. The last glimmer of life, leaving his body, the perp thought. His machiavellian smile engulfed his face, his lips curling up at the ends, showing genuine pride. He watched with amusement. He ran his gloved fingers over his victims knuckles and sighed. 'It didn't have to be like this.'

He knew the kitchen knife would cut through living bone. Still fresh and less tough than dead bone. He read in his book about how bones dry out after death, which made it appreciably tougher to cut through.

He didn't just want his knuckles, he wanted it all. The knife worked perfectly; he didn't need the saw on the work bench. He was nearly done. Cutting the last piece of flesh, he smiled and put his trophies into a plastic bag. *I must clean up. Can't let the workers come in tomorrow morning, having to clean up after me, before they start work. I'm not that cruel.*

Before tidying up, he slid his hand in the blood and lifted it up and used it like paint to mark his next direction on the garage floor. His arrow pointed East. Simple move from here.

Placing the plastic bag in his rucksack, he looked around and gasped. *Gosh, I nearly forgot again.* The number 3 counter had to be placed. He stood, observing his handy work. *Now where would be the greatest place to show off my craftsmanship. Here?* Looking to see what it would look like near the front tyre of the corolla. *No, too out the way. How about…here? Perfect.* He placed the beautifully carved purple 3 counter, centre of the blood. *The colours compliment each other,* he thought and tilted his head to look again. The dice came out of his pouch. He knew the last number was 2, but he wanted to throw it anyway. He threw it at his feet, just slightly away from David's blood. '4…3…1, this can't be happening,' he rolled it again, '4…God, please help me,' he looked up as though he was talking to his saviour, held the dice tight in his palm and dropped it. '2…I knew you would shine through for me.'

Picking up his dice, wiping it clean on his jacket, he took the slip of acrylic painting paper out, which he acquired and put it near the car jack. He had written, "3 down one to go, you're paces behind and proving too slow." He lifted his shoes and walked out the back door, breathing in the cool night air. Rain was just starting to lightly fall. He locked the back door. *I don't want anyone taking anything from the garage. That would be dishonest and stealing,* and then put on his shoes.

Heading back to his vehicle, he felt a huge sense of empowerment. His move had been a success, he had kept himself under the radar. He was a pawn knocking his opponents off the board one at a time. The combination of all his favourite games were proving to be masterful. He was untouchable, unnoticeable and he understood his direct communication with God was powerful, getting stronger. He felt like he could almost touch him, feel his presence all around him, right here on Patton Street itself.

His vehicle, still parked in the store's parking lot, looked like it needed a wash. *You're in this with me, I need to look after you too.* He entered the store, carrying his rucksack over his left shoulder. He strolled down isle 12 and found all the car parts, air fresheners, sponges and vehicle shampoo. Taking his time smelling the different fragrances, he decided to go with Bubbalicious products. Placing them in his basket, he made his way to the cash registers. He waited his turn.

'Excuse me darling!' A lady's voice came from behind him.

Turning around he saw a little old lady in her late 70s, pushing a filled shopping cart to the back of the queue. Her expression was one of concern. 'Something is leaking in your bag son. You've left a puddle on the ground. Is your juice in your bag leaking?'

His eyes glared at her, then down to the ground behind him. A small pool of blood had formed between them. Just enough for his anxiety levels to rise. 'Damn juice. I 'preciate your observations ma'am. Thanks kindly. I left my bottle in the ice box by mistake and it must have cracked it open,' he lied.

'I know son, y'all know that I'm forever losing my mind, doing things like that more and more as I'm getting older,' she replied with a smile.

He bought his goods and left the store, holding his rucksack on its side, making sure no more blood dripped out over his clothes, over the parking lot. He couldn't afford a trail, a fault in his game. Turning around he saw one of the cashiers cleaning up the thick bloody juice. She wasn't concentrating on the task, instead she chewed her gum and chatted away to one of her colleagues, oblivious to the spillage in front of her.

I'm a stupid fool. That could have lost me the game. The plastic bag inside my rucksack must have a tear. He placed it in the trunk, leaning it up against the side. He started the vehicle and headed home. His mind was racing with feelings of anger, stupidity, but also elation. 'That has been the only mistake I've made so far. All gamers fall at some point, but its all about the recovery that matters, I've won again tonight, I'll celebrate by displaying my newest trophies alongside the others.'

Arriving home, he exited his vehicle and took his winnings inside. *I'll wash the vehicle tomorrow evening. I've a night off.* He strolled over to his sink, unzipped his bag and tipped the contents into the bowl. A large bucket sat in his laundry room. He filled it up with hot water and detergent, dumping the bloody rucksack in and leaving it to soak. He threw the useless, plastic bag into his garbage bin.

I need to get that rucksack cleaned for my last opponent. Number 2, she was always better than the rest of us. Studious, bright and Ma's favourite. Head always in her books. I remember when she used to read to me. She spoke of how books enlightened her life. Then she was told not to waste her breath and energy on me. To take her books away from me and read by herself. I heard her reading out aloud. Knocking on her door to let me in and getting shouted back at, to go away. I just wanted to talk, a conversation. But no! She will pay now, no more reading out aloud for her. Georgina Miller you have to die.

Moving back to the sink, he looked into the bowl. A gold wedding band sat tightly on the fat, chubby wedding finger. Egyptians considered the circle of the ring to be a symbol of eternity. Eternal love. He laughed at the thought. His life would soon be eternal, not David Torres's. His life was over.

He used his nail brush to clean under the fingernails and cut off excess-stringy sinew dangling from the muscle connecting the bone. *Reminds me of Genesis 32:32 and Job 10:11 The Children of Israel, not eat the sinew of the hip, which is upon the hollow of the thigh.* His thoughts drifted in and out of the different verses in the bible, as he finished off his accomplishments and achievements sitting in the bowl.

His vintage 5-gallon glass jar was stored in the cupboard, waiting patiently for something to hold, to show off and keep safe. He had learnt from his biology book, page 72, about how organisms can typically be preserved and stay intact by just pouring in either, alcohol or formalin. He chose the latter.

Finishing off, displaying the jar in the green cupboard, which he needed to restore tomorrow, he admired his work. The man went back up to his kitchen and put the kettle on the stove. He ran the hot faucet, placing the knife underneath to wash it. He walked over to the refrigerator. He was dying for a coffee and something to eat.

Chapter Eighteen

Packing her bags to head home, Clara wondered if she would still have a job when she returned back to Durant. She knew, herself and Adam had worked well together, she was hoping he would write up a good report on her conduct and intelligence work. They seemed to have bonded towards the end. It was that little bit of hope she clung to.

Putting in her last pair of folded pants, she zipped up her bag and sat on the bed. Perez said he would knock when he was ready to make tracks. She glanced at her watch. *What's keeping him?* She sat for a little bit longer. It was these times when her anxieties raised to the surface, she thought about the drink. Her legs started to twitch. She stood up and paced around the room. Her mind went straight to her mama, who was lying in Butler hospital, dying. She knew she was heading home, not by-passing the hospital. *I'm not ready to see her. I'll come back, maybe with Frank to Rainer Lake. Try and say my farewells to Grayson.*

The knock on the door came. *About time!* 'Come in.'

Special Agent in Charge, Adam Perez, stood in the doorway. Clara noticed he hadn't any luggage with him. 'You not ready yet?' Asked Clara, eager to get home and see her best friend.

'There's been another murder,' he said solemnly.

'What? Are you kidding me?'

'I'm afraid not. A man's body was found this morning by his employees. It's our killer's M.O. We're heading there now. Get your coat, it's bitterly cold out there.'

They headed downstairs, telling the girl on reception they wouldn't be booking out just yet.

Getting into the SUV, they headed over to Patton Street, Clara navigated as usual.

'So, we got it wrong? Joseph Martin isn't our killer?' She asked.

'Looks like it. He's in the cells. Our victim was last seen alive at 17.00hrs yesterday evening by his work crew. We'll hopefully find out more. Dr Cameron is on scene as we speak. Martin is in jail awaiting a trial hearing in front of Judge Trueman. He won't be seeing daylight for a very long time.'

'Who's our victim?' Clara asked. She felt dizzy with the annoyance they got it wrong, that her investigatory capacity was all wrong. *What will Miller say now?*

'His name is David Torres. He owns the car dealership and garage. Done alright for himself so I hear.'

'It's as though our unsub is jealous. All his victims have owned high-end homes and achieved good jobs.'

'Yep, after the initial crime scene visit, we're heading straight to Torres's home in Lavaca. He has a wife and son. Officer Carter and Sheriff Harris are there now, doing the inevitable job of informing them.'

Parking up, they headed towards Torres Car Dealership. Officer Asher was standing at the main door, to the front of the building. The scene was chaotic. Camera crews and reporters had got wind of what was going on in Butler. The gathering, pushing and shoving their way forward to get answers from the officer. Clara noticed his face was one of terror.

'Please get back. We have nothing to report. Please. We are trying to do our jobs. Step away from the entrance!' Asher repeated, his words falling on deaf ears.

Clara and Adam had no choice. Straight through the middle with their heads down. Officer Asher spied them, lifting his arm for them to duck under. When they were through, he slammed the door and took a deep breath. 'The place has gone crazy!'

'Which way is Dr Cameron?' Perez asked, putting his hand on Asher's shoulder to calm him down.

'Down the corridor sir. Straight through the door in front.'

'Thanks. And don't open the door. Let the vultures freeze out there,' said Perez.

Reaching the connecting door, they saw a box of protective clothing. Suiting up, they entered. Dr Cameron looked up. 'It's definitely our killer. Same M.O. but this time he's cut off both hands from the wrists. The two agents saw the white car jacked up, David Torres body lying in a pool of blood and vomit. The stumps at the end of his arms, oozing. 'Again, like Mrs Parker, he has been hit over the head, pre-mortem by a large object, of which has been left on scene. A torque wrench. He hasn't even bothered to clean it after use. He is either getting sloppy or his confidence for not getting caught, is building.'

'The injury to the front of his skull? Where has that come from?' Asked Clara.

'Combing the scene when we first arrived, we think he was struck on the back of the head over there, near that bench. He fumbled to the ground, hitting his head off the floor. Your unsub has dragged him over, placed him here and amputated his hands whilst squashed beneath this Toyota. The cuts are clean and precise. Very professionally executed.' Dr Cameron reduced the whole act, which had happened last night, in a nutshell. 'Counter 3. Purple. Looks like the same materials were used to make it, as the others. The written slip is actually written on acrylic paper. Something an artist would use. Come to think of it, I have seen this in Joseph Martin's studio when we searched. He had a stack of it and the top sheet was torn. Don't ask me why I remember, I just do.'

'How's that even possible? He's been locked up since yesterday afternoon,' Clara was feeling disappointed not getting results.

'He's going to strike again agents. You need to up your game,' said Dr Cameron, showing both of them the slip of paper. The direction of his next kill is East from here,' they looked over at the painted bloody sign on the ground. 'If I find out more, I'll let you know. Oh, and Eleanor died from blunt force impact and hypothermia. No indication of toxicity in her blood. Her stabbing was carried out postmortem.'

Throwing their coveralls in the trash bag, they collaborated and decided to look around David's office, it was all part of the crime scene. They asked one of Dr Cameron's assistance for some evidence bags.

On entering, they noticed his chair was pushed away from the desk and Clara saw his reading glasses sitting on top of invoices, centre of his desk, indicating he probably left the room without a struggle. 'How did he get from here to the garage? Do you think he was forced? Did he get up of his own accord, hear the killer in the garage and then met his own death?' She asked Perez.

'It looks that way. Everything in here looks in its place, no signs of struggle.' Ten minutes into sifting through David Torres's filed paperwork in a grey filing cabinet, situated at the back of his office, he pulled out an A4 invoice with the corner ripped off. Showing it to Clara, he slipped it into an evidence bag. 'Could be a match to the slip of paper found at Eleanor Parkers crime scene. We take anything that looks connected.'

'There's no correspondence between this victim and the others, or any of our suspects. Oh wait. What do we have here? William Parker had his car serviced the day his wife was murdered. Do you think that has any bearing on our investigation?' She asked her boss, rummaging through the copious amounts of paper.

'Bag it!'

Clara picked up a handful of invoices and flicked through them. She found the flyer the police had posted through residents doors informing them of the situation and to stay safe. 'Obviously Torres never even read this,' she said lifting it up and showing her boss. 'The car dealership had some minor repairs done, toilet replaced, some new cladding fitted,' She ran her finger down the list, 'the lunchroom painted, new carpet laid, the invoice is from Arnold and Davis. Is that Michael and Eli?'

'Not sure, look I've found something else. David Torres was in debt. There are bank statements here. Wow, thousands of dollars worth of debt. No wonder he was trying to balance his books last night,' Perez bagged the information. 'Think we need to go pay Mrs Torres a visit.'

They headed back to the main doors, Officer Asher still watching out for the local press. He opened the front doors for the two agents. Reporters were in their vans, defrosting. They spied the two agents and clambered from their vans. A throng of men and women headed for them, microphones and cameras in hand. Clara and Adam were more agile on their feet, jumping in the SUV, throwing the evidence in the back seat and speeding off. 'Which direction?' Perez asked, out of breath.

'I'll get the details from Hannah.' She lifted her cell and dialled the sheriff's department.

'Butler Sheriff's office. Officer Hannah Young speaking.'

'Hannah, it's Agent Strong. I need David Torres address. Is Sheriff Harris and Officer Carter still at his home?'

'No, they're on their way back, but wanted to go and check on William Parker and Benjamin Johnson first. They are trying to figure out what is going on and get their alibis from last night. He asked me to phone you to let you know. Sorry I've been swamped, I'll send you the location now. Agent Strong, are we safe? I'm currently here on my own. Michael is in the office, fixing the door, apart from that..?'

'Just make sure you have the main door to the police department locked. You'll be fine. I'll speak later.'

'West Pushmataha Street, straight onto the east side, left onto Meadowlark rd, then right onto Lotts Ferry road. Their house, according to Hannah, is on Bandit Drive. She seems pretty spooked about the whole thing.'

'We can't let him win this, we need to be in front, catch him before he kills again.'

'Back to the starting line. We need to cross reference every single detail. We should check out the Pentecostal Church Eleanor and Evan attended when they were kids. Think it was on…I'll have to look it up back at the office. All the files have been stored.'

'Be interesting to know if David Torres attended there too. It could open a new lead. We need to look at this from every angle, regardless of whether we think it's relevant,' Agent Perez spoke up. 'Give Hannah another call and get her to check.'

Clara got straight on it. They needed to find out before arriving at the Torres's home. 'Hannah is definitely proving to be helpful. Norton Pentecostal Church, Norton Street. It's just off South Mulberry Avenue.'

'Good job. As hard as it's going to be, we need to get as much information from his wife as possible. She probably won't be up for talking much, but we'll have to stipulate the urgency of her help,' he said quickly, as they entered into Bandit Drive.

The home was large, with its centralised fountain in the driveway. There was a show of garish garden ornaments surrounding the manicured lawns. Clara thought it looked ostentatious, but knowing their financial problems, it looked more pretentious. They didn't have time to take in the rest of the views. There was a serial killer out there needing caught.

A young 17-year-old teenager answered the door. 'Yeah, who are you?'

'I'm Special Agent in Charge Perez and this is Special Agent Strong. May we come in?'

The young teenager just opened the door, walking away. He headed to the large room on the right and sat down. 'What y'all need from us? Can't you see we're in a mess?'

'We're so sorry for landing on your doorstep so soon after, well after the tragic loss of your father. We are really desperate to talk to your mother. We need to ask her some questions before this happens to another family,' Perez explained.

'What use is that to us? It ain't gonna bring my pa back any!' He wailed.

'We understand, we can't undo what has been done, but please, we need to catch this son of a bitch and we need your help,' Clara snapped.

The young teenager looked up at Clara. He nodded his head. 'Okay.'

'Is your mother in? Can we talk with her?' She continued.

'She's upstairs being consoled by Noah. I'll go fetch her.'

The agents peered over at one another. Moments later, a fit looking woman walked into the room. She was wearing green sweatpants and a tight black shirt, defining her curves and muscles. 'You wanted to see me?'

Perez introduced himself and apologised for her loss. 'We understand your husband was having financial difficulties. Did he owe anyone a substantial sum of money? Can you think of anyone that would want to see your husband harmed?'

'He was always in debt. God only knows what he did with his money,' Mrs Torres replied. Clara looked around the room at the outfits Amelia Torres and her son Hudson were wearing. *At least 3 months rent on my apartment hanging around her wrists and neckline alone,* she thought.

'Did he seem anxious or cross paths with any of his clients? Mrs Torres, I hate to be the bearer of bad news but…. we believe your husband may have been a victim of a serial killer.' Perez's words echoed around the room; the sound of his voice penetrated through the whole house. Amelia Torres fell to her knees.

'Pray to God, why on earth would he be involved with someone like that?' Her eyes welled and the tears came. Her son lifted her from the floor, sitting her close by his side on the yellow and white gingham velvet couch.

'How do you know this?' Asked Hudson. His body shaking with shock.

'He is leaving the same crime scene behind. There are details we can't disclose, but trust me, it's definitely the same guy,' said Perez.

Just then a tall, muscular man with tight jeans and an athletic white t-shirt entered.

'I heard you crying. Are you okay?' He asked.

'Can I ask who you are?' Clara inquired.

'This is mum's boyfriend, Noah Cooper! Big time hot shot from out of town!' Hudson said, mocking the man with sarcasm and a tone of condescension.

'Enough! He's a friend of the family!' Amelia shouted. 'I don't understand what is going on.'

'We are trying to connect the 3 victims. Did your husband drink at Alabama South Avenue Bar & Grill?'

'He frequented there a few nights a week. He took his workers, you know, to keep them sweet. He knew some weeks he couldn't pay them, so he use to get them drunk and they would be pally, they would suffer the financial burden for a couple more days. It didn't happen every week,' David's wife explained.

'Did he ever mention a woman called Eleanor Parker? She was an elementary school teacher in Butler. Her maiden name was Garcia,' asked Clara.

'Eleanor Garcia, that name sounds familiar. But I have so many people attending my classes, she could be one of them. I'm sorry. I can't believe this is happening to us.'

'Mrs Torres, have you ever had a family portrait done by an artist named Joseph Martin?'

Her expression changed to confusion. 'Why yes, we had to go and get our photograph taken first at his studio. It's hanging up in our bedroom. Why d'you ask?'

'Unfortunately, we can't explain, but it's helpful,' she replied.

'Did your husband ever attend Norton Pentecostal Church on Norton Street, Butler?' Perez piped up.

'Why all these peculiar questions? What's that got to do with my husband's…' she couldn't finish the sentence.

'Please Mrs Torres, can you just answer the question?'

'I believe his folks used to attend that church when he was a young boy. A lot of strange goings on inside the church doors. It was almost like a cult,' wiping her tears, she stood up. 'Now if you don't mind, I need to lie down, I'm feeling extremely tired.'

'Thank you, Mrs Torres. Again, we are truly sorry for interrupting you at this ungodly time.'

The agents left the Torres's home and headed straight to the morgue to drop off the evidence sitting on the back seat. They knew Dr Cameron would look through it after finishing processing the third crime scene.

'We'll head back to the police department. We need to clear the board and start from the beginning,' Agent Perez told Clara.

Chapter Nineteen

Officer Hannah Young had retrieved all the case files and placed them on the agents' small desk, in their makeshift office. She used yellow stickers to document each file with the date, contents and put them in chronological order.

A tray of croissants and pastries sat beside two cups of black coffee. Cream, milk and sugar at hand. Hannah knew it was going to be a long day in the office, for everyone.

Pleased to see Officer Young had used her initiative, the two agents hung their coats to the back of the door and took a quick sip of the caffeine fix, which was essential.

'What did you make of Noah Cooper? Amelia Torres so-called boyfriend. I wonder if her husband knew what was going on. We should maybe do a background check on him too,' said Clara.

'We'll get Hannah to do it later. First, we need to forget everything we know and start from the beginning. We'll work through what we think his M.O is, his victimology, the crime scenes themselves in detail, and start building up a profile on him with the evidence and not on guess work. We need to look at all the different angles of his killings. Is he doing it because he knows the victims or are they random or,' he paused to think, then continued, 'has it nothing to do with the people, but their wealth and achievements. Is he simply jealous?'

Rubbing the whiteboard clean, Perez wrote, "unsub" in the centre and circled it. He drew a line from it and marked "M.O".

'So, his distinct pattern, signature or manner he is using is, 1 leaving numbered counters, 2 leaving messages, 3 leaving his next direction of the next kill, 4 targeting specific areas of the body. Anything else?' He asked Clara.

'He is only killing at night, undercover. Nobody has seen anything. He is meticulous to a point of obsession and all his kills are premeditated. He has thought about every detail. He must be local to the area to have studied his victims. He uses a knife to do his work and Dr Cameron said the unsub has excellent fine motor skills. He has an artistic eye for detail.'

'You know your stuff Agent Strong. He also kills them before he does the unforgivable. He has to make sure they are unconscious, at least. Maybe he has feelings for them, and he can't amputate or carry out the removal or stabbings while they are aware of his actions, watching him. Each event shares multiple similarities and is connected in more than one way. These connections mean something to him. Counters, gaming counters? The numbers on them; we now know 4 people are his attended target. His last note said, "one more to go." Did these 4 people wrong him in the past? Old friends, acquaintances, colleagues, school friends? His desire to kill could stem from a series of environmental and internal factors in his personal life. The eyes, the hands, the pregnancy. I know from previous cases many serial killers have a loss of function in the part of the brain that generates feelings of ethics and empathy. Along with family history of violence and a childhood devoid of love and affection, it can be a combination of disastrous outcomes. I'm not saying this is our unsub, but we need to think on a broader scale,' Agent Perez took a breath, then continued, 'Maybe he despises these people for wronging him.'

'Is he taking the parts for trophies? Eleanor Parker's was different. He stabbed the area of the developing foetus, but William's statement indicated her coat, hat and gloves were missing,' said Clara. 'Also, I don't understand why he left the torque wrench at the garage? I bet forensics won't find any fingerprints again.'

'I think he's getting cocky and believes he won't get caught. Serial Killers normally escalate their attacks, but he seems to be biding his time, making sure he doesn't make any mistakes or slip ups,' answered Perez, still scribbling on the whiteboard. 'He's almost what you would call a spree killer. Not much time in between kills. He wants to get it done or he's enjoying the act of killing, doesn't want to wait too long. He's on a mission.'

Clara noticed Perez was talking away mostly to himself, rather than to her.

'But why the notes? Is he taunting us and playing with our heads?'

'Think he's just having some fun in the process. Making himself more attractive to us feds,' he explained.

'So, his victims. Two males, one female.' Clara spoke while Perez drew another line from the central unsub heading. "Victimology". 'Different backgrounds, not related, different ages. Evan 39. David 38, Eleanor 32.'

'All married, white American and in their thirties. All successful in their choice of careers, but also quite vulnerable at the time of their death. Evan drank and wasted money. Eleanor, pregnant and suffered from early signs of depression. David, up to his eyes in debt,' Perez added. 'Was he putting them out of their misery? He thought they were suffering and wanted them to be at peace.'

'Did this all stem from when they were younger? We know the three victims attended the same church with their parents. Did they rattle someone's head back then and stir up trouble?' She asked.

'Ask Hannah if David Torres attended the same school as the other two? But we should head over to the church ourselves and start digging around.'

'I'll go and ask her. I need to stretch my legs,' Clara left the office and went next door. Officer Hannah Young was typing away on her computer. She looked up in surprise. 'Ma'am?'

'We need to know if David Torres went to the same school as Evan and Eleanor. Do you think you could get into records and search?' Agent Strong asked.

'Yes, I'm catching on fast. I'll let you know.'

'Also, can you find out anything about Noah Cooper. I don't think he is a resident of Butler or Lavaca, so it might be tricky to track his info down. He's a friend of David and Amelia Torres. If you keep going the way you're going, you'll be after my job,' Clara said with a reassuring smile. Hannah blushed and put all her energy back into the search platform.

'Agent Strong, glad I've caught you. I've spoken to William Parker and Benjamin Johnson. They both have alibis. William's is solid, his parents have been staying with him and can vouch for his whereabouts, but we are still digging into Johnsons. Said he was with his wife all night, but something tells me different,' Sheriff Harris said.

'Did you know David Torres?'

'Only through the garage. I never knew him personally. I tend to keep my distance from folk on a social level. I know how they can manipulate people of the law, for their own gain,' he replied.

Clara recognised that look. Harris must have been hurt in the past by someone close.

Returning back to Perez, she poured them both another coffee and sat back down behind the desk. 'She's searching as we speak. Parker and Johnson look to have alibis for last night and Sheriff Harris didn't know David Torres, so can't give us a heads up on who he was.'

'Great! None of the victims were known to the Sheriff, so they've never been in trouble with the law. Three people just going about their business. Not knowing they were being watched by their killer. Does he know them personally, just biding his time to attack? Did he befriend them years ago as kids or now in adulthood? Before we move on, we need to try and write up a clear profile of our killer. We don't have any sightings of him, but we have quite a good understanding of who he is. Can you write it down as we go Agent Strong?' Perez asked.

Picking up a notepad and pen she nodded. 'Ready.'

'Our unsub is of a fit physical build. Estimated height between 5ft 10 and 6ft ,' Perez said.

'Sorry, but how do you know that?' She asked.

'Because of all the scenes we have attended, what we've seen, his strength and M.O, it is a rough guesstimate. I can't see him being any smaller, especially after all the lifting and dragging he has done. Trust me, I've been at this game for a few years, you get a good understanding of human anatomy by piecing together bits of evidence.'

'Okay, just thought I missed something.'

'So 5ft 10 to 6ft. Quite shy or keeps low key. He is probably a loner, lives by himself and not married. A local to the area, maybe he has lived here all his life. Employed, physical job I believe, to keep himself fit. His job may also be a skilled profession seeing as he is good with his hands. His cutting skills are precise, so could work in a meat industry, hospital, lumberyard. He's focused and confident with his abilities of killing. He is dangerous and calculated. I believe he's in it to the end. He needs to finish what he's started.'

'Sir, look! The numbers on the counters.'

'What about them?'

Clara was staring at the victims' detail sheet, perched at the side of the desk.

'Evan was the eldest 39, counter 4. David second oldest 38, counter 3. Eleanor, the youngest, 32, counter 1. So, our next victim will be counter 2. Agree?'

'Yes, but what are you getting at?'.

'Our next victim will be between 32 and 38 years of age. His pattern. Its age related. He hasn't killed in order though. Why? We need to get everyone to inform the residents of this age group, east of the car dealership.'

Clara jumped to her feet and rushed out to find Harris. 'Gather everyone up. We need to talk to them, now!'

Clara's adrenaline rushed through her body. She had found something concrete. At last, they had started to understand their killer's M.O. The officers shuffled into the room. All eyes on Perez and Strong. 'We have found out the killer's methods of selecting his victims, he's playing some sort of sadistic game. He's selected four people for his target. As we know, three have been brutally murdered, but if we work efficiently and together, we might be able to stop him before he targets his last victim.'

Perez brought the map in. He unrolled it on a desk, telling everyone to move closer. 'We are focusing our search starting from the car dealership and heading eastwards. So, E. Church Street, across South Mulberry Avenue, over to South Academy Avenue and Roger's Street. Pass the woodland here, to Pickens Avenue, Harrell Avenue, Ida Drive and Woolley Avenue. We believe he's going to target someone between the ages of 32 and 38 years. We aren't sure if the next victim will be male or female at this stage. We need you to split yourselves up, knock hard on these residential and commercial properties. Our unsub is about 5ft 10 to 6ft. If you see any male acting out of the ordinary, call it in. Do not approach him.'

'What do we say to the residents?' An Officer asks hesitantly.

'Tell them to stay home, preferably not on their own and don't answer their doors for the next 48hrs at least. Almost like lockdown,' Clara stated.

'Sheriff Harris, Agent Strong and I are going to follow up on some more leads. Can we leave you to hold the fort?'

'What can I do to be of help?'

'Hannah was checking to see if David Torres attended the same school as the other two victims. Maybe call his wife and ask. Quicker than the system. Also, can we find any information about Noah Cooper, Amelia Torres's friend?'

'I'll phone you if anything comes up. Where are you two headed?'

'Norton Pentecostal Church here in Butler,' said Clara, anxious to get going.

Leaving the department, heading to Norton Street, Adam asked Clara if she knew what pentecostalism actually meant? He explained he didn't follow any faiths and knew little about what each religion believed in.

'I believe it's a movement within Protestant Christianity. It emphasises the gifts of the Holy Spirit.'

'Meaning?' His curiosity stirring.

'Meaning, they believe in the likes of the supernatural healing and other manifestations of the Holy Spirit.'

His eyebrows furrowed. 'Do you believe in all that stuff?'

'Nope. If there was a God, then why are people murdered? It's not to give us a job in law enforcement. Too much suffering. It says here on my phone, the fundamental requirement of Pentecostalism is that one be born again. The new birth is received by the grace of God through faith in Christ as Lord and Saviour. It also says that, in being born again, the believer is regenerated, justified, adopted even, into the family of God, and the Holy Spirit's work of sanctification is initiated.'

'I'll let you do the questioning at this one!' Perez announced.

Pulling up outside the church, they saw it was well maintained. The building was in excellent condition with new windows displayed to the side. Clara looked at Adam. Entering the church, the agents heard a choir of women singing at the very front. They were practicing songs for the Sunday gathering. The angelic chorus sent a wave of emotion through Clara, her skin tightened with goose bumps. Her gaze was cut short.

'Can I help you?' A voice came from their left.

'Yes, we're from the FBI. We were hoping to speak with the Pastor.'

'Then you have found him. How can I be of assistance?'

He stood about 6ft tall, back straight, hands clutched together, wearing smart but casual clothes. He held his stare, waiting until one of them answered.

'Would we be able to speak with you somewhere a bit quieter?' She continued.

'Does the singing not please you officer?' He retorted.

Clara was just about to explain she wasn't an officer, but an agent. Her head told her to push forward. Ignore his ignorance.

He raised his hands, 'Follow me.'

The room he led them into was big enough to accommodate Clara's whole apartment. She couldn't help it. She did it every time. 'What's this about officers?'

Perez could tell the Pastor was rubbing his partner up the wrong way.

'We're concerned for residents' safety here in Butler and the surrounding towns. We're investigating three murders and need help finding answers.'

'You've come to the right place. God's willing answers everyone's questions,' Pastor MacArthur said, satisfied with his answer and smiled.

'We were hoping maybe you could help. Have you been preaching at Norton Pentecostal Church for long?'

'I was part of the congregation years ago. My father was an Elder later on in my life. He encouraged me to take my exams and become a Pastor. So here I am. I've never looked back.'

'Back in the days, do you remember three children that attended here. They would have been in the company of their parents. Their names are Evan Thomas, David Torres and…'

'Eleanor Garcia! Yes, everyone remembers those three. I was a bit older than them. Their parents used to bring them along, but they had no interest in the Holy Spirit. All they wanted to do was run around and create chaos,' he finished.

'How odd you remember them so vividly. We're talking twenty plus years ago,' she turned to look at Perez. Her heartbeat rhythm changed.

'Nothing odd about it my child. The whole congregation probably remembers them. They used to torment other children when the sermon was spoken. We preach through storytelling using worshippers' testimonies of miracles and how the Holy Spirit has supported their lives. I remember this one particular story being told, it was interrupted by the three in question and they had to be removed. I know we were all young and foolish but what they did to that poor young boy,' his eyes reflecting pure hatred. 'It was really the two older boys who instigated most of the horrendous things happening in the church. Eleanor just happened to know them, sat next to them at every opporcune moment.'

'This particular day. Can you recall what happened?' Asked Perez.

'Yes.' Pastor MacArthur looked up and took a deep breath in. 'They sat behind another young member, cut his clothes with a sharp knife, slicing through the back of his neck. All the parents were too engrossed to notice what was happening. The children denied it. The child had to be admitted to hospital. Get stitched up. It was quite harrowing. His family never attended this church again after that.'

'Pastor, this is an important question. Do you remember the name of the child that was hurt?' Clenching her hands and waiting for an answer.

'Yes, it was Eli…Eli Davis.'

Chapter Twenty

'We need to put out an APB on Eli Davis. All officers should be aware he maybe armed and dangerous. Shit! Is he at the Sheriffs department working. I didn't even notice. Did you? Hannah, I need to phone Hannah,' Clara's panicking made her breathless.

'Agent Strong, look at me, you need to calm down. We'll find him. You aren't going to get anything achieved in this state. Officer Young will be out with the others. We gave them a job to do, remember?'

Sitting in the SUV, she put the window down. The freezing air hit her face.

'We'll head to the station. Eli maybe working and we don't want to spook him. We'll play it down, approach him as usual but with caution,' uttered Perez calmly.

Clara nodded. She didn't understand why she was so riled up and being protective over Hannah and the young officers. Was she trying to make things right because of what occurred with Grayson. Her coping mechanisms were starting to shut down. Her mouth was dry, she needed something to take away the bitter taste. *God, where are you Jack Daniels when I need you?*

Arriving at the courthouse, doors now unmanned, they spied Michael. He was in the corridor that led towards the sheriff's office, painting the skirting boards on his knees.

'Michael, has Eli turned up for work today?' Remarked Perez. Not giving anything away at this point.

He placed the paintbrush in the pot of gloss and stood up. 'Nope he sure ain't. I had a feeling he wouldn't show up. He's been acting suspicious lately. Don't know what's going on in that head of his.'

'What do you mean suspicious?'

'Well, his been acting cagey. I ask him what's going on and he won't answer. Shrugs his shoulders and turns his back. I can hear him talking away to himself, muttering things about God and how he needs his help. He isn't sleeping at night. Says he needs to cut down on the caffein,' Michael divulged.

'If he isn't at work, where would he go?'

'We're supposed to be finishing off a job this afternoon. A bunch of fence panels blew down in that wind, over by the grocery store. Looks like I'll be at it on my own.'

'He's missed a few days from work, is that right?'

'Yeah, sure has. Can't recall every time, but I know he didn't show the morning after that poor gal was killed, come to think of it, nor the morning of the first murder. That was the morning you folks just arrived and asked me where the sheriff's office was. Is he in some kind of trouble?' Michael's face showing concern.

'No, we just really need to talk to him. Would you know his address off hand?' Said Perez.

'I sure do. It's a bit of a drive. You'll be glad of your vehicle I can tell you that. He's over at Desotoville Avenue. Head out on North Mulberry Avenue and its sign posted to the left. If you come to Cherokee Avenue, you've gone too far. Signposts round here need a sprucing up. Can't read nothing. His place is impossible to find. Sits beside a swampy lake, no one to talk to but those pesky gators.'

Clara got her cell out and pulled up google maps. She zoomed in on Desotoville Avenue and showed it to Michael. 'Can you show me on here?'

'Holy crap, how does your cell do that?' He pointed to Eli Davis's house, perched on the side of a lake, surrounded by acres and acres of forest.

'Thanks Michael. Do me a favour, if he shows up here can you say nothing, but give us a call. Here's my cell number,' Clara interjected.

'I'll have to use the Sheriff's landline. I don't know where I've put mine.'

'That's fine, I'll let Sheriff Harris know. Thanks.'

'Anything I can do to help, just let me know.'

Coming out of the courthouse the two agents were inundated by hoards of news reporters, flashing lights and microphones hurled into their faces.

'What can you tell us of your investigations on the Alabama Murderer? Have you got any suspects that you are holding for questioning? Why is it taking you so long to catch the so-called Alabama Murderer? Agents. Do you have anything to say?' A young lady reporter verbalised.

'We have a number of leads we are following. We will be doing a press release soon. We have interviewed a number of people of interest and closing in on the perpetrator as we speak. Now if you don't mind, we have a job to do. Thank you,' Special Agent Perez conducted himself professionally, jumping into the SUV with Agent Strong. Flashing lights indicating all eyes were on these two now to close the case, to catch the killer.

'Damn press. Like leeches sucking on an open wound.' Agent Perez took the wheel, calming down from the entourage of charging bulls and headed for Eli Davis's home. The blue crisp skies slowly disappeared, getting left behind as they headed up Desotoville Avenue, that runs centre of the abundant forest and wetlands of the Coastal Plain. The gentle slopes of the rivers and streams here over time, have developed broad flood plains, shaped by the wide seasonal fluctuations in the rivers. It is home to a diverse habitat of native birds, plants and animals. It was like driving into a world that time forgot.

The density of the trees thickened; the avenue slowly disappeared to reform as a dirt trail.

'We are heading in the direction on the map?' Perez questioned. Their vehicle was feeling the uneven ground. Clara bounced around in her seat, holding onto the handle above her head.

'It's showing this way. Let's trust technology,' she said.

A sign up in front read, "State Wetland Activities Authorised. Permit Holders Only."

'Eli must be a keen hunter if he lives out here. Where the hells the turning? Slow down, our location is showing here. We need to park up and head through that trail by foot.'

'Where's his vehicle? There's no sign of it.'

Clara and Adam got out. They were engulfed by swamp oak and red maple trees. The tupelo gum trees with their broad stout branched trunks, sat in the flooded areas to the side. Partnered with the bald cypress, creating a plethora of root stems, which was habitat to a multitude of wildlife. To the agents they would be pure hell to manoeuvre around. The smell of damp shallow root systems dominated the air. Its magnificent beauty was captivating, with the flock of hooded warblers and their songs roaming the forest canopy, leaving the river otters and wood stork to forage in the swampy waters below.

'We need to tread carefully, the ground is unforgiving, follow my footsteps and you'll be fine,' Clara said to Perez in a whisper. He nodded. 'Watch out for the gators, they hide just below the surface.'

Perez smirked. Clara put her finger to her lips and pointed down to the water. A gator, waiting for its prey to arrive, lay still and unmoved.

'Shit!'

The landscape in front of them started to open up. A small wooden structure sat almost camouflaged against the backdrop of the trees. The coloured leaves turning with the season, floated softly to the water's surface and drifted away with the ripples created by the slight breeze.

Reaching for their weapons, they covertly moved forwards. Perez signalled to Clara to go round back. He ducked below the front window, then knocked hard on the door. 'Eli Davis, it's the FBI. We need you to open up and step outside with your hands raised above your head. Do you hear me?'

A wooden outhouse in the rear yard sat close to Eli's home. Its door was open. Clara held up her Glock and checked inside. The sight before her made her stomach convulse. Dead animals hung from the ceiling by chains and ropes. Unrecognisable creatures, with their blood dripping into buckets, situated underneath their poor lifeless bodies, rattled Clara's senses. Two of the creatures were completely skinned and left hanging to dry. She recognised the rope, it was similar to that found underneath Eleanor's jetty, tying her body to the posts. Clara knew Eli was their killer. She waved her arm around her head to swipe the flies away. She stumbled out into the fresh air, gasping.

Noticing the door to the rear of the house was slightly a jar, Clara tapped her foot gently against it. The door's opening made a slight noise, she peered through the gap and saw nothing. Tapping it open some more, she placed her foot inside, her Glock poised against her thigh.

She entered.

She noticed inside, the house was neatly furnished. A total contrast to the exterior. She lifted her arms to waist height and moved forward. She heard Perez shouting from the front. Maybe she shouldn't have entered. Maybe she should have stayed outside. But her adrenaline levels were sky high. *I know you're in here you son of a bitch. Show yourself!* She wanted to face him, pull the trigger, so this would all be over.

The floorboards creaked as she manoeuvred forwards. She froze. *Fuck!* She waited then advanced towards the stairs. The rail was handcrafted, painted a creamy white, reflecting Eli's skills. *It's him. We've definitely got him. Now come and show yourself.* Thoughts raced through her head of all the different scenarios that might arise. Moving up a step at a time, she paused at the top. Shoving a door open to her left and seeing the room empty, she carried on down the hallway. The sound of something dripping from the next room, caught her attention. Slowly and steadily, she reached for the door handle.

'FBI! Come on out with your hands above your head.'

Nothing. No movement. No one responded to her demands.

She kicked the door open. Lying in the bathtub was a dead hog, its legs tide together and surrounded by its own blood. The faucet was dripping slowly into the murky water. The hog's eyes, with its dead stare made Clara's stomach turn. She had seen enough dead animals; she even caught them when she was younger, but this. This made her feel nauseous. She left the room and checked the bedrooms. Nothing.

Lowering her gun, she returned to the ground floor. She unlatched the front door from inside and opened it.

'It's me, don't shoot!' She shouted.

'What in God's name are you doing inside?'

'The door was open, I thought I heard someone moving around inside,' she hated bullshitting to her boss but needed to keep herself right.

'No sign of him then?'

'No. Just a hog corpse in the bath.'

Perez gave her a look of confusion. Putting his gun away, he entered the house. 'Try not to touch anything with your hands. We need to scout the place for any evidence.'

'The outhouse round the back, there's rope similar to that found at Eleanor's crime scene.'

'Jesus Eli, why would you do this?' Perez thought out loud.

He took his gun back out and used it as a tool to move items. Clara entered the laundry room. Everything had its place. She felt it odd a single man would live like this. All her male friends were disgusting with their hygiene standards and organisation skills. *So why is he meticulous about the way his home looks? Out here. The middle of nowhere.*

'Anything?'

'No, just organised rooms. They all have decorated handmade furniture. Everything has its place,' she said.

'It reminds me of Joseph Martin's home. Eli definitely looks after his things. It could be to make his home like his victims, but on a smaller scale. His castle. It says a lot about him. He's organised to a point of perfection. He's creative with the rooms and being disorganised would throw him off kilter. But where the fuck is he?'

'We should call Harris and ask him if he knows anything. He may know something about Eli we don't.'

'Get on the blower and see. I'm gonna keeping looking. I'll bag up the rope. We should maybe get forensics out here when we have more evidence.'

Taking herself outside, Clara dialled the police department. *Come on signal. Not now. Work you stupid phone.* Moving it around in the air, she had no luck. She stepped back inside the house, shouted out to Perez she was going back to the vehicle to try get a signal, hoping he heard.

Her feet were soaked, tramping through the wetlands was no longer fun. As a child, her and Grayson lived for the moment, trying to find crawfish and other food sources. Now she was an FBI Agent trying to get a signal. She remembered George teaching them how Alabama was sometimes known as the Aquatic State. What with the countless streams, rivers, lakes, swamps and bogs, she could see why. Her thoughts moved to her mum as she stared at her cell, wishing a signal would appear.

The slip of one foot on a protruding cypress root, was all it took. Twisting her weak left ankle, falling over on her side, she tried to grab for a low branch. Her body fell too fast. She felt the cold sensation of the water, taking her breath away. Her head dropped below the surface, striking against a rock on the way down. Blood. She saw blood floating above her, as her body lay under the water's surface. Panic set in at the realisation of her surroundings. She heard muffled sounds of movement beside her. *I'm gonna die. I don't want to die! Grayson help me!*

A hand plunged into the water, gripping the front of her jacket. Pulling her up, Perez dragged her back from the water's edge to a safe distance, far enough from the prying eyes of the gators.

'Clara, can you hear me? Clara.'

'Frank?'

'We need to get you to the hospital. Can you stand? Clara, listen to my voice. You need to stand.'

Her hair was matted in blood. Soaked to the bone, she held onto Perez. 'I...I don't know what happened...my head,' She reached up feeling the gash, her hand covered in blood.

'We're nearly at the vehicle. Stay with me Clara.'

Chapter Twenty-One

The distant sound of sliding doors opening and closing, air conditioning systems running on a low frequency, people talking in low voices, was what she could distinguish. Lying still, she opened her eyes to see where she was. The light above her shone a sickly white light in her direction.

'Lie still. You've got a nasty gash to the back of your head. The Doctor has stitched the area up. It's not as bad as we first thought, nevertheless it's still pretty sore looking. We had to shave a little area of your hair; it'll grow back.'

Clara moved her head to the side, wincing with the pain. An old looking nurse peered down at her. 'Darling, would you like some naproxen? It will help you to relax and reduce the swelling.'

Clara nodded gently. The sound of throbbing, still prominent in her ears. Sitting up with the nurse's help, she consumed the painkillers, wanting to remain sitting up in bed. Noticing her wet clothes had been removed and dried off, she turned her attention to the man sitting to her side.

'George? What are you doing here?'

'I heard you were brought in. News travels fast in this hospital. I blame it on Cheryl from reception. I was in visiting…' he cut the sentence short. 'Heard you fell in gator territory. You sure were lucky. Not many folks have come out alive to tell the tale. How ya feeling?'

'I'm fine. I'll be back on my feet in a couple of hours. No good taking up a bed for someone who needs it.'

'Always the true hero. Your Partner told me to tell you he'll be back. Lucky for you he pulled you out. Didn't I teach you anything?' He laughed.

'Never had cell phones back then.'

'What's that got to do with swamp survival?' George's puzzled look comforted Clara. She smiled at him with admiration. She still loved him, even though he was visiting her mama.

'Have you been to see her?' She asked reluctantly.

'I was just on my way, when I heard you were admitted. I'll check on her shortly. She is two corridors along if you want to see her?' Clara could see he wanted to say more. He held back.

'Did my partner say where he was going?'

'To dry off your phone. He said you held onto it; he couldn't get it out of your grip.'

She reckoned it was maybe to do with the fact it was her only communication to the outside world. To Frank.

Agent Perez came into view; he had changed his clothes. 'Good to see you back in the land of the living Agent Strong.'

George vacated his seat. 'I'll be seeing you then. Look after yourself. I'll let your mama know you're okay,' with that he bent over and kissed her gently on her forehead.

'Your mama? Is she…?' Perez knew this wasn't the time to ask personal questions. He sat down beside her bed and shook his head. 'Ironic really. City boy rescues country gal. Nothing to it wrestling gators and the likes,' His southern Alabama accent needed practice she thought.

Clara was thankful for some good humour. God only knows she needed some right now. 'What about Eli Davis?'

'Sheriff Harris has informed his officers to keep a look out. If they see him, they need to call it in. Act as though things are normal. He doesn't want him flipping out on his team. He doesn't believe that Eli is capable of the murders. He's known him for years. He actually supported him back when he was going through a divorce.'

'Eli Davis was married?'

'Yeah, she took to the bottle and ended up having a miscarriage with their first child.'

'Is that why he attacked and killed Eleanor Parker, because she was pregnant? You and Dr Cameron both agree the killings are personal to him,' Clara uttered.

'Sheriff Harris is adamant about Eli's innocence. He would put his life on it. Strong words from a man of the law.'

'Where's his wife now?'

'Madison Davis packed up and went north. Took Eli years to process what had happened, why his wife took to the drink in the beginning. That's why he moved to his home in the swamps. Wanted nothing more to do with folk. He works, but that's about it. Harris said he has an elderly father who adopted him, lives up near Pennington. I'm heading there now.'

Clara pulled down the sheets and swung her legs over to stand.

'Whoa, hang on there. You aren't fit to be going anywhere.'

'I'm coming with you. I can rest in the vehicle. Can you pass my clothes?'

'I don't have to remind you about your injury?' He said with conviction.

She looked up, staring into his eyes. 'I'm truly thankful you rescued my sorry little arse, and fixed my phone, but I'm coming, sir,' for a split second she looked over his shoulder. 'Eli Davis. He's just walked past my door.'

Perez spun his head around, seeing no one. 'You're still concussed.'

'Listen to me, Eli Davis has just walked up the corridor. I'm not hallucinating. Please, you need to go and check.'

Turning on his heels he left the room. Checking the rooms one at a time, peering through the small rectangular windows, he spotted him. Sitting by the side of an empty bed in room 7. He slid his head back so he wouldn't be seen and grabbed the attention of a passing trainee nurse.

'Can you tell me who is admitted in room 7?'

'Sorry sir, that's confidential information. I can't divulge patients details to strangers.'

He reached for his I.D. 'Look, I really need to know who is in there. I wouldn't want to arrest you for obstructing an investigation. Name?'

The young trainee flushed with embarrassment. She held her clip board up and scanned the page. 'It's a Mr John Oliver Brown.'

'Who's his next of kin?'

The nurse checked the patient's details. 'Mr Eli Davis, his son. The reason they have different names is due to adoption.'

'Where is he?'

'He should be in his room,' she peered through the window. Eli looked up. 'He maybe using the bathroom. I'll go and check.'

Her movements were too quick for Perez, he didn't have time to protest. She calmly walked in. 'Is everything okay?'

'Yeah,' Eli motioned his head to the bathroom door.

'Okay, just doing the rounds to see if you are good,' she exited the room. 'He's son said he's in the bathroom,' she walked away, carrying on with her duties.

Perez called Sheriff Harris, asking if he had anyone spare to stand by the front doors of the hospital in case his suspect decided to run. He knocked on the door. Eli got up to see who was there. 'Agent Perez, isn't it? What brings you here?'

'It's a bit sensitive. Is there anyway we could speak in private?'

'Do you mind if we stay here? Pa needs all the help he can get. Whatever it is you need to say, you can say it in front of him, his hearing is a bit impaired, so fire away.'

Just then, a frail elderly man appeared from the bathroom. His walking frame providing him with mobility, which he clearly needed. He looked up to see his new visitor. 'How do.'
'Pa this is my friend, Agent Perez from the FBI.'
He nodded. Clearly not hearing what was being said. Perez knew there was something not right about this situation. Trying to quickly process Eli Davis and his body language, he said, 'We're asking local folk to provide us with their alibis for the three nights in question, Sunday 12th, Tuesday 14th and Thursday 16th.'
''That's easy. I've been here every night since Pa got admitted on Saturday. Isn't that right Pa?'
His adoptive father just smiled, randomly asking his son questions about why there was a strange man in his room. Perez was struggling to understand Eli and this whole situation. 'We understand that you knew the three victims.'
'Three? I didn't know someone else had been,' he moved his head to indicate the missing word. He didn't want his Pa getting cross wires from his conversation.
'Last night David Torres was murdered. You knew him. And the others.'
'I'm sure a lot of the people in Butler and the surrounding towns knew all three. What's this really about?' Eli was starting to get annoyed.
'The times you needed off work. During the day. Where were you going?'
'That's my private business. I don't have to tell you anything.'
'When I'm investigating three murders, it would be in your best interest to cooperate Mr Davis. I can arrest you here and now, take you down to the police department in handcuffs on the suspicion of three murders,' Perez explained.
Eli glanced over at his Pa, who was lying in his bed staring at the ceiling, just existing and no more. 'He hasn't got long. His mind

is deteriorating, his cancer has spread all over his body and I'm the only one left in his life. How can I be at work? Do you have family Mr Perez?'

Adam Perez kept professional. 'Can the nurse's back up your alibis?'

'I've been trying to sort out his finances. He has left everything to me, his truck, his home, his debt. My head has been all over the place. God help me through this shit time, is all I can say. Go check. Butler town bank will let you know of my visits. God only knows I've had loads. My head wouldn't be able to cope with anything else, and you're telling me I'm a murderer,' he guffawed and turned back to hold his father's hand.

Perez stood up. 'Until we can identify all possible evidence that can prove you were at these places, on these days, I need you to stay in Butler. Do you understand Mr Davis?'

'Whatever you want. Now if you don't mind, I want to be with my Pa. Close the door behind you,' Eli didn't show any emotion as Perez left the room.

Going out to the main doors, he saw Deputy Dubois. 'Hope you're feeling fit to work?'

'This? It's just a graze.'

'Do me a favour. I need to check Eli's whereabouts during this whole investigation. He's in room 7 now with his adoptive father. If at anytime he leaves, tail him. Don't let him see you and report back to me. Can you do that?'

'Eli? What's he been up to?'

'He's a person of interest,' answered Perez.

'Eli Davis, a person of interest! Sorry sir, but you're definitely wasting your time there. I've known Eli since elementary school age, and he hasn't a bad bone in his body.'

'That's what sheriff Harris said as well. Until we can prove his whereabouts, I want you to treat him as a suspect. Okay?'

Yes sir. Should I stakeout his home, if he goes there later tonight?'

'That would be a good idea. I'm still unsure of his story, it sounds too wholesome and practiced.' Perez went to go back in to update Agent Strong.

'Agent Strong has already left!' Deputy Dubois shouted.

'When?'

'Just before you came out,' he looked at Agent Perez, pleading his innocence in her leaving.

'Do you know where she was heading?'

'Something about a Noah Cooper. She found out he works for Oak to Interior, Jackson's lumberyard. She took my car. Officer Young phoned her, gave her the information.'

'You stay here, call me if he moves. Call Sheriff Harris to see if he can get you some transport!'

Agent Perez sped off, leaving dry dust engulfing the parking lot. He dialled her number. It rang. 'Answer damn it!' The night skies were darkening. The lumberyard would be shutting its doors soon, maybe earlier seeing as it's Friday.

The engine purred as he floored the SUV through the stop sign in Butler central. Other drivers breaking hard around him. Tearing up East Pushmataha Street, he reached Dansby Road and eased off the pedal. Perez calmed himself at the wheel, reaching his destination and seeing a Butler police vehicle parked outside the large building.

He surveyed the area. The majority of lights inside were switched off. Three administrators congregated in front of the main desk, talking about their weekend plans. 'Excuse me, I'm looking for my partner, she's about this height, long blonde hair, maybe a bandaid to her head.

'I saw someone of her description in the sawmill outback. Just past the wood yard. You'll have to go round front, everywhere is locked up in here.'

Outside, Perez couldn't see his outstretched hand in front of him. The yard lights were starting to dim down and switch off. He had to use his cell for a light, his maglite was in the swamp back at Eli's place. His chest was pounding. He was fuming his partner had snuck out to follow a hunch. She could still have concussion. It was at this point he thought she could be in some serious trouble. Collapsed somewhere and no one would know. Another yard light switched off.

'Clara!' He could feel the cold air creeping through his clothes. Why was he even caring what happened to her. She was reckless, unpredictable and damn right impossible.

One of the wooden shed doors were still open, a centre light shone above a workbench. The space inside was immense. 'Agent Strong, you in here?' Walking towards the centre, cell light on, he shone it around. 'Clara are you in here? Answer me God damn it.'

The shed door slammed closed. Perez couldn't see if anyone was there. 'Hello, I'm with the FBI, who's there?' Clanging of chains were heard in the distance, his heart rate quickened, he reached down for his weapon. The noise got louder. Another door slammed to the right of him. 'If you're trying to scare me, it sure isn't working. You need to do better than that!' The cold he embraced earlier turning to warm beads of sweat.

Two large piles of wood chip sat next to a huge piece of machinery, the front of which held a big industrial log saw. Manoeuvring around, arms poised, trying to hold his cell light in front, he heard footsteps running on metal steps. 'Stop FBI, show yourself.' Double doors lead out to a side corridor. The stairs were at the end, heading to another floor above. Perez continued to follow the sound of the footsteps. They were getting quieter; he was getting away. *Come on Adam, think. Concentrate. Stay alert.*

A scraping sound echoed from the room above as he started to ascend the metal steps. He took a few steps at a time, Glock still at arms length. Twisting with the shape of the staircase, he turned his head looking up in front, then checking to see if anyone was following. Double metal doors at the top opened. A tall, dark figure stood, something large in his arms. He dropped it at his feet, running back the way he came. Taking the rest of the steps two at a time, Perez reached the metal doors. Shining his light to the ground he saw the large package. 'Clara!'

Chapter Twenty-Two

'Strong! Strong wake up.' Her hands were tied to the front, mouth taped with duct tape. He shook her, lifted her eyelids and shone his cell light in her eyes. 'Clara,' he checked to see if she had a pulse. He had to slow his own heart rate down, to feel for hers. Taking deep breaths, he inhaled slowly. 'Thank god.'

The decision to leave the perpetrator and take care of his partner was an easy one. He called it in.

Sitting her upright, holding her head, he slowly peeled the tape from her mouth and untied her hands. He slid down behind her, comforting her, pushing her hair away from her eyes. 'You've gotta stop disobeying orders,' he said jokingly. His hand stroking her hair. 'Medics are on their way. Are you hurt. I mean he didn't touch you?'

He felt her head shake from side to side. 'I'm sorry,' her voice faint with despondency.

'You've a death wish Strong. You need to nip it in the bud, before it really does destroy you.'

'I know, I just can't see how,' she murmured.

The two agents sat in the dark, only the light of the cell to keep them company. Quietness between them felt natural, there was a strange bond forming, they were becoming closer. He cared about her; she was his partner on this case.

'I got his neck,' a weak voice said.

'What?'

'I scraped his neck with my nails, see if we can match his DNA,' she sounded sleepy, a bit disoriented.

The sound of the main lights switching on downstairs raised their spirits. Adam could hear Sheriff Harris's gruff voice calling out.

'We're up here!'

Harris, the medics and Zachariah Jackson stood for a second, taking in the scene before them. The medics attended to Agent Strong, taking her slowly down the steps to their rig. Harris took Perez by the hand and pulled him to his feet. 'You okay?'

'Yeah. He was here. He saw me and fled,' Looking at Jackson, he asked, 'I don't suppose your yard sensor lights are working yet?'

'Actually, they are. Got them fixed two days ago.'

'We need to check surveillance footage,' Perez looked at Jackson. He had a small nick to the side of his face. 'You've been in the wars yourself by the looks of thing,' pointing to his cheek.

'Oh that, I cut myself shaving. I'll take you over to the office and we can have a look,' he led the way. The two men followed.

Scanning through the footage, they caught sight of Clara making her way to the sawmill. All lights were on at this point. Two-yard lights after a minute of her showing on screen turned off. She entered the building. 'Stop, rewind. There up in the top left-hand corner. Who's that? Can you zoom in?'

'I can but it goes grainy, the quality is poor I'm afraid. I don't recognise him. It doesn't help he's wearing a black hoodie and gloves.'

'Doesn't really give us much to go on,' Harris sighed.

'Can you tell me if Noah Cooper works for you?'

'Noah? Yeah why? One of my best workers. Bit of a ladies' man but harmless,' Jackson said.

'Was he working today? I saw him this morning, but later on?'

'I can check on our systems,' Zachariah Jackson typed away on his keyboard and brought up the day's rota. 'Look, there. He had a large delivery late this afternoon. He's gone to Tuscaloosa, just below Birmingham. He's there for the night, back in the morning. He is booked into a motel. Knowing Cooper, he'll probably find other accommodation.'

'He definitely went?'

'Yep, they have to phone our administrators here, once they arrive at their destination. The receivers mark on our systems that delivery has been completed.'

'Was Benjamin Johnson working today, here on site?'

Checking his screen, Jackson nodded. 'He has been on light duties, something to do with a swollen ankle. Should have clocked out an hour ago. It's saying here he hasn't. That's strange he's normally switched on enough to make sure his hours are recorded.'

'If you get anything more from your surveillance footage, call me immediately,' said Perez. 'I need you to wait here. We need to take a look around. Have you got a couple of flashlights?' Zachariah unlocked a cabinet by the side of the reception area, bringing them over two industrial ones. 'Lock the door after we leave.'

Outside Harris turned to Perez, 'David Torres's wife said he attended schools outside of the area. So, no connection.'

'It's got something to do with that church,' Perez told Harris.

They decided to split up. The sheriff walked over to the storage warehouse and loading area for deliveries. Six large trucks lined up, ready for the morning shift. Shining his light, he pulled himself up on the steps of the cabins. Searching each one thoroughly, waiting for the inevitable to happen. It didn't.

To the rear of the lumberyard sat the wrapping and packaging sheds. The doors were locked. A yellow forklift sat with a stack of lumber, waiting to be shipped out. The yard lights flickered on above. 'Benjamin! Are you there?' He continued to search the area. Nothing.

Perez went back into the sawmill. He retraced his steps to the rear, passing a large debarking machine, up the metal steps and through the metal doors. Chairs and tables scattered everywhere; half filled vending machines fringing the room. The powerful light swept through the space. Adam retrieved his weapon. 'Benjamin, show yourself. Let's talk about this. You don't want to be running, we'll just catch up with you.'

The noise of a crashing trash can was heard from across the room. Arms poised; Adam moved forward. Light directed in front. He could feel the pressure. The can rolled, revealing a large raccoon scrambling out of sight. 'Damn! How'd you sneak in?' He lowered his Glock, heading back out.

'He's not here.'

'He can't be stupid enough to head home.'

'That's probably what he will do,' Perez stated.

Harris and Perez both drove back to the hospital first, to check on Deputy Dubois and lend him Sheriff Harris's cruiser. He was standing inside the foyer, chatting to the nurses on duty. Perez slipped off for a few moments to check which room Clara had been taken to.

'Jeremiah, everything okay?' Harris asked his colleague.

'Yeah, just asking if Eli Davis is still with his father. Didn't want to spook him by peering in. Apparently, he's been given permission to stay the night beside his pa's bed.'

'Ask the nurse to call you if he leaves anytime during the night. You've got the wagon, it's a bit of a ride to his place so go easy if you have to follow him. We're heading to Benjamin Johnson's place over at Lisman,' Sheriff Harris saw Adam returning. 'Is she good?'

'Yeah. She's sleeping. Would you mind asking the nurse to call me if she needs anything? You've got my cell number.'

Deputy Dubois said he would check on her before he made tracks. 'All the residents have been spoken to east of the car dealership,' Dubois quickly remembered, telling Harris. 'Hopefully folk will stay in.'

'Okay, hold the fort here and at the station. Make sure everyone on duty gets supper. Bill it to the mayor's office. He said if there was anything he could do to help,' Harris smirked and followed Perez back to the SUV.

It was getting late; streetlights glowed a dull yellow and most folk were thinking about calling it a night. 'Do you think Benjamin Johnson is our guy? He doesn't seem to fit the bill.'

'William Parker's parents are with him 24/7, Martin is in the cells. Johnson is the only one who has the freedom to come and go. We'll know if it's him or not when we see him! Clara scratched his neck to identify him. Quick thinking.'

'I'll call Dr Cameron to get over there now to scrape a sample. God damn Clara. Even when she's in trouble, her head doesn't switch off.'

Perez concentrated on the route while Harris rang Cameron. 'He's already there. She told the medics in the rig on the way over, to call him.'

'We maybe need him to check over Eli's place. We'll leave it until the morning. Let's see what Dubois reports back first.'

Driving slowly down Martin Avenue, only side lights turned on, they pulled the SUV over to the tree line opposite the house. Out of sight to anyone advancing along the road. 'How are we doing this?'

'His vehicle isn't there, so let's just sit it out for a while, see if he turns up,' Perez said, reclining his seat, trying to rest his body.

'Take ten minutes, I'll keep watch.'

Agent Perez wasn't going to argue. He closed his eyes.

Harris checked his watch. An hour had passed, when a vehicle light shone through the trees as he looked in the rear mirror. 'Adam, wake up. We have a visitor.'

He sat upright. 'Is it him?'

'Can't see.'

The porch light came on. A figure wearing a black hoodie opened the door. 'Bingo! Let's go.'

Perez knocked hard on the door. Harris had gone round the back. The dog was quiet, asleep in its hut. 'Benjamin Johnson, open the door! We know you're in there, we have your house covered, so don't think about running.'

'Come on out Mr Johnson. We will force entry. You don't want your wife to be here by herself with a broken front door. Mr Johnson, I'm going to count to five. One...' He stood there with his hands above his head.

Perez approached him, pulling down the neck of his jumper both sides. 'Mr Johnson you are under arrest for the assault of an FBI Agent and the suspicion of murder of Eleanor Parker, Evan Thomas and David Torres. Turn around and put your hands behind your back.'

'Who the hell's Torres?'

His miranda rights were read.

Sheriff Harris returned to the front yard after hearing all the noise. Johnson's wife came out screaming, she was high as a kite, she hadn't a clue what was happening. Sheriff Harris escorted her back inside, came back out and closed the door. 'She can sleep it off.'

They put Johnson in the back seat and drove to Butler police department. He remained quiet, he didn't protest.

Agent Perez's phone buzzed. He didn't want to put it on speaker with Johnson in the back. He put the cell to his ear. 'Dr Cameron, tell me you have something for me?'

'It looks like your killer is playing you. The note at Evan's crime scene was written on paper found at Eleanor's house, the note found at Eleanor's crime scene was written on the A4 invoice paper found in David's office, you know what I'm going to say next?'

207

'The acrylic paper beside Torres's body is a match from Joseph Martin's studio! Son of a bitch. He's been gaining access to their homes and taking items to lead us a stray.'

'My team and myself are calling it a night. I've been over to see Agent Strong and taken samples. I will process it tomorrow.'

Perez waited until they were out of the vehicle to relay the information to Harris.

'It's one sick game!'

Officer Carter was in the office with Hannah when they arrived with their suspect. They both looked exhausted.

'Why don't you two call it a night. We're going to process Benjamin Johnson's details and then call it a night ourselves. He can spend the night in the cells. We'll interview him first thing tomorrow.' Perez took Johnson away.

'Where's Officer Asher?' Harris asked.

'He's on his way over. He's on night duty,' answered Carter.

'When he gets here, you two head off. We'll need fresh heads tomorrow.'

Harris's phone rang. 'Sheriff Harris speaking.'

'Sheriff, Eli has settled down for the night in the hospital. The nurses on duty have my number if he makes a move. I'm heading home,' Dubois explained.

'Same here. See you back here in the morning, early.'

The police department closed up for the night. Martin and Johnson locked up in their cells. Officer Asher stared at the monitors, drinking coffee to keep himself awake through the night. Everyone needed to get some rest, recuperate and be ready for the next day's workload.

Perez drove Harris home. 'I'm going to check on Clara first thing tomorrow, then I'll be down to interrogate Johnson. Do you want to sit in with me?'

'I would like nothing more than to see him fall apart and own up to all this crap,' Harris's tiredness was getting the better of him. 'I'm getting too old for this shit!'

Perez pulled up outside the Sheriff's home. He drove back to the motel, looking at the empty passenger seat. *See you in the morning Agent Strong.*

Jeremiah Dubois landed home. He threw the keys down on the sideboard, sat down at his dining room table and took his boots off. He had been standing up most of the day. He rubbed his toes and massaged the soles of his feet. His cell phone rang.

'Shit. Please not now!'

He was reluctant to answer, but he knew he had no choice.

'Hello, Deputy Dubois.'

'Hi, its nurse Gonzalez from Butler hospital. Just wanted to let you know, Mr Davis has decided to go home as his father is comfortable and sleeping.'

'I appreciate you phoning. When did he leave?'

'About two minutes ago,' Nurse Gonzalez replied.

He sighed, put his boots back on and lifted the keys from the sideboard.

Chapter Twenty-Three

He arrived home and probed around. Most of the rooms were filled with beautiful things he had collected or handcrafted, they were aesthetically pleasing to the eye. They filled him full of pleasure, stirred his emotions and heightened his senses. He rubbed his finger on a shelf in one of the spare bedrooms, looking down at the tip of his index finger, he noticed dust. He shook his head, annoyed with himself for neglecting his household chores.

The two china ornamental vases with detailed lids, decorated with blue and white Japanese patterns were alluring and fascinated him. He picked one up, opened the lid and looked inside. 'Mother, you should have protected me from the day I was born. You didn't even know I existed. I was an embarrassment to you, a burden from hell. The wickedness of wrath is a deadly sin, but I can never feel vengeful hatred or resentment towards you Mother. My siblings have to be avenged in order for me to meet my saviour. While it is a natural reaction to be angered by your wrong doings, I must stay vigilant and not become a slave to my emotions, instead respond in a rational manner as God commands. When he visits me in my home, presenting me eternal life, he won't judge me. I have listened to his words. He has guided me through my journey, played my moves and will reward me for my efforts as I took part in the game.'

He closed the lid of her ashes, looking at his father sitting next to her on the dusty shelf. He doesn't remember how they came to their fate. His memories were normally clear, but this event was hazy. He remembered being with them on his own in their home the day they died; his four older siblings had fled, left home to start new lives without him. They didn't even look back. One by one, they walked out the front door, down the path and out into the big wide world.

He felt himself getting annoyed, but he didn't really understand why he was experiencing these emotions. God would tell him why when he visits. His mind bounced back to the dust on the shelf. *I need to scrub every surface, dust every corner and make sure everything is cleaned for him coming.*

He left the spare bedroom and went to the kitchen. Filling up the bucket, the one which previously contained David Torres's metacarpals and flesh, he poured detergent in, to make it smell nice. He knew fragrances had a direct relation with the spirits and that the universe's bounties are manifestations of divine beauty and signs of the universal creator. He read in one of his books sitting in his favourite room, the smell of incense represented prayer going up to heaven, which God loves. He smiled, turning the faucet off.

Scrubbing the kitchen floor with a scouring pad felt great, he was getting rid of the things that depicted sin and evil. Cleansing his home was paramount. He remembered from the bible Jesus even cleansed his own house when he cleansed the temple. When he walked through the temple, he got rid of the things that were not honouring God. *I'll do that, I'll go into every room and check. First, I need to get this blood out of the floorboards.*

As he was on his knees he thought about Georgina Miller. He knew that wasn't her real name. Just like Evan, David and Eleanor. Did they think he didn't know. He knew who they were.

His fingertips started to bleed with the intensity of his scrubbing. He slowly licked the blood, tasting the rich protein, which gave the blood that metallic taste. He carried on cleaning; he knew there had to be sacrifices.

Looking at the clock on the kitchen wall, he realised he had been working on the floor for over two hours. He stood up, poured the last bucket of sin down the drain and put the kettle on the stove.

He sipped his coffee, thinking which room he needed to concentrate on next. He would clean the kitchen cupboards tomorrow after the floors dried out properly. It was getting late, but he knew tonight he would work into the early hours of the morning, to achieve his desired goals.

Time was running out for him. He wanted to play his last move now, but he will have to wait until Monday night. He couldn't access his last opponent's place until then, it wasn't open at the weekend, it was now Friday night. He would go to his work tomorrow as normal, show his face and see what was happening.

He tipped the remains of his coffee down the drain, filling his bucket back up with fresh water and suds. He stood for a moment to think. *Where would my saviour appear when he rewards me?* 'The living room is probably the best bet.' He hadn't stepped foot in there since he decorated it all those years ago.

He started emptying the biggest cupboard in the room. It was full of so-called antiques that were collected by his father to make him look important in the community back in the day.

'Crap, that's all it is. Nothing but cheap china from the grocery store on the corner,' he recollected the times his dad traipsed to Henry's store to see what antiquities he could find in the back, piled up high in the wooden crates. He lifted a coin and rubbed it with his thumb. 'Cheap American tin!' Tossing it in with the other trash he turned back to remove the items from the next shelf down. A photograph.

It was in a white wooden decorative frame. Dust had covered the glass, so he wiped it softly with his wet cloth. He stared down, feeling perplexed at the sight in front of him. His eyebrows furrowed as he continued to gaze, open mouthed and confused. He didn't realise the cloth had fallen, and he perched himself down on the armrest of his floral couch. His mind was stuck in time, his body distancing itself from him. His forefinger slowly and gently moved across the photograph, stopping at each subject in turn.

His father stood tall and upright, wearing his Sunday best, smiling with pride at the others around him. His mother's green eyes glaring at him through the half-cleaned glass, hidden secrets kept from other attendants of her precious church, behind those eyes. His heartbeat was all he heard and felt. His older brother standing in between his parents looking important, grinning with pretend pride. His other brother sitting on a wooden chair, centre stage. His fists tightened slightly as he held the frame, remembering. His two sisters stood either side, hair down to the middle of their backs, wearing plainclothes so not to attract the attention of the boys at church.

And himself, where was he in the photograph. His eyes scanned the picture, face tensing with confusion. He shook himself from his unpleasant reverie, picking up the cloth, scrubbing the glass impetuously, staring at the photo again. He was willing himself to appear, to be standing next to one of his sisters. Rubbing harder, he stood straight, took a deep breath and looked down again. His anger stirred and riled his mind. Throwing the frame to the floor, he stood on it, crushing their smiling faces and their perfect world.

He had to take deep breaths, dig deeper than he had ever delved before to find the air in his lungs, to feel the sense he was a live. He slumped down on his knees, glass cracking beneath him as he knelt. He closed his eyes and slowly calmed his heartbeat.

The sensation of tears was new to him. He hadn't cried since his brother hit him outside in their yard when they were kids and he fell to the ground, banging his head off the pathway. Nobody came. Nobody helped him rise from the ground, to assist him with his injuries. He remembered lying there cold and frightened, blood seeping from his wounds. No one cared, no one came. His head always hurt after that day.

The brush and dustpan were stored in the cupboard off the kitchen, rubbing the tears from his eyes with his forearms, he started to tidy up. *They've all paid with their lives, bar one. I'll see her Monday night. I'm tired playing, tired of righting the wrongs from the past. God, promise me you will never leave me alone, never leave me to lie on the ground by myself or ignore the words that come from my mouth. I trust your wisdom and power to make my life better.*

Picking up the broken shards of glass that wouldn't sweep up, he cut his thumb and forefinger. He went back to the kitchen sink and ran the water over the pieces of glass stuck in his flesh. Rubbing his digits together feeling if it was all out, he put his hand up to the light, then put his finger and thumb in his mouth to taste the blood. He felt his whole body relax, calm and rejuvenate his soul.

He would carry on tidying up over the weekend. But now he needed to visit his favourite room. He needed that familiarity, which made him who he was.

Maybe this will be Gods choice of rooms. That would make sense. He has been playing my moves and talking me through my strategies. Why didn't I think about it earlier. He felt his spirits lifting. He felt elated and excited about his meeting with God. *I wonder if he will have another game for me to play. Carry on doing his work here, on earth. I am tired, but with my new eternal life, I will feel better and energised to kill the evil of this world.*

Sitting in his gaming chair, pulling out a blanket from the bottom drawer, he placed it over his body and tucked it up over his shoulders. He glanced up at a picture on the wall that meant everything to him. It was two feathers crossed over and, in the middle read, "When the time is right The Lord God will make it happen. Isaiah 60:22." He smiled shyly, closed his eyes feeling exhausted from the night's events and fell into a deep sleep.

Chapter Twenty-Four

The sound of muffled chattering and rustling noises were keeping Adam Perez up. He peered out the window from his motel room. Three raccoons were running around the trash cans, hunting for a tasty meal. Beer cans and cigarette butts were turning out to be their choice of supper.

He lifted his phone to check the time, 3.03am. He settled back into bed, fidgeting, turning continuously, he finally fell asleep.

His alarm on his phone rang. 'What the hell!' He peered down to see the time. What he thought were literally minutes, were actually three hours of solid sleep.

Jumping in the shower, he heard his cell ringing. 'Damn!' Wrapping the towel around his waist he answered his phone. 'Hello, Agent Perez.'

'Is that Adam Perez?' The voice on the other end asked.

'Yes, who's this?'

'I don't think you know me, but I'm a neighbour of your father. I'm afraid I've got some bad news.'

'Mrs Foster. Is that you? What's happened?'

'Your father has been taken into Durant Major hospital. He had a heart attack this morning around 3am. He is okay, but I knew you would want to know.' The line went quiet. 'Mr Perez, are you still there?'

'Yes, sorry. I'll comeback up today. I just need to tie up a few loose ends here, then I'll go and see him. If you are speaking to him, could you tell him I'm on my way. I appreciate your call Mrs Foster,' Perez got changed and headed to the hospital.

He hated this part of the job, torn between being loyal to the job or putting family first. He knew they were close to finding their killer. He also knew the inevitable had to be done.

Butler hospital was busy, especially for a Saturday morning. Adam parked up and noticed Sheriff Harris's cruiser in the parking lot. Walking towards Clara's room he spotted Jeremiah Dubois leaving.

'Everything okay Deputy?'

'Morning sir. Just checking on Agent Strong before I head home. It's been a long night. Followed Eli to his house like you said. Nurse here called me and gave me the heads up. He didn't move from his home, he stayed put. I had an eye on his vehicle, it was parked up all night. He's back here now with his pa.'

'Okay. Before you go, get one of your colleagues down to keep an eye on him. Just in case.'

'No worries. Are you questioning Johnson shortly?'

'I'm afraid I have to go back to Durant. I'm just here to check on Agent Strong.'

'If I can be of any assistance to Agent Strong, please get her to contact me.'

'You could find something out for me. See if Eli has alibis for the times of the murders and also during the days when he wasn't working at the courthouse. Check Butler bank and here at the hospital. He said he was in between these places all week. We need to eliminate him from our inquiries or charge him,' Perez said. He knocked on Clara's door and walked in. He was pleasantly surprised to see her dressed and sitting on the chair.

'Well, I didn't expect to see you up and about.'

'Yep, just waiting for the nurse to discharge me and then I'm good to go.'

'You've been through a rough patch. How are things? I'm gonna have to ask you, did you get a good look at him, when you scratched his neck?'

'He knocked me out, I was trying to wake up and I grabbed hold of him. I didn't see his face.'

'We've arrested Benjamin Johnson. We think he attacked you yesterday. He has a scratch on the left side of his neck. Dr Cameron swabbed under your nails for DNA, so we will hopefully hear back from him today. I've arrested him on the suspicion of the three murders too. He has a lot of explaining to do.'

'I wanna question him. I don't want to be a victim in all this.'

'I have to head home to Durant. It's my father. He's been taken into hospital, heart attack. I need to see him. Can you hold the fort until I get back tomorrow or Monday? I wouldn't ask but…'

'Yes. Go. I can take it from here. Give my love to him.'

'I'm on the phone, so call me whenever. Sheriff Harris was going to sit in with me today. Are you up for it?'

'Yes. I'll head over as soon as my release papers are signed. Actually, I'll walk out with you, tell them I have to go,' she smiled at Adam. 'Thanks for, you know, last night.'

'You're my partner Agent Strong,' he said, giving her a wink.

The two agents exited the hospital. Perez drove Strong to the police department. 'Ask Harris to lend you one of his vehicles. I'll get back as soon as I can.'

'Drive carefully and I'll let you know what happens.'

Perez sped off, breaking all trafficking rules to get home in time, to see his father. Clara waved to Michael and entered the sheriff's office.

'What in tarnation are you doing here?' Harris asked.

'Agent Perez had to leave on personal matters, he should be back tomorrow. Looks like you and I have the pleasure of chatting with Mr Johnson.'

'Are you sure you can face him?'

'Absolutely, I can.'

Harris asked Officer Carter to escort Johnson to the interrogation room. 'Tell him he can have an attorney present.'

'Has he been charged with not holding a hunting licence yet and possession of cannabis?'

'All in the system, being processed as we speak. Things take time down here.'

'Can we get Dr Cameron and his team over to his house. We already have a search warrant which still holds?' Clara asked Harris.

'I'll phone him now.'

Agent Strong, Sheriff Harris then entered the interrogation room. The cold air circulating above their heads. Benjamin Johnson sat in his usual spot and his representative sat close by his side. It was the same attorney William Parker used. Being a small place, attorneys were few and far between.

Clara entered from behind Johnson's chair and sat down. His face went white, his whole body froze, he clearly wasn't expecting her to be here. She could feel herself starting to shake slightly. It wasn't noticeable to anyone else, but she could feel her insides shudder. 'Mr Johnson. You were arrested last night for the assault of an FBI Agent. You struck her from behind, gagged her mouth and bound her hands together,' Clara put her fingers on her lips feeling the sores. 'Have you anything to say Mr Johnson?'

His attorney had obviously instructed his client to mention nothing.

'No comment.'

Clara tried the same tactics Perez and herself used with Joseph Martin. 'You have also been arrested on suspicion for the murders of three people, on the nights of the 12th, 14th and 16th. We are collecting evidence as we speak, connecting you to all three crime scenes.'

'You've arrested my client without evidence? What kind of circus is this?'

'His hunting traps were found at the first crime scene. He works with longleaf pine wood. The chain found at the first crime scene, stolen from his place of work.'

'All just weak connections. Nothing solid to even begin with. That's very lame Agent Strong,' Johnson's attorney said, with raised eyebrows.

Always a waiting game. Come on Dr Cameron, find that bloody clue, link this son of a bitch to all three crimes. She continued. 'Where were you Thursday 16th October?'

'Home, with my little old lady.'

'Can anyone else clarify that?'

'We weren't up to threesomes if that's what y'all think. Just me an' my pretty old Sarah. Fine woman, don't you think Sheriff?'

Harris stared. Controlling his temper, breathing through his nostrils slowly. Clara's phone rang. She stopped the interview and took the call. She was glad to be out of there. 'Agent Strong.'

'Agent Strong, how are you? It's Zachariah Jackson here, from Oak to Interiors lumberyard.'

'What's up Mr Jackson? I'm a bit busy at the minute.'

'This morning, I decided to take a look around the sheds and warehouses, here in my yard. Well, I found something, and I thought you should know.'

'Mr Jackson, slow down. Tell me clearly what it is you've got?'

'Benjamin Johnson has been using my establishment to run his own racketeering business or should I say businesses. I don't want my lumberyard being connected to all this crap.'

'Mr Jackson…'

'Johnson has been storing, then shipping out illegal drugs and….' There was a long pause. 'He has been distributing photos, photos of children.'

'Are you sure its his gear?'

'It's definitely his. The boxes were packed by him, his initials on the sides. We found them in the rafters above his locker. You wouldn't notice them; he had tarpaulin draped over them. I can't afford my business to be ruined by him. Please you need to sort this mess out.'

'Don't touch anything else. We'll need your fingerprints to eliminate you from the items, but we'll send someone over now to get them,' She dialled Perez's cell.

'Clara, how's it going?'

'Johnson is distributing illegal drugs and pornographic child pictures. We haven't got anything solid on the murders apart from the traps and Dr Cameron hasn't got back. Do we detain him until we hear, or shall I charge him now with the possession of child pornography and drugs?'

'Hold him in the cells. Keep gathering up as much information against him as possible. Don't charge him with anything yet. Stick to your guns and play the game. Let him stew for a little longer. If he's behind bars and he is our killer, then Butler residents will be better off. Keep digging. Get Cameron's team to dust for fingerprints again at the car dealership, check to see who Johnson was sending that gear too. We'll probably find Joseph Martin is behind all this.'

'Okay. On it.'

'Did Deputy Dubois get a chance to check Eli's alibis? I know he was heading home first for a Kip.'

'I haven't seen him at work yet. I'll get in contact with him shortly.'

'Christ this bloody weather. It's getting worse. Hope it's not torrential downpours all the way to Durant.'

Clara could hear the rain penetrating Perez's SUV through her cell. 'Take it easy, I'll speak later,' she said her goodbyes and returned to the interrogation room, terminating the interview for the day. Johnson was taken back to his cell, while Harris and Strong went back to the office.

'What the fuck am I not seeing!' Clara shouted. 'Three killings and no shred of damn evidence.'

That feeling was stirring in her chest. She needed a drink, to calm her nerves. She poured herself a black coffee and kicked the desk leg in frustration. 'I'm going to head to Lisman and Johnson's place. Patrick should still be there. I'll give him a call to let him know I'm on my way. Can someone pick up Johnson's shipments from Jackson's lumberyard? It's evidence so handle with care.'

'Do you want me or one of my team to come with you?' Asked Harris.

'No. I'm fine. I just need the lend of a vehicle.'

'Jeremiah returned mine this morning, here take these.' He threw her his keys. 'Don't be beating yourself up. We're all in this, we'll find him.'

'If Dubois turns up for work, tell him to call me asap.'

'Everything okay?'

'Yeah, just following up on some leads,' she sighed, walking out of the courthouse, jumping into Harris's police cruiser. She knew the way to Lisman, she had done it enough times in her life.

Clara thought about this morning before Perez turned up, she was debating whether to visit her mum down the corridor in hospital. She hadn't seen her for years. Knowing what to say would be difficult. *Hi ma, it's me, the daughter you disowned. Thought I would see you before you passed!*

She rang Patrick Cameron; told him she was ten minutes away and not to pack up until she got there. Her thoughts were scattered. She didn't even know why she needed to see Johnson's place. Was it to clarify her suspicions about him. She didn't know what they even were anymore. She drove until she came to Lisman signpost, her whole body felt weak, and she collapsed behind the wheel.

Chapter Twenty-Five

The vehicle swerved off the main road, descending under the force of gravity into a highway gully. The SUV rolled over onto its side, lodging itself tight amongst the rocks. The rain persisted, hitting the side of the vehicle, sounding like a cacophony of deafening beating drums. The noise and vibrations of the engine, still humming quietly in the background. Wipers still racing in full swing across the bulletproof windscreen. His body lay still against the ground side of the vehicle. His breathing shallow, his vision blurry, like mist passing in front of his eyes. Visibility on the roads had been limited, but he wanted to get back to see his father. Highway warnings trying to force the users to slow down, but he didn't want him being alone; being without someone who really cared. The rain, the wipers, the engine, the sound of other traffic users driving down the road, was what he could hear. He couldn't move. His body was wrapped around the seatbelt, arms tight against the side of the body work, not knowing which direction was up. Adam Perez was alone, just like his father. No road users would see him because of the horrendous downpour. His vehicle was hidden, out of sight, away from the mindset of other drivers. All he could do was hope and wait.

***

Turning off the main road to Martin Avenue, Clara parked her vehicle behind a white forensics van. She knew her lack of concentration nearly caused her to veer off the road. She took a moment to herself before getting out. A young man kitted out in a white suit combed the outside area. Lifting trash and items as he walked. Inside she called out to Dr Cameron.

'Agent Strong,' the man looked exhausted. Dark rings below his eyes. 'Suit up!'

'Is his wife Sarah here?'

'Yes. Pleasant lady. Likes to talk a lot and throw her weight about, she's in the living room, smoking her lungs out.'

'Have you checked his basement again? His hunting stuff, knives, guns?'

'Mason is down there now. Too small for a two-man job, best leave him until he surfaces. We've found his computer. Strange, a man like him owning a computer. Anyways, we're bring it all back with us. Examine it thoroughly,' his cell buzzed. 'Excuse me, I really need to take this call. Give me a second.'

Looking around Clara could see nothing out of the ordinary. Stack of newspapers, tin of biscuits. She opened it, biscuits turning mouldy sat on the bottom. Dirty clothes strewn over the bannisters; wood piled up beside a rusty old log burning stove. Dr Cameron returned from his call. 'Agent Strong, that was Maggie back at the morgue. She ran tests from your scrapings and samples off Johnson's comb. She hurried it through and it's a match. I'm sorry to be the bearer of bad news.'

Clara didn't react. She had a feeling it was him. 'Thanks Dr Cameron.'

She wandered off around the house outside, thinking about last night. Johnson's dog was clipped to a long chain, attached to a freshly painted kennel.

Now why is that the only thing fixed and restored in this place? Her head was thinking outside the box. It had to, they needed answers.

The matted golden looking dog barked as she approached. Clara dropped to her knees, letting the dog move towards her. It was hesitant at first, then dropped to its belly, scraping it along the dirt to move closer. She put her hand out for it to smell, keeping still, letting the dog sniff her scent. It's tail wagged and began to lick her hand excitedly, rolling onto its back, waiting for that all important belly rub. She shuffled closer and the two began playing on the ground, like old friends.

'What are you guarding in that kennel of yours boy? Are you going to let me see? There's a good boy,' the dog brought over an old shoe and dropped it at her feet. 'You wanna play? Go get,' she threw it, proceeding to the small wooden kennel. The paint was still fresh. She thought hiding something here would be extreme, but she had learnt over the years anything was possible, especially if the person was desperate.

Retrieving the shoe, the dog dropped it beside her as she knelt back down in front of the doghouse. Not looking, she picked it up and threw it behind her, keeping the dog occupied she stuck her head inside. There was an old threadbare blue carpet and two empty bowls. *Poor thing*, she thought. The floor was slightly raised. Pulling up the carpet, the wooden MDF board underneath lifted up. 'What do we have here?'

Putting on latex gloves, she pulled out the bag stashed under the board. She unzipped it, pulling out the contents. Small individual bags of white powder, indecent photographs of children and a plastic bag containing one tube of red and one of yellow acrylic paint, identical to those found in Joseph Martin's studio, which matched the paint from the counters at the first two crime scenes. 'You are going down Johnson for a long, long time you sick bastard.'

Clara felt the dog pushing against her as she knelt. He looked up at her wanting attention. 'You're a sweet little boy, you don't deserve this kind of treatment.'

Packing all the contents back into the bag, she got to her feet, finding Dr Cameron. 'It's stacking up against him.'

'Mason found blue rope inside a hunting rifle case in the basement too. Looks like a match. We don't know how we missed it last time, we swept through the whole basement; we are certain all cases were checked,' Patrick scratched his head looking puzzled. 'My team are thorough and professional. Something isn't right.'

'We also found the same rope in Eli Davis's shed. Is it a common sell at Parts & Parts store?'

'I know we are stretched with bodies and crime scenes but....' His voice echoed off.

'I'm gonna head back to Butler. See you back there, later? Dr Cameron, see you back at the morgue this afternoon?' She repeated.

'Yeah, yeah whatever you think.'

Distracted by the search, Patrick Cameron decided to take a look himself down in Johnson's basement.

Clara headed straight to the living room to find Sarah smoking a cigarette and drinking a can of beer. 'Mrs Johnson, we've found evidence hiding out back with your dog, which connects your husband to our case. Think very carefully before you answer my question. You don't want to incriminate yourself just to protect a man who gives you those bruises,' she pointed to Sarah's wrists.

Pulling down her sleeves she quickly responded. 'You haven't got a clue what you're talking about. You and your flashy suit, get out of my house, you bag of shit! My husband's a good man, you don't know what y'all talking about. Mangy old dog needs a kicking, flee beaten piece of shit!' Her voice trailed off.

'So, the coke in the kennels is yours and the indecent photographs of vulnerable young children? If he's such a good husband, they must belong to you.'

Sarah looked up at Clara, her expression changed from a sarcastic drunk, to one of sobering concern. 'You think you're so clever, standing there in your expensive suit, looking smug and treating me like trash. Well, you don't know the first thing about me lady,' she swigged her beer, banging it off the table. 'I used to be all fancy like you,' pointing her drunken finger up and down Clara's body. Her alcoholic tones getting the better of her.

'Mrs Johnson, the items, are they yours or your husbands?'

'My Pa told me he was the wrong sort. He chucked me out of our home, told me I was nothing but a dirty, drunken whore,' her voice lowered; her eyes glazed. She slumped back on the couch. 'Well, they sure ain't mine!' Her eyelids were heavy, she clenched them together and drifted off to sleep.

Clara looked at the sorrowful sight on the couch. Copious amounts of empty tins, strewn across the table; burn marks decorating the drab couch. *You haven't a clue. I pity you, Sarah.* A sudden realisation of what alcohol can do to a desperate person, hit Clara in the face. 'Fuck!'

She left Sarah to waste away her life and headed to her vehicle. She placed her hand on the door handle, then stopped. The wind picked up, blowing the tops of the trees, shaking the dead leaves to the ground. Her hair blew into her face, and she felt a cold breeze engulf her body.

The whispering sounds of the trees in the wind reminded her of Rainer Lake. It was close by, just behind Johnson's house. Her inner child wanted to go and explore, see the lake one more time. Benjamin Johnson wasn't going anywhere, and she had to wait for forensics to do there processing, she had time. It wasn't an easy decision. Clara had thought about this place every single day of her life.

Moving through the forest, she heard the sounds of the birds above. She could almost hear the laughter of her brother, as he ran down to the lakeside to catch a crappie for his supper. Her stomach knotted; her face still cold. Her legs carried her to the opening where she arrested Benjamin Johnson previously.

Standing at the edge of the lake, she stared into the darkness of the water. The wind created ripples that flowed her direction.

She remembered George always saying, "There's more truth in a ripple of water than in a clear day." She laughed at the memory. Sitting herself against a rock, Clara gazed up to see the birds in the trees. They were trying to find food. She listened to their chatter and tried to identify the species.

Her brother was always good at identifying native plants, animals and birds, she was always worried about keeping him safe to notice what was happening around them. Her face warmed, her eyes began to fill with tears. She wasn't afraid to cry here by the lake. She wanted to, needed to.

The air current grew stronger, riding across the water. She felt her brother's presence. 'I'm so sorry Grayson,' as she spoke a great blue heron landed beside her. She kept still, so not to disturb it wading through the water. It turned and faced her; it looked like it was staring in her direction. The moment lasted for a few seconds and then it took flight.

She new every Fall, millions of birds left North America and flew across the Gulf of Mexico to spend the winter in South and Central America and the islands of the Caribbean. All the knowledge George had introduced them to, came flooding back.

She felt herself calming, sitting by the lake. She absorbed the quietness of her surroundings.

Her memories of that day were vivid. Grayson had vanished without a trace, without a sound. Clara closed her eyes, trying to recall the sounds she heard on that particular summer's day. The birds, the otters playing in amongst the trunks of the tupelo gum trees, the distant call of a black bear. One of the books George gave them stated that black bears rarely ate meat that they lived off grasses, fruits and herbs.

They always heard them near the lake. It was disappointing if they didn't. She managed a smile as she reminisced.

The wind settled down, almost disappearing with the great blue heron. Clara's tears stopped falling and she felt a warmth within her heart. 'Love you Grayson. I will find the truth of what happened to you.'

She stood up and wiped the shingles sticking to her clothes. The sun of the Fall shone through the trees, lighting up the path as she made her way back to Sheriff Harris's borrowed vehicle through the forest.

She glanced over to the dog. It lay on its belly, with saddened eyes and a forlorn look upon its matted face. *No, you can't! You live in an apartment that doesn't allow pets.* She found herself uncoupling the chain and lifting the dog bowls.

Clara had forgotten about the case for just a few moments, and it felt good. She needed that time to begin her healing process. Now she had to fight the demons of alcohol. Opening the door the dog automatically jumped in the backseat. She looked up in her rear mirror, the dog was staring back. 'Have you lost your mind Clara Strong?' She said as she drove away.

Coming out of Martin Avenue she saw the sign for Edwards Avenue.

Her hands on the steering wheel turned left. She drove down her old haunt, feeling anxious being back home. She knew her Mama was in hospital, which made the visit bearable.

The front of the house was shabby and neglected, it looked smaller than she remembered. She slowly drove past, turning her vehicle at the dead end where George's house sat. Her window was down, and the sounds of the surrounding area were familiar. Her 10-year-old self appeared in front of her vehicle, kicking a ball against the curb. Grayson sitting on the lawn to the front of the house trying to find worms for his fishing rod, which he made with Jeremiah Dubois.

She pulled up outside her mother's home and exited the vehicle, grabbing her parker. The dog jumped out with her, frightened she was going to leave him on his own. She slowly walked up the path to the front window and peered in. As far as she could see nothing had changed, it was the same furniture, the same carpet, the same dreary curtains that hung above the window.

Taking the side path to the rear she noticed the flowers in the raised beds were dying off. The chill in the air made her zip up, the dog at her feet. 'You need a name,' he was already loyal to a fault. His ears pricked up and he bolted round the back. Clara could hear him barking.

Following the dog, she heard a man's voice trying to calm the animal. 'Good boy, stay!'

'George! What are you doing here?'

'Jesus Clara, is this your dog? Get it to stop.'

'Dog! Come!' She clicked her fingers, it responded to her commands immediately. 'Impressive! You can stroke him.'

George bent down and the dog growled. 'I think I'll leave it if you don't mind.'

Clara didn't want the dog to be protective of her. 'A lot of training needs to be done with you boy.'

'I'm round to tidy up your mama's yard. She hates to see it overgrown and messy. It gives me something to do.'

Clara didn't understand George. She thought she knew him. But here he was, helping the woman who used to stand by and watch her kids get a beating. 'Why are you really here George?'

'What do you mean?'

'You visit her in hospital, you clean up her mess! Have you forgotten about what she put me through, what Grayson had to endure, day in, day out? How can you push all that to the back of your mind?'

'You have no right to say those things to me.'

'I have every right. You were like a father to us. So, what happened?'

'Clara, you have to understand. It's not easy being on your own. Your mama and I needed the company out here, at our age it's hard.'

'Bullshit!'

'Clara, please. Listen to me. Your mama was also a victim. She suffered and was scarred from your father's abuse.'

'Again George, bullshit!'

The dog could sense Clara's anger and started to bark at George. He was persistent and wouldn't let up. 'Come on boy. This was clearly a big mistake coming here.'

'Wait. Clara come back, we can talk about it. Clara, please!'

She could hear his pleads and knew this whole situation was never going to move forward or get resolved. The pain was too deep. She started up Harris's vehicle with the dog in the back. He licked the side of her face, as she sat crying. 'Let's get out of here, what d'you say!'

Chapter Twenty-Six

Sheriff Harris sat behind his desk, exhaustion manifesting itself. He picked up the photo on his desk, studying his wife and two grown up kids. 'Getting too old for this shit.' There was a knock at his door. 'Come in!' He placed the frame back in its usual spot and noticed Clara. She wasn't alone. 'You can't bring that filthy animal into my office!' He protested.
'I couldn't leave it to starve. Animal welfare doesn't give a shit, so he's with me. That reminds me, I need to clean your jeep out. Is there a place around here I can give it a wash. I need to keep busy. I'm waiting on Dr Cameron's reports.'
'Just take it around back of the courthouse. There's a do-it-yourself car wash called Eddies.'
She sat opposite Harris. 'Found, what looks to be Florida snow sachets and child pornographic material up at Johnsons.'
'Jesus, are Johnson and Martin in this together? And have been from the beginning?' Harris asked. 'Is that cocaine to simpletons like me?'
Clara nodded, 'We believe there's only one killer. It's all been too well orchestrated to involve two people, things tend to go wrong when more than one perp is involved. Our guy is methodical and meticulous. There was blue rope from Eleanor Parker's death found in the basement too. Dr Cameron isn't convinced. Too many players in this game, but only one killer. Blue rope found at Eli Davis's too. We have evidence connecting Martin and Johnson to some of the crimes too. Red and yellow acrylic paint were found at Johnsons. David Torres's counter was purple, that colour tube was missing from Martin's studio along with red, yellow and green acrylics.'

'It's like a freaking game of Clue!' Harris commented. Rubbing his brows, he pulled out a box of painkillers from his drawer. 'Want one?'

'Na, I'm good. Head still throbbing, but I'll see if Patrick will redo my dressings,' she felt the back of her head, the sensation of feeling her shaven head gave her goosebumps. 'The thing is, if one of these two men is our killer, we will soon find out. If they are both behind bars then..,' she shrugged her shoulders to finish her sentence.

'Do you think one of them is?' He asked, desperation in his words.

'I wish I could say yes. The complexity of this case is throwing up too many lines of inquiry.'

'Well these two will be going away. Hopefully Judge Trueman will throw away the bloody keys. Talking of criminals, had those goddamn reporters in the courthouse, first thing this morning. Told them we were following leads. The pressure from above is firing up. They are looking for answers and want this wrapped up as soon as. Do we need to call in reinforcements Agent Strong?'

'I'll give Agent Perez a call shortly. He should be back in Durant in..' she glanced at her watch, 'a couple of hours.'

'Eli is still at the hospital. Officer Carter is keeping watch. He hasn't moved from his father's bedside. The nurses and bank staff all confirm his whereabouts on his days off, and his visiting times during the evening at the hospital all square up. Does he need watching? Our manpower is stretched as it is. I can just get the hospital to keep an eye out.'

'There's still the matter of finding blue rope in his shed. I'll go over to Parts & Parts store again, see if they have a record of who bought some. We need all officers to be vigilant up and down the east route. Keep an eye open for a tall male, acting suspicious. Tell Carter to leave his post and join the others but inform medical staff of the situation. We don't want to cause a panic, but we do have a duty of care.'

'Right. Will do.'

'Our killer has left no DNA traces anywhere. He's good, I'll give him that much. What are we missing sheriff? Have the officers found anyone of that age range we think is his last attended target? 32-38yrs old. Their counter will be 2 and green! We're sure of that, not that it matters. If we find them, then its too late, he would have killed his fourth victim already.'

'You can appreciate the number of residents and workers in Butler and beyond. I can assure you; my team are working tirelessly to make sure everyone is informed,' the tension in his sentence was palpable. Clara knew everyone was physically and mentally drained, herself included.

'Look, we'll get him. He'll slip up somewhere and we'll be on him,' the dog sat beside Sheriff Harris's chair and put his head on his lap.

'Hey boy, you're filthy,' he tapped the top of his head.

'He likes you, Strange.'

'What is?'

'Nothing, inner voice escaping from my mind. I'll get your cruiser cleaned then head over to the morgue. Dr Cameron should be back by then. Is it okay if I still use your vehicle?'

'Use away.'

She walked down the corridor of the courthouse with the dog in toe. *Why did you growl at George and not Harris?* Her mind started wandering and she had to pull it back. 'Wash for you too dog. I'm sure the car wash won't mind me lathering you up,' the dog whined as though it understood what was being said.

The scruffy mutt started barking. Michael was up ladders, rolling the ceiling with fresh paint. 'Shush boy,' Clara told him.

'Probably thinks I'm a threat with my roller,' Michael interjected. They both shook their heads and gave a little laugh. 'I'll let you pass, then I'll move again. Don't want him getting stressed out.'
'Cheers. Come on boy.'
Clara ran inside the store, just off Hendricks Avenue, near David Torres's car dealership, which was all closed up and would be until they caught whoever was doing this. She went inside the store, picking up some cheap dog shampoo, a new leash, collar and a plain chicken and bacon sandwich to share with him. She overheard an old woman chatting away to one of the store assistants at the cash register. 'It's a shame, all these killings in such a small area. And what are the police doing about it, nothing. They haven't even looked into it if you ask me. No good useless..'
Clara's insides boiled. 'For your information ma'am, Sheriff Harris and his team have been working round the clock. So, I would kindly suggest you stop your idle chit chat and hurry up and pay.'
'Well, there's no need for bad manners now is there!'
Clara pushed past, hurling her money on the counter. 'Friggin good for nothing old biddy,' her stomach churned. She was going to prove these people wrong.
The exterior of the cruiser was spotless. Her pent-up frustrations proving to be useful when it came to polishing. The dog shampooed and dried with the blower looked like a new breed.
Cleaning inside she felt something under the front seat, pulling it out, a small bottle of hard liquor sat in her hand. Her heart sank. *Sheriff Harris had said he had given up.* Then she remembered Deputy Dubois had apparently borrowed the vehicle last night. *Could it be his?* She wondered. Holding the bottle, her hand started to shake. Temptation to open the lid was overwhelming. It would be unfathomable to think about taking a swig, to feel

the liquor on her dry lips. She stood contemplating the idea. Her insides were screaming for the taste of alcohol one more time. She quickly stowed it back, putting the dog in the open trunk and drove to the morgue.

'You need to stay in the vehicle. You have water and the window is down. I won't be long,' he winced at her words, but settled down after his traumatic experience at the car wash.

Placing her fave mask on she looked through the double doors of the morgue. The smells were still prominent and caught Clara's chest as she entered.

'Agent Strong? My name's Mason. I'm one of Dr Cameron's assistance. Please to finally meet you in person. I've heard so much about you.'

'Like wise,' she lied, but spoke kindly as she wanted answers. 'Mason, do you have anything that'll help me catch this god-awful madman?'

Mason turned to face her. 'Madman you say. Interesting choice of words. I think he's extremely clever and is outwitting his opponents. He isn't leaving any traces behind and knows exactly what he's doing. Very smart guy if you ask me.'

'Well, I'm not!' Clara snapped. Not understanding why this forensic scientist was so delusional.

'Oh, I didn't mean to upset you. I just meant he's clever in his game but I'm sure you will catch up with him,' he looked away, knowing he had annoyed her.

'Do you have anything of interest to help me catch this clever unsub?' Her tone uncaring and unfriendly.

'White substance found, cocaine the class A drug. We also found ketamine, mephedrone and some class B drugs, amphetamines. He has been shipping it out to businessmen, who must believe they're untouchable. Maggie has been following up with the substances found at the lumberyard and found out where his boxes of goodies were heading. The rope fibres from his basement are identical to the ones we have back in the evidence room. The photographs, well we are still trying to get into his computer to see if he is distributing these like Joseph Martin is. If their computers are compatible, we'll soon know. It's a web of confusion, you will have to untangle Agent Strong.'

She didn't like his tone. His demeanour was intimidating to say the least.

'David Torres's and Eleanor Parker's toxicology reports have come back. No acute poisoning or any high concentrations of drugs or toxins were detected in either victim. Dr Cameron has written here that death occurred first, with all three victims before the unsub detached body parts or penetrated. Sounds like the chap you are after has a conscience.'

'No fingerprints, DNA at any of the crime scenes? Nothing?' She was waiting for a response from Mason, describing the killer as being proficient and an expert in his line of work.

'Not a hair, clothing fibre or footprint. Shall I continue?' He stood, reading from his clipboard looking smug. Clara's body tensed. She really didn't like this man. He was pretentious, but he wasn't impressing her. If he wanted to sound important, then that was his choice. She just thought he was a jerk.

'Agent Strong!' She heard a friendly voice entering the morgue.

She turned her back on Mason, 'Dr Cameron, how are you holding up? You must feel completely fatigued.'

'Like you agent, I'm just trying to do my job and get results. Thanks Mason, go get a break.'

'It was good to meet you Agent Strong. I'm sure we will meet again very soon.'

Not if I can help it! She was tired. She needed food and a strong coffee.

'Do you have a plan Agent Strong? To catch him?' Patrick asked. He stood in his lab whites; splashes of blood patterned the middle where his stomach protruded.

'Without fingerprints or DNA evidence the courts will just exonerate Johnson and Martin. Their attorneys would defend their innocence from being wrongly convicted without substantial evidence. All the leads we have are circumstantial. They will both go down for their crimes, but for murder, I don't have enough to use against them.'

'I'll keep looking.'

'Thanks Dr. I'm going to check who bought blue rope. It's all I have. I'm running out of ideas and time. I nearly forgot, would you take a quick look at my stitches and clean it up. I don't want to go back to the hospital because…,' she stopped. Thoughts of her mama and George came to the forefront of her mind.

'Of course I will. Sit over there and I'll see to it now.'

Dr Cameron had a very steady hand. He was very comfortable around dead and living people. He placed a new dressing over the wound and gave Clara some of his private painkillers.

Walking out the door, Mason approached her. 'Agent Strong. I was wondering if you would like to go out for dinner this evening. With me?'

'I appreciate the offer, but I already have a dinner date tonight,' she was looking forward to sneaking her new four-legged friend into the motel and eating junk food. She needed a rest; her body was running on empty cylinders plus anything sounded better than spending an evening with this pompous prick, she weighed up in her head and inwardly grinned.

'Oh, another night then. I can't do Monday night, I have other commitments, but maybe some evening after that?'

'I think it's best to leave it strictly professional between us, don't you think,' it was a rhetorical question and she left him standing, sipping his coffee.

She was pleased to see the dog was still sleeping in the trunk of the vehicle. She jumped in and drove over to Butler Specialised Parts & Parts to see Mary Louise. *I must phone Perez afterwards.*

Not being disappointed, Clara saw Mary Louise the shop assistant flirting with two young men, near the rack of nails and screws. Glancing over at Clara, she gave her a nod. 'I'll be with you darling in two ticks.'

Clara looked around the store while she waited. 'Blue rope,' she whispered. 'Where are you kept?'

'Hello there. I remember you. Are you on your own today?' Mary Louise looked around to see if she could find the handsome one.

'Yep. Do you sell blue rope?' She didn't want to waist anytime with niceties.

'We sell a lot of rope. Do you want to purchase a length of…'

'No, no I need to have a look at the different types. Can you show me where it's kept?'

'Over by the paints and gardening section. You'll find it.'

Clara got the feeling Mary Louise wasn't going to be helpful. 'Thanks.'

Slipping through the cracks of the stacked items, she saw gardening tools, paint pots, brushes and rope. It wasn't organised in a proper manner, which frustrated her.

'Are you thinking of helping me?'

She looked around and saw Michael lifting paint from the shelves. 'What?'

'I said are you gonna give me a hand, back at the courthouse. Seeing as Eli is off again, I could do with the help,' he smiled.

Clara hadn't really noticed his smile before, but it lit up his whole face. His eyes were a piercing blue colour, and she looked straight at them. Realising she was staring, she shook her head and turned back to the stacked items. 'Oh! I wish I could help, but my partner has also left me on my own. Looks like we are in the same boat.'

'That's a shame. You should take it easy otherwise you will burn yourself out.'

Is he flirting with me? I would rather go on a date with him than Morgue Mason! She inwardly laughed.

'I'm trying to find some blue rope; these are all natural colours. It says here, lockstitch construction rope suited for blocks and pulleys, this one double braided for extra strength,' she lifted each one up and set them down. 'I just want simple blue rope. This place is so disorganised.'

'You've got to know where to look. If you've been in here as much as I have, then its easy to put your hands on things. Blue rope is the other side of this so-called, man-made isle,' he said, gesturing over the top of the shelves.

They both laughed, looking at the chaotic arrangements of goods randomly placed.

'Thanks, I would've been standing reading about ropes all day if you hadn't come to my rescue.'

'That would be a sorry sight to see Miss Agent,' his smile was quite infectious, he gave her a nod and purchased his paint with Mary Louise.

Her eyes spotted what she came in for, she took down the number and went over to the old counter. Michael waved as he left the store. Clara felt a slight flutter. She told herself she was being silly that she needed some food to get back on track.

'Can you tell me if anyone has purchased the blue rope, numbered RP4374?'

'Let me see.' Mary Louise flicked through the purchasers' details. 'Nope. Not the blue.'

'I thought you said you sold a lot of it?'

'No. You asked me if we sold a lot of rope. Not blue.'

'So, you haven't? Not even in the last year?'

'That's what I said. Now if you don't mind darling, I have customers to serve.'

The conversation wasn't amounting to anything. Clara took her frustrations outside and paced the parking lot. She noticed the dog was awake, sticking its head out of the back window. She stroked the fur from its eyes, 'D'you fancy a burger and fries' boy?'

Chapter Twenty-Seven

The TV was playing some sitcom from the 70's as Clara and the dog lay on the motel bed. Empty food wrappers and containers strewn across the blankets. It was evening time. She must have fallen asleep for 3hours after devouring her cheap dinner. She leaned over and picked up her cell from the side cupboard. She dialled Perez's number. It rang out, so she tried again. The same thing happened. Looking at the time on her cell phone, 7.30pm, she thought he maybe visiting his father at Durant Royal Hospital.

'Do you fancy a walk dog? Can't keep calling you that,' he jumped off the bed and sat by the door. 'You were trained at one point, so how did you end up with the Johnsons?' He barked. 'No! Shush you're not allowed in here remember?'

The girl on the desk was filing her nails, feet on the counter, watching the same sitcom. They snuck past, exiting out into the cool air.

Outside seemed quiet. It was a Saturday evening, *where was everyone?* she thought. They walked along the street taking in the fresh air and the faint smells of the Fall. Some of the shops' window displays were replacing autumn colours for Christmas ones. Clara hated the Christmas period and Thanksgiving. They never celebrated like other families when she was younger, they were lucky to even get a secondhand gift. Passing Evan Thomas's bar, she saw Jeremiah Dubois coming out. He looked like he had been drinking for a while. 'Jeremiah?'

'Clara, I mean Agent Strong. What are you doing out?'

'Clara, please. We know each other well enough to be on first names outside of work.'

'See you have a new partner. Better looking than the last,' he sniggered, looking down at the dog.

'Yeah, Agent Perez had to go back to Durant. We needed to stretch our legs, so here we are.'

'Do you fancy joining me for a drink? Dogs are allowed. Joe's a good egg. He takes all different strays in that bar!' He chortled again. He was on the verge of being really intoxicated.

'I'm okay. I don't think it's a good idea.'

'Why not? I could do with the company. Please, we have a lot of years to catch up on. Just one!' He looked like he wasn't going to give up. He held his hand out, giving her a solemn smile.

This was a pinnacle moment for her. She would either accomplish her greatest achievement or go down that path of drinking herself to oblivion. Her career would be over. The dog looked up at her and pulled her towards the bar doors.

'See, even he wants a drink,' Dubois commented.

Inside the bar the fire generated warmth that was much needed. Seats were vacant and the normal buzz of the place was missing. She sat in a booth with Dubois, taking her parker off. The dog laid down at her feet under the table. 'What would you like?'

Her eyes scowled the bar. Amber coloured rays shone against the bar lighting. Her thoughts raced to that smooth harmonious taste and the different flavours that triggered her emotions. The sweetness, spices and smoke were the perfect balance of a good whiskey. The Jack Daniel's bottle sat two bottles from the end on the top shelf. It was easily drinkable, and she craved that smooth sensation in her mouth. Joe the bartender reached over and brought it down to the bar. Three men who looked to be locals, sat on their stools consuming her favourite liquor.

'Clara! What would you like from the bar?' Dubois repeated.

'A coke and ice would be great, thanks.'

'Come on, join me for one.'

The dog got up from the floor, placing his paw on her lap. He looked straight at her, his amber coloured eyes wide and alert. 'Nope, I'm good thanks Jeremiah.'

She stroked his head and reached down to kiss his nose. 'I have you to look after now, JD,' she couldn't help but smile. 'Perfect name for a perfect companion.'

Joe the bartender came over to her table, bowl of water in his hand for the dog. JD curled his tongue and plunged it into the water. A pool of the liquid formed around the bowl, which he also devoured. Clara and the four-legged Jack Daniel's were getting acquainted with one another, and she knew he's table manners needed some work.

'Dog looks familiar. Is he yours?' Joe asked inquisitively.

'Yeah, found him wandering the streets. Looked starved and dirty. Couldn't just pass by him poor thing.'

The dog was contented, sat by her feet and licked the back of Joe's hand. 'How's the case going? Heard you had another death. Agent Perez is away I hear.'

'Yeah, I just needed to get out for some air. Head overloading with information. Dubois pulled me in for a drink. Grateful really. It's cold outside.'

'Jeremiah is a good man. I've known him since this high,' putting his hand at knee height. 'He was really good to me. Kept me company and we use to play in his yard, everyday over the summer break. We went to the same elementary school. There was another kid too, but apparently something happened to him. Someone said he was murdered by his father, down by the lake.'

Clara jumped up from her seat, heart beating out of control. She couldn't breathe. 'Are you okay?'

She pushed him out of the way, grabbed JD's leash and ran outside. Arms swinging in all direction, she felt sick and lightheaded. The dog barked. 'I'm okay boy, give me a minute.'

Descending down the front steps of the bar, Clara turned to walk back to her motel room. Slowing her breathing down, she steadied her pace and zipped up her coat, putting her hood up, to hide from the outside world. 'Come on boy let's get back.'
She crossed the road to Smith Street, walking past Lou's coffeehouse and Butler bank. Her steps were now coordinated, feeling relieved to be away from Alabama South Avenue Bar & Grill.
She knew Joe was none the wiser to who she was, she didn't blame him. Clara couldn't seem to get away from her past in this place. People after eighteen years were still talking about the boy who disappeared. She didn't cry, she didn't have anymore tears left inside. That was the first time she heard her father was to blame. She hadn't even considered the possibility. She took her cell phone from her pocket to check the time. 'It's not too late if I hurry.'
Turning the key to lock the door behind her, Clara left JD to sleep in the motel room. She had to be somewhere before visiting times were up. She took Sheriff Harris's cruiser and sped over to Butler Hospital.
'Can I help you?' A freshly, dressed nurse asked, her nightshift just about to start.
'I'm looking for Mrs Strong, Mrs Alice Strong. She was admitted a while back.'
'Are you a relative? I'm only asking because she is having limited contact with visitors. Due to her health.'
Clara couldn't find the words. It was too painful to admit who she was, not only to the nurse but to herself. 'Yes, I'm a relative.'
'Okay, can you sign in. Visiting will be finishing in about half an hour. Mrs Strong is in room 57. Two corridors down, turn left and you will find her in a room on her own, on the left.'
'Thanks.'

The nervousness returned in her steps. Her hands and legs shook. She pushed through the first set of double doors and continued down the sterile white corridor. A wheelchair sat next to an infusion pump machine at the end, next to the second set of doors. She moved around to the right, glancing unintentionally through the glass of another patient's room. *Eli Davis.* His hand sat on top of an elderly man's shoulder. The nurse in the room nodded at Eli and pulled the blanket up and covered the man's face. 'Shit!' Clara felt guilty intruding on his privacy. He was a person of interest, a suspected Killer but here he was, consoling himself with grief.

She found her way to room 57. She stopped. Was this even a good idea, the thought weighing down on her. *I want to know.*

Knocking on the door, she entered. A frail lady lay in the bed over near the window. The sound of numerous machines bleeped in synch with one another. Her mama turned her head on the pillow, to face the visitor. Her body unable to move independently. Wires were hooked up to her, drips hydrating her fragile frame to keep her organs functioning.

'Ma,' her determination to find answers disappeared at the sight of her. Her dark brown eyes, sullen and rimmed with thin skin, stared at Clara. 'Mama.'

She tried to slide her hand along the sheet to reach her daughter. 'Don't move. Stay still.'

'Clara,' she whispered softly. 'Is it really you?'

Clara smiled and took her mama's hand. Words were unspoken between them. The silence in the room was unexpectedly peaceful. Her mother tried to squeeze her hand. 'I'm here mama, I can stay for a while.' Alice closed her eyes, turned her head and coughed.

'How have you been?' She managed to ask.

'I'm good. I'm doing just fine. Rest up,' Clara returned the hand squeeze, making her mama smile.

'I'm sorry for what you went through,' her coughing intensified.

'It doesn't matter. I just want you to rest.'

'He beat me too. I should have protected you both. He wouldn't let me take you.'

'Grayson, what happened to him?'

Alice turned her head to face the window, taking the moment to squeeze Clara's hand again. 'I don't know.'

'Was it Pa? Did he hurt him?'

The coughing persisted making one of the machines bleep louder. A nurse rushed in and checked all the equipment and wires. 'I'm sorry but she needs to rest. You can come back tomorrow; she just needs a good sleep. I'm sorry but you'll have to cut your visit short.'

Clara went to put her hand on her mama's shoulder and kiss her goodbye but froze. 'See you tomorrow mama.'

Alice Strong had no energy to reply. The nurse controlled the machines and showed Clara to the door. 'Come back in the morning.'

The door to room 57 closed and Clara watched the nurse through the glass settle her mama. She still had no tears to shed. Her numb body felt detached.

Walking past Eli's father's room, she noticed he had gone. The lights were turned off, the bed already taken away. *Patrick will be depleted with so much going on.*

She decided to leave the cruiser and walk back. She needed the fresh air to her face and some alone time. It wasn't too far to the motel. Clara felt the rain to her face, she didn't care. Her hood stayed down, she needed to breathe, to think about everything that was happening in her life, with her career, the case, her dying mother, Grayson. She dug deep, bringing her memories of her upbringing in Lisman, to the forefront of her confused ruminations.

There was an undercurrent of emotions she couldn't seem to access with her mind. She had solved other cases, deciphered problems other FBI Agents couldn't. She felt she was so close to unraveling the murderer's identity. *It's there Clara, think. Nature versus nurture? Just like my own upbringing.* She knew her perception of people was strong, but why not now?

She thought about her childhood, the unknown of what happened. Her father's fury every time he had a drink. *Maybe the killer's background was also intense. He felt neglected, unloved or otherwise treated. We've been concentrating so much on the victim's lives, maybe we should be focusing more attention on his mental state and the acts he's committed. See if we can check out anyone from Butler that had an unpleasant upbringing like mine.*

She knew her traumas came from her past. She could have turned out so differently, but she had some inner control to exceed in life, to keep moving forward and not to look back all the time. The latter was the part that turned her to the booze. *Our unsub is struggling to contain his anger, he has no self control. He wants to punish those who wronged him. Just like I wanted to punish my mama, ask her why she didn't care.*

She crossed the road to the corner of Smith Street and Hendricks Avenue. Her concentration was fixed on her case now. She had taken a wrong turn. She doubled backed on herself, she had the feeling she wasn't alone. Her back felt cold, under her warm parker. Glancing over her shoulder she saw no one. *For fuck's sake Clara, you're being paranoid.*

The sound of trash cans grated across the streets, making her feel uncomfortable. She pressed on, turning her head at every given opportunity. Shadows, she saw shadows. The wind started picking up, the rain was falling heavily on her face. Her feet moved quickly, to get back to the dirty but safe motel, wanting desperately to be with her companion, JD. Clara needed more sleep. She knew tomorrow they would be one step closer to catching the killer. But first she would try phoning Perez.

Chapter Twenty-Eight

He drew back the green and blue chequered curtains in his bedroom. There was a storm brewing. Dark clouds were forming over Butler town. The thick smoky clouds rolled in, consuming any spec of light visible to the naked eye. His room, filled with old antiques from his father's collection, courtesy of Henry's grocery store on the corner of Sheffield Street and Grandview River Park, sat like a king's trophy collection.

He picked up a small porcelain doll, which sat on his wooden dresser and combed his fingers through her hair. He was wondering about his day ahead. The idea of attending church for the very first time since childhood, rang in his thoughts. *It's Sunday and it feels appropriate. I'll meet my saviour tomorrow night, after my final opponent has been sacrificed and given to him, so cleansing my thoughts today would feel appropriate.*

He looked at his clock on his bedroom wall. The wheels and moving parts were powered by weights that turned the hands. It was cased, so not to get damaged. He didn't know if it was worth anything or if it was even an antique. He kept it in his bedroom to help him fall asleep with the sounds of the moving components. He wound it meticulously every other night so it wouldn't stop. *One hour before the church doors opened,* he thought.

Changing into his best outfit, he glanced at himself in the full-length mirror, which stood in the corner of his room by the window. He would hang it up after church and wear it tomorrow night when he returned home from his last victorious move. He used his clothes brush to take off any access fluff. He smiled to himself, leaving for church in his vehicle. If it rained, he didn't want his suit to get ruined, it wasn't a designer brand; it was a roomier regular fit from Slater's store in Pennington. He bought it for special occasions, like tomorrow night.

Norton Pentecostal Church doors were already open. He parked his vehicle on the road and walked inside. His skin tightened with excitement and gave him an overwhelming sense of empowerment. He could sense the Lord speaking to him separately from the rest of the congregation. He was the chosen one, picked out from all the other members to do God's work. Self adulation welled up inside. He noticed the Pastor greeting his members as they congregated in the foyer area. Standing up straight, taking a deep breath, he shook his hand as he entered.

'A new face. You are very welcome. Please find a comfortable spot and I hope to see you attending again,' Pastor MacArthur said to his new church goer.

'Thank you kindly. I'm sure the Lord will give his blessing for me to return and maybe offer me a front row pew next time,' Pastor MacArthur smile didn't look genuine, which slightly disappointed the killer. *He'll be sorry next Sunday when I return, having received my gift from God.*

After the Pastor had emphasised the Acts of the Apostles; the fifth book of the New Testament, the congregation prayed aloud using their gift of tongues and creating too much noise for the perpetrator's liking. He was secretly praying for this sermon to be over, he had somewhere else he wanted to be. Pastor MacArthur finished off the service by talking about the preaching of the church's belief, in acting like a hospital where individuals can come to heal, to grow and to be made whole. Sitting on the hard seat the killer laughed inwardly, immense satisfaction warmed within, he knew he was going to be whole tomorrow night.

Pouring out of the church at the end, a young woman was handing out flyers. He didn't notice who it was until she handed him one. 'Georgina! I didn't know you attended here,' his heart started racing with excitement.

'Why hello stranger. I haven't seen you for quite a while. You stopped your visits to my work. Have you read everything on the shelves?' Georgina's face lit up as she spoke.

'I've been busy working; everyone wants my attention.'

'Well don't leave it so long next time. Actually, this is an invitation for the opening of the new wing. We received a substantial grant from the mayor's office to complete it quickly. It's tomorrow night at 7.30pm. I would love you to see the new collection of books. Will you come? I'm there this evening arranging the layout of the rooms. There should be a good crowd coming.'

Dry mouthed and in a state of confusion, he couldn't answer. *This wasn't the way I had planned it with my maker. Why is she ruining my game?* His head felt light, making him keel slightly to his side.

'Are you okay? Do you need to sit down?' Georgina Miller asked.

'No, no. I'm fine. I just need to go home,' he took the piece of paper from her, walking away without saying anything.

She shouted after him, 'See you tomorrow evening then!'

He sat in his vehicle, hands shaking, clutching the steering wheel tightly thinking about the now horrific denouement to a well detailed plan. He stared at the words printed in front of him. 'No!' *An open night was not happening.* His rage was intense, he ripped up the paper and threw it onto the passenger's seat. He heard God's voice in his head telling him to act tonight, his work had to be completed so he could be rewarded. He was yearning for this last move. He was ahead and Georgina Miller wasn't going to let him lose.

He waited and watched. After the last person left Norton Pentecostal Church his opponent shoved the leftover flyers in her bag and walked over to the last remaining car in the parking lot.

He needed to follow her to make sure she wasn't heading there now. He wasn't ready. He would have to go home and gather up his winning components. The man switched on his engine and proceeded to drive slowly at a distance behind her.

Her red car, vibrant against the dark clouds above turned onto South Mulberry Avenue, heading south. He knew then she was going home, but he had to be sure. She passed Ararat Road, putting on the brakes to turn up Pickett Creek Road to her home. Relief flooded him with the realisation he still had time to go home and organise himself. He parked up out of sight and watched.

Georgina unpacked her car from the morning's service, unlocked her front door and was out of the killer's sight, until later. All he could do now was to head home, collect his thoughts and talk himself through the night's events, which he had to execute with precision to win the game.

He turned the vehicle around, put his foot to the gas pedal and headed back to his castle.

The first thing he did was put the kettle on the stove, followed by making himself a tuna salad sandwich, lashings of mayonnaise and black pepper. He was hungry.

Entering his bedroom after his lunchtime meal, he threw the ripped-up flyer in the trash. *How dare she change the way it should be played,* he felt angry, frustrated with apprehension roaming around in his head.

His good suit hung from his old wardrobe as he changed into leisure wear for a while. His clothes he would wear for the kill were already sitting folded neatly on his ottoman at the foot of his bed. He needed his games room to think about this evening's kill.

The access to his basement was perfectly hidden, only he knew how to enter and descend the stairs. The room smelt clean, fresh and ready for his visitor. The sound of thunder rumbling outside made him think God was already on his way. A jar sat on his desk waiting for a piece of Georgina Miller's arrival, later tonight. *I must label them properly with neater handwriting,* he nervously sniggered.

Sitting in his gaming chair, flash memories from his childhood containing his parents kept coming to the surface. He remembered his siblings fleeing from the strict upbringing, leaving him alone with his Christian parents. Life for him consisted of mental abuse and neglect. There was never any conversation or interaction between him and his parents. His friend Dubois tried to visit but was unable to get past the first hurdle. Life was intense for him. Sometimes he would encounter blackouts, finding himself positioned in a completely different place to where he was originally playing.

He had a blackout the day his parents disappeared. He was of an age he could defend for himself, make his own meals, wash his dirty clothes. It was the smoke in the backyard which caught his attention that day back in the summer break. Flames then started to spread across the trash, a large pile in the centre burnt fiercely and out of control. He remembered staring, wondering who had started such a blaze. He went in the house to tell his father, but he couldn't be found, his mother also left him alone in the house.

It was then God told him to scoop the ashes from the fire and place them into two vases, they would remind him of his mother and father. And he should keep the ashes to look back on them one day and tell himself he has grown in strength without their crushing hands upon him.

The state recognised he was 19 years of age, which was over the majority age in Alabama and Nebraska to defend for himself. The authorities assumed his parents being devoted Christians, left to preach and spread the word of the Pentecostal faith. They were known to the residents of Butler as strict believers and unpleasant people.

His thoughts trickled back to the very start of his game, he didn't understand or remember how God approached him at the beginning, but he was pleased he did. His saviour's company has been his prized possession for the last 6 years. He has treasured every moment, hoping he will continue to have that close relationship with him after the end of the game.

The thought of being ignored again by someone didn't sit well with him. *God won't abandon me; I have faith in him.* Convincing himself of that thought was crucial, especially for performing later. Focus and motivation pushed his confidence up a notch.

He could hear God's presence outside; his words were louder and clearer than ever before. *I need to speak to him properly, face to face prior to Georgina's sacrifice. I need to cleanse myself in the storm and be clean for entering my new life with God.*

He closed the back door, walked over to the trees at the back of his yard and stood out in the rain. He raised his arms towards the sky, lifting his head to face heaven. His body was covered by his clothes, this wouldn't do. He needed the rain to touch his body, his skin, his soul. Pulling off his jumper the lightning bolted beyond the trees, the electrifying experience gripped his chest, he felt aroused with excitement. He stripped naked and straddled his body like Jesus on the cross. Rain poured down his front and back like torrents of water in a river that had burst its banks. He spoke clearly and said, 'God take me. I am a sinner; I ask for forgiveness. Jesus died for my sins and rose again. My relationship with you is pure and mighty. I have done your work and seek eternal life this night.'

Electrifying lightning raced across the afternoon skies and clouds were darkening. Intensifying tensions of light surged down to earth. Rain pelted his body; he embraced every inch of pain. The storm was powerful, he knew God had answered him and his soul was cleansed. His joyous screams echoed across the skies like a wild cat calling out to its colony.

He shook his hair, short golden locks curling with the wet and lifted his sodden clothes from the muddy ground. Entering his home feeling like a king and not the small insignificant pawn anymore, he surveyed his castle, ascended the stairs to the bathroom, dried his hair and purified body with a fresh white towel.

Caressing his hanging suit with his hands, tears appeared in his eyes. Emotions of love for his Lord conquered his life, making him the happiest man alive. He decided to dress in his chosen outfit he pieced together for the special occasion this evening. Tonight, the red jumper under my jacket and black pants were to be worn.

Passing the kitchen, he felt ravenous. Finishing the rest of the tuna and making a coffee, he slipped away to his favourite place and waited.

Chapter Twenty-Nine

The phone kept ringing out. 'Why aren't you picking up!' She was becoming irritated with Perez. She needed to talk to him about the case. She felt alone, completely abandoned down here in Butler. JD was lying down on the motel floor, biting his back paw to keep himself occupied. But she needed to have a conversation with another human, about a serial killer.

Picking up the dog's bowls and placing them in a plastic bag, she clipped the dog's leash onto his collar and snuck past the old man who had the Sunday graveyard shift on reception. He was partially oblivious to her presence, waving to her without lifting his head, not noticing the four-legged animal by her side. Peering at her watch, seeing the morning had disappeared, she opened her umbrella and ran to the sheriff's vehicle situated in the motel parking lot. Rain pelted the windscreen as she jumped in. JD sat in the back on some old blankets she found in the trunk yesterday, whilst at Eddies car wash.

Butler was quiet on a Sunday. The wave of church goers, commuting to and from their choice of religious organisations were the only people Clara had encountered on the way to the department. Realising she hadn't eaten or fed JD yet, she pulled over to a gas station, purchased some dry dog kibble and what looked to be a cheese and salami salad sandwich.

The courthouse parking lot was virtually empty. Sheriff Harris had allocated some downtime for his team in the morning, he wanted them back this afternoon feeling refreshed, ready to filter through the case files.

Officer Hannah Young was already sitting at her desk. She was in early and sifting through vanilla-coloured files, searching her computer, drinking a can of soda.

'Afternoon.'

She jumped from her seat, 'Afternoon ma'am.'

'What are you hunting for?' She asked, with inquisitive curiosity.

'I was wondering if Benjamin Johnson or Joseph Martin had any more connections from their past. Nothing promising yet. Joseph had an older brother who went off the rails when they were younger, done time for aggravated assault, theft and possession of firearms. Sounds like a nasty piece of work, I'm going to keep looking,' Hannah turned back to her computer, sipping her soda.

Officer Asher entered, followed by Sheriff Harris and Deputy Dubois. The consensus was they couldn't be at home doing nothing while there was a killer on the loose. JD ignored the gathering of law enforcement officers and snuck under Hannah's desk by her feet. He was quivering with the sounds of the storm. Hannah lifted her issued work jacket, placing it over his body to act as a security blanket.

Jeremiah Dubois's demeanour looked similar to the dogs. His face was timorous, turning it away from Clara, probably wanting to forget how intoxicated he was last night.

'Right, everyone, it's just us. As some of you know Agent Perez was called away on personal business, I'm hoping he will be joining us again later today or tomorrow. I want all our concentrations focused on catching this sadistic son of a bitch. put him behind bars, hopefully before he returns.' Two other officers opened the door and joined the group. 'Is that everyone?'

'Officer Carter phoned in sick. He said he must have caught some kind of viral infection while he was watching Eli Davis at the hospital, he sounded terrible,' Officer Hannah explained.

'Does he normally take time off?' Agent Strong asked trying not to sound like she was being smart, throwing out accusations.

'No. This is his first time sick,' Sheriff Harris jumped in, trying to defend Carter's reputation. He was loyal to his team and Clara sensed it.

'I need to talk you through where we are with this investigation. Our makeshift office is small, but I need you all to come next door. I want you all to look at the whiteboard with fresh eyes, tell me what you see. I need to hear your thoughts.' Agent Strong took control. She had too. Agent Perez had gone off the radar.

The sound of thunder clattered through the building. The rain relentless, hitting the building's roof like pellets. A flash of lightning filtered through the large window to the rear of the room, lighting up the office, making some of the officer's flinch.

Perez's notes were still on the whiteboard. The "unsub" word central, with all other headings surrounding it. The officers stared at the scribble, trying to unravel all the information and make sense of it. The truth and answers were up there somewhere. 'Forget everything we have spoken about and tell me what you see.'

'He's targeting thirty-year-olds,' Officer Asher began.

'He's playing some sort of game, as he kills,' Hannah read from the M.O and signature.

Clara noticed Deputy Dubois sat with his coffee, brows furrowing, staring at the board.

'Do you think he's angry with friends or does it go deeper than that? I'm only asking as it's the way he kills first, then does the inevitable things to them,' Hannah piped up again, her confidence had exceeded in such a small period of time.

'We're thinking along the same lines. We need to do background checks on any residents who had history of any confrontations, serious injuries etc with family members. Like Joseph Martin. Hannah, keep looking into his family background. Did he only have one older brother?'

'Okay ma'am.'

'Also, we should do family checks on William Parker, he's still a person of interest and delve deeper with Eli's adoption history,' Clara explained.

'I'll get onto that,' the other woman police officer volunteered, who stood more reserved to the back of the room.

'Great. Anything else?' She continued.

'A lot of the action seems to be centred around the lumberyard up at Dansby Road. I know Johnson's stash of paraphernalia was found up there, but things just don't seem to add up. Too many loose ends and no answers to tie them together,' Sheriff Harris interjected.

There was a sudden sound of something falling and hitting the ground. Deputy Jeremiah Dubois's fingers had slowly unclenched the side of his coffee mug, dropping it at Clara's feet. A few officers gasped, their nerves already on edge with the storm. He stood, but not to clean up the shattered pieces of ceramics strewn across the floor. He instead inched towards the whiteboard. The whole room fell silent. All eyes were focused on Dubois. He lifted the cloth from the shelf directly below the board, his stare recognising something in front of him. He didn't say a word, rubbing everything off apart from the victims' names and ages.

'Oh my god. It can't be,' all his concentration fixated on the three names. He reached down for a marker, drew a line next to Evan's name and slowly wrote with a trembling hand, Elijah. Underneath he saw David's name and shook his head, disbelieving his own thoughts. He drew a line from it and wrote, Daniel. He left a gap then gazed at Eleanor's name, 'Christ please tell me I'm wrong,' he drew a line next to hers and wrote, Elizabeth.

The silence in the room was palpable and hauntingly quiet, no one spoke or moved. The air pressure reduced as Dubois lifted his hand again to write on the whiteboard. He began filling the gap between Daniel and Elizabeth's names. Hand to pen he started to scroll out a new name, Grace.

The pen fell, landing next to the smashed ceramic mug on the floor. He couldn't breathe. He put both his hands on his head looking up to the ceiling.

'Jeremiah,' Clara put her hand on his shoulder, 'What's going on? Who are these people?' The tension in the air was masterful, consuming everyone who was present.

'I need to sit down,' falling onto a chair, his hands covered his face.

They could hear the storm worsening outside, rolls of thunder heightening the intensity within the room.

'How do you know them?' Clara asked with a shaky voice.

'He thinks they've returned to Butler, after all those years being away. I befriended him back then. I tried to make his life easier by talking to him every time I saw him. I got him the job here, in the courthouse. He's always been so grateful, kind. I don't understand.'

'Jeremiah please! Who are you talking about?'

'You have to remember I was just a neighbour. My parent's encouraged me to try and play with him. And then later on in his life his parents just packed up and left him, just like his siblings. He found himself alone, but he turned his life around, educated himself, learnt new skills to pay bills,' his body trembled; his heart rate pulsated uncontrollably.

Clara knelt down, taking Dubois's head in her hands. 'Look at me. You need to calm down and tell me his name.'

'It's Michael, Michael Arnold. The victim's names begin with the same letters as his siblings. He must be confused about their identities.'

Clara's head lowered; her own body tightened. The news came like a bolt from the blue. To her consternation her own mind struggled to process what Dubois had just revealed. The rest of the team, who remained quiet during Dubois's realisations, stood frozen to the floor.

'Michael? The guy who has been painting inside this courthouse? Are you sure it's him?'

'The ages are identical to his siblings. I don't know why I didn't see it before, if I had then Eleanor and David would still be alive.'

'Look at me. Listen to me Jeremiah. Don't go down that road. You've just made the connection; I really need you to step up and help me find him.'

He was still in a state of shock as though he had been struck by a thunderbolt but nodded his head.

'Grace, what age would she be? It's important.'

'Michael is 4 years older than me; she was 3, no wait, 4 years older than him, so 34.'

'You're sure Jeremiah?'

'Yes! God what have I done.'

Lightning was striking quicker between intervals, adding more energy to Clara's determination.

'You've done nothing wrong. Befriending people is a skill, not everyone can do it. You were there for my brother too.'

'Yeah, look what happened to him,' the crowd of officers studied the two, looking puzzled. It was out of him before he realised. 'Shit! I didn't mean that, I just can't believe Michael would be capable of killing innocent people.'

'But you said it yourself, he thinks these people are his family members, returning.'

'His pa and ma used to neglect him, throw the bible at him while he sat playing in the front yard. He didn't deserve any of it,' his eyes started to bleed with tears. He didn't want any of it to be true.

'I need you to think about what he did to each of his victims. I need your help finding out what he is intending to do next. Please, think. We're running out of time.'

'His life was full of abuse. His brothers tormented him all through their childhood. Daniel got physical with him, he never admitted it to me, but I saw it happen, his body was always covered in bruises. His youngest sister Elizabeth fell pregnant at a young age. Everyone in church said it was their fathers, but we never knew for sure.'

'What about Elijah? What happened between him and Michael?'

'Elijah never had any dealings with Michael when they were growing up. He acted as though he didn't exist. His Ma and Pa practically worshipped the ground he walked on; Elijah loved the attention. You could see the pain in Michael's eyes, he was so lonely.'

'Grace, what happened with her?'

'Grace! She was close to him, she used to spend her days reading to him, tell him stories, read him passages from the bible, help him with his schoolwork. Then she just stopped. She didn't go near him again, something happened. I remember watching him tare out pieces of her schoolwork from her books so he could teach himself. He wanted to learn. Teachers never helped him; they were just as guilty.'

Clara turned and faced the board. 'The counters! 4 siblings, Eleanor or in his case, Elizabeth, represented his 1st sibling, the youngest. The counters are in order of their place in the family.

Elijah being the oldest, that's why he put counter 4 on Evan's body.'

Sheriff Harris's office phone rang from next door breaking her concentration. It was just audible over the pelting of the rain. He vacated the makeshift office to answer it, returning sharply, he glared at Clara.

'Agent Strong. There's a phone call for you. I think you better take it!'

'Wait here,' she instructed Dubois.

She picked up Harris's landline. The voice on the other end could just be made out, 'Agent Strong is that you?'

'Deputy Miller? I can just about hear you. If you're phoning for a progress report, now isn't the time.'

'Listen, it's Agent Perez. His SUV was found in a gully by workmen trying to access drains in the storm. He has been taken to Durant Royal Hospital, he's in a critical condition. I'm going to send down Agent Ferendez to give you a hand.'

Clara couldn't believe this was happening. 'Is he going to be, okay? His father is in the same hospital. Did you know that? Christ, why did it have to rain,' she paused for a second to think. 'Don't send anyone down, we've just identified the killer and are working on a solution to wrap this up, with hopefully no more victims. I'll keep you updated as soon as we have made an arrest. Please keep me posted on how Adam is doing.'

'I will Agent Strong. You're on your own then. It probably would be too dangerous for Ferendez to travel down on his own in that storm. Don't fuck it up Strong. You know what the future holds if you do,' Miller finished the call. Clara took a moment to reflect on what was happening and to absorb his threatening comment. She had to concentrate on Michael, then she could return home to see the people she cared about.

265

Chapter Thirty

He was ready. His time had come. 'My sheep hear my voice, and I know them, and they follow me: and I give unto them eternal life; and they shall never perish.' His voice was loud as he read John 10:27-28 from his blue bible in his basement. He closed it over slowly, breathing in the air of the room for one last time before his life would change forever and placed it neatly on his gaming desk.

He swung around, opening the green cupboard door to beam at his collection, his trophies. *One more and then it's over. I've won. I get to embrace the feelings of winning, belonging.* Inside one of the cupboard doors hung a sign. He caressed it with his bare hands. "Deuteronomy 20:4 – For the Lord your God is he who goes with you to fight for you against your enemies, to give you the victory."

He stretched to the ceiling feeling alive, put on his rain mac, gathered up his tape, blue rope, knife and green counter, stuffed them in his rucksack and left his castle. His basement light left on for his return.

The coldness of the rain tinged his face as he ran to his vehicle. A large flash of bright light erupted the nights sky. *I'm ready.*

He knew where Georgina's house sat, but he wasn't going there tonight. He pulled out onto West Pushmataha Street and turned right, heading to the centre crossroads of Butler town. Visibility was difficult but he didn't care about the weather forecast, his mind was on a whole different ball game. The lights turned green; he drove straight over the crossroads trying to avoid the trash hitting the sides of his vehicle from the wind that stirred. His wipers were on fully, he could just make out the road signs to his right. *Oscar Gray Road, no. Pickens Avenue, no. I'm close.*

He put his indicator on to turn up Harrell Avenue. He knew it was a waste of time, no other road users would be silly enough to venture out in this weather. Still, he felt he needed to abide by the county road laws.

The building was quite large, it was a T shape and had two parking lots either side of the main entrance. It was in need of a lick of paint. He thought he might volunteer for the job after he had finished the courthouse, he would drop Eli and go solo, he mused to himself.

Butler County Choctaw Library stood amongst blowing trees. Leaves gathered up around the perimeter of the building. He reached for his rucksack, put his hood up and made his way to the main entrance. His outer layers soaked from just a short time outside made him feel cold and uncomfortable, so he took his mac off and placed it in the corner of the foyer as he entered.

Georgina always left the doors opened for anyone to access the library if she was working there out of hours. She would always be delighted to accommodate passing foot passengers to use the facilities. That's how Michael befriended her. Her presence lit up the room the first time he set eyes on her 7 years ago and she seemed familiar to him. He could never push aside the fact he already knew her. Then the realisation hit him, it was Grace, his sister who wronged him all those years ago. He had to include her in his planning at the beginning with Gods blessing.

The foyer was dark. Head statues of George Wallace, a governor of Alabama and James Buchanan Jr, an American lawyer, diplomat, politician and the 15th president of the USA, lit up with each strike of lightning. Straight ahead, Michael noticed two enormous carved wooden doors. One was open, shining a dim light, slightly reflecting off the hard wooden parquet floorboards. He could hear music playing. Georgina's favourite composer,

Vivaldi was blaring out The Four Seasons concerto from the old library's tape deck.

He hummed to the sounds, crossing the threshold to his next kill. The room he next entered was the hub of the grand building. Darkness was still present, but he could see where Georgina's new extension had been built. Another set of new modern doors, lay wide open at the end of the rows of desks and surrounding chairs that cascaded along the ground floor. Above were two more levels.

A plethora of books, old and new, filled the spaces with ease. He could make out the section titles and grimaced. The smell of old book covers dominated the air in the room. He walked towards the light, rubbing his hand over the different genre of literature on the shelves. *Fiction.... Nonfiction.... historical fiction.... literary realism. My word what a load of nonsense. Magical fairy telling trash. People need factual information to stimulate their minds.* His gaze left the shelves and concentrated on the double doors ahead.

He stopped and watched from behind the door. His opponent was standing by a desk organising new editions to the library's collection. She piled them neatly and swayed her body to the instrumental composition. He heard her crooning, trying to keep up with the concerto's tempo. She had to die. She treated him with so much contempt, it made his heart bleed. Her time had come to repay her sins.

The new extension inside was modern, he hated modern. Computers laid out on desks as though they had all the answers, it was his idea of hell. The shiny cream tiles felt cold and uninviting. *They would look well with a splash of colour,* his thoughts now drifting to his last move of his game.

Opening the door, he made himself visible to his victim, placing his rucksack down by his side. 'Hello Georgina,' his voice low and disconcerting.

She didn't hear him. Vivaldi's mandolin concerto now blasted through the speakers. He walked over to the tape deck switching it off. Georgina turned, looking to see what happened to her beautiful music. 'Michael! You scared me. The opening isn't until tomorrow night, it said on the flyer.'

'I know,' he stood gazing at her. Her beautiful brown hair, still long and uncut moved with the pulse of her heartbeat. Her brown eyes wide with traces of in-trepidation. She could sense he wasn't himself.

'Michael, are you okay? You look pre-occupied,' she tried to shift the tension between them. 'Do you fancy giving me a hand, now you're here?' She turned and carried on piling the books on the desk for tomorrow evening's opening. 'You could start by opening that box. It's got a new collection of poetry books in it. You like poetry don't ya Michael?'

He went back over to the tape deck and switched it on. Georgina smiled nervously at his odd behaviour. 'I only read factual books about real people, real events. You should know that.'

'I..I thought your interests in books were diverse. I must have misread you.'

'You never took the time to see who I was, to see what I was interested in. You left me alone like the others. You and Elizabeth laughing behind my back. Yeah, I heard ya.'

'Elizabeth? I don't know any Elizabeth. Michael, you've got me mixed up with someone else,' Georgina shifted her stance away from his body and closer to the doorway.

The light was bright enough to carry out his mission, to kill for his Lord's glory and to finally restore his life.

'Just answer me this, why did you stop reading stories to me?'

'Michael, I have always read snippets of new books, especially the new ones we received into the library. Remember last year, you visited every Friday afternoon until I finished the whole book. I wanted to read it myself and you suggested that you would join me. It was the Anne of Green Gables novel by, who was it by?' She stumbled on the author, her mind was elsewhere, like the main doors.

'Lucy Maud Montgomery!' He yelled back at her. 'Half of it was factual, the other was just the authors life fused into the story.'

Georgina was an educated woman; she had read enough true crime novels to know what to say that would make him calm down. 'You're right, stupid story.'

'You haven't answered my question.'

To deny his claims would be damning and dangerous for her. She had to think on her feet. 'I read to you a lot. Don't you remember?'

'But then you stopped. Was it Pa who told you to?'

She started to understand the situation she was finding herself in. He had just taken it to a new level of some sort of mental instability, and it terrified her. She knew she couldn't show fear in front of him. Georgina was so scared to say the wrong thing.

'Pa? Why do you think it was Pa?'

'He despised me, and you sat there reading your books ignoring me, shutting me out of your life,' he was getting angry with the memories.

Georgina had to find away to defuse the anger he was experiencing. 'Michael, do you remember when you joined the library and you always sat in your favourite seat to read and look up interesting facts? Do you want to go and sit there now? I'll go with you.'

He looked at her with utter confusion. He looked around the room.

'Not in here Michael, it was through there near the book section, True crimes,' pointing through the new doors out into the old main room, where the space wasn't so claustrophobic. He turned his head to look. 'Remember?'

His forehead scrunched up as he turned back to look at Georgina. 'Nice try, but I think I would have remembered my favourite place. It certainly isn't here in the library,' Michael sensed he was losing control of the game. He slowly moved towards his opponent. 'I'm so sorry, but you really should be more careful who you let in the main doors.' He suddenly grabbed her arm, spun her around and pushed her against the desk she had just spent arranging. Books fell from the top of the piles.

'Please Michael, you're scaring me. If you let me go, I won't say anything to anyone, I promise.'

'You won't be able to speak after I finish with you. You deserve to die, and you'll never be able to hurt me again,' he looked around the room to see what he could use. The plan he penned was more precise, but she had thrown a spanner in the works by holding some stupid event for useless, uneducated fools.

He saw what he needed sitting on the shiny cream tiles in the corner of the room. He dragged her along with him to reach the ceramic vase on display. Lifting it up high, he heard her scream out loud. It was working. Michael had moved forward one more step to the finishing position.

The sound of her head colliding with the vase was loud, her body dropping to the floor in a heap. Reaching for his rucksack he pulled out the duct tape and wrapped it tightly around both her hands to the front of her body. The tape deck still blaring out concertos.

Splatters of tiny blood particles sat on the cream tiles. He had to remember what he had penned in his planning regarding her death. Michael reminded himself he was a champion game player and his thoughts returned to the last page of his game plan.

Georgina was out cold. He hadn't killed her, that would be too simple. Dragging her back over to the display table he swung her hands against a table leg and tide them tightly with the blue rope. He had purchased it from Parts & Parts Store, asking Mary Louise to not write it in that damn logbook. He promised her dinner and all the attention she desired. The thought sickened him, but it was all part of the process. She really wasn't his type. All his love was devoted for his Lord.

He lifted up her head with his gloved hands. He wanted to see her face before he carried out his actions, his duties. Stroking her hair and cheeks he thought how his whole life was about to change. He prized opened her mouth and stared at her tongue, caressing it softly as she sat unconscious, looking like his porcelain doll in his bedroom. He waited for her heartbeat to slow and then he would perform. 'Oh Grace, you should have been a good sister to me. Read me literature of old and new, but you wronged me like the others and now you will have to pay. Your storytelling will end now, your tongue will never unravel those latin words you found hard to pronounce again,' he laughed.

Chapter Thirty-One

Butler police department was a hum of activity. All officers at their desks looking for a 34-year-old female at one of the addresses along the eastern line. 'Don't forget employee names at any of the commercial buildings also need found,' Special Agent Clara Strong shouted out. 'Jeremiah, do you know where he lives?'

'He's still in his parent's house along Tom Orr Avenue.'

'We need to go, now! Sheriff, can you call us if your officers find a name? JD you'll have to stay.' He didn't even notice her; Hannah's coat was working perfectly.

'I'll have police backup waiting. Just be careful, you know what he's capable of.'

Deputy Dubois said very little. He checked his weapon, police radio and slipped on his coat. 'I'm ready.'

The storm was still raging in the night sky, lightning struck as the two law enforcement officers approached the cruiser. It was Dubois's turn to navigate. Branches lay across the road; the wind coming from all directions. Turning off South Mulberry Avenue onto county road 24, Clara was told to slow down. 'There!' Dubois pointed to the left. 'Just past Spear Creak and we'll see his vehicle, if we're lucky.'

Driving slowly down Tom Orr Avenue, Clara shifted the vehicle into a slow crawl. His home was in darkness, his vehicle gone. 'We need to still check if he's in or not. He could have parked round the back.'

Clara could see the Deputy getting agitated. 'You good to go?'

He nodded his head, 'He can't get away with what he's done, friend or not.'

'I'll take the back door,' she told him. 'Be careful and watch your back.'

Around to the rear of the property she shone her light and noticed some old outbuildings but made her way to the back door. Her hands cold to the bone as she clutched her weapon. With her back leaning against the house, she turned around to peer through a window. The place looked to be empty, there were no lights on inside that she could see.

Reaching for the door handle she turned to see if it was unlocked. Her frustrations grew and she knew she had to break it open. Looking around in the pouring rain, she spied an old milk churn by the outbuildings. Kicking it over to empty it, she grabbed the handles and slammed it hard against the backdoor. 'Break you fucking piece of shit!' Her second attempt managed to bust the lock, manoeuvring inside. 'Michael! Michael it's Agent Strong. Can you hear me? I'm coming in. I just want to talk to you, nothing else!'

She had a feeling she wasn't going to find him. Thunder rolled outside as she searched for a light switch. The kitchen remained in darkness, her eyes trying to focus, covering all directions. 'Michael, it's Clara from the FBI. I just want to talk!'

The floorboards creaked below her feet as she walked through to the next room. A long hallway was filled with antiques, stuffed animals hung on the walls, lighting up with the strikes of the storm.

Her concentration was focused on her surroundings, when she saw Dubois's shadow to the front of the house. A large wooden front door situated off to the right at the end of the hallway had a single key in the lock. Turning it quietly, she let Dubois in. She signalled for him to carry on checking on that level whilst she headed upstairs.

Clara turned on the landing lights. Upstairs felt cold and uninviting, there was a feeling of sadness about the place, which manifested her soul. She couldn't quite figure it out, but it was there. 'Michael, it's Agent Strong,' she whispered softly, 'I've just come to see if you are okay,' she felt being sympathetic to his needs maybe the best solution to get him to come out, as to posing as a threat. She entered the rooms, one at a time.

Everything had its place and was spotlessly clean. She opened the door to the last room upstairs, quickly raising her weapon. 'Michael! Put your hands up where I can see them!' Heart racing, she ran one hand down the wall, switching on the light. There in front of her hung a suit over the wardrobe door. Lowering her weapon, she told herself to calm down.

The room was colder than the rest of the house. The windows were closed, yet she felt uneasy and creeped out by her surroundings. Making her way back down to Dubois, he showed her a photograph sitting on an old fire mantel. It was torn in places and crumpled. 'Take a look at this,' Jeremiah told Clara. 'It's his family, except he isn't in it.'

'I hate my job sometimes, my heart goes out to him as a child, but now as an adult, he needs to pay for what he's done,' Clara commented. 'He's not here.'

Heading back towards the kitchen, Clara watched her footing as she manoeuvred around the kitchen table. The floorboard's creaked loudly beneath her feet. Shining her maglite on the ground, she detected a small hole in the wooden planks. A tiny glint of light radiated through, catching her eye.

Stopping Deputy Dubois in his tracks, she pointed between the table and bottom kitchen cupboard. Putting her finger to her lips, she slowly slouched down to feel the boards. Using her palm, she pushed down on the planks to see if they would move. The creaking noise informed her she had found what she was looking for. Pushing harder, the plank and several others connected to it, shifted slightly.

Dubois placed his fingers underneath, pulling the hinged trapdoor open. It was an entryway to another lower level. Clara took the lead, stepping carefully as she descended the stairs into the basement. 'Michael, it's Clara.'

She had to catch her breath as her eyes wandered around the room. Dubois circled around Clara, looking at the shelves, which were full to capacity with board games and books. 'Holy cow,' he reached over to touch them.

'No, don't touch anything.'

'But I've never seen such a collection,' his eyes transfixed on the plethora of diverse games dating as far back as the 70's. 'What is all this?' He stepped closer, captivated by the pristine boxes. His jaw dropped, 'Sweet Jesus. It can't be.'

'Jeremiah, what?'

'These games. My parents gave him these when he was a young boy. Look at them, they still look brand new,' Dubois was overwhelmed with guilt and anger. 'I need some air.'

Clara continued to search, she needed to find anything to direct her to his next move, his next victim. She rolled her jacket sleeve down to use as a shield so she wouldn't leave her fingerprints and opened a green cupboard door sitting by his gaming chair. Hand to her mouth she gasped for air. Struggling to comprehend what she was seeing, she turned away, trying to regain her composure.

She took out her cell and called Harris. 'We need Patrick and his team up here now. Tell them to drop whatever they are doing and get here asap.'

The rain persisted, hitting the roof of the cruiser as they sat waiting on forensics to show. Clara's cell phone buzzed in her pocket. She put it on speaker, 'Strong.'

'It's Officer Young. I've got two females coming up on the system in that age bracket and one male. One of the females lives east of the dealership, on Woodley Avenue; the other female's home address isn't in the area we're searching but her workplace is. I can't imagine her working on a Sunday evening though. The male lives on Pickens Avenue.'

'Hannah, give me their names.'

'Sophie Calder, Georgina Miller and Lucas Andrews.'

'It's her, Georgina Miller,' Dubois told her. 'What's her address?'

'Butler County Choctaw Library on Harrell Avenue.'

'Hannah, tell Sheriff Harris we're heading over there now. Tell Dr Cameron the house is accessible. Can you do that? Then get two of the officers to head over to Georgina's home address to make sure she isn't there.'

'Yes, on it.'

'It makes sense, a library full of books. He's planned this all by himself,' Dubois was feeling anxious. 'God, hope we aren't too late.'

Clara drove through the crossroads ignoring the traffic lights and sped off up East Pushmataha Street. Turning down Harrell Avenue, they spotted Michael's vehicle parked near the main entrance. 'Shit Michael, why?' Clara muttered.

Pulling up their hoods they jumped out and ran to the front of the building. 'We go in together. You cover my back,' she whispered.

Dubois nodded. Entering the dark main foyer, they heard music coming from inside. They couldn't waste any time, they had to move fast. Swiftly advancing forwards they entered the main room. Lights shone from the rear of the library whilst the music played on full volume.

Stepping carefully around the desks and chairs, reaching the doorway, they stood either side with their backs turned. Signalling to Dubois she will go in first, she turned herself slowly around and entered the room.

'Michael, it's Agent Strong,' Dubois followed.

He was crouched down beside the table leg, rubbing Georgina's face and prising her mouth open.

'Michael, I need you to stand up slowly, put your hands above your head. Then turn around very carefully and face me,' the music was loud, but she made herself heard.

He stayed crouched down caressing Georgina's unconscious face. Blood on the ground indicated she was hurt, maybe even dead.

'Michael, it's me, your friend.'

His caressing hand stopped. He didn't move. 'Listen Michael, you know you can trust me, I want to help,' Jeremiah told him.

Clara nodded, indicating for him to carry on. Michael slowly stood up and turned off the music. 'Why are you here?' Michael's voice sounded solemn, his soft tones expressing confusion. His back still facing them. 'Don't come any closer to me.'

'We won't Michael. We are here to help you through this. We know what you went through as a child,' Jeremiah continued.

'You don't know any of what went on. But this bitch does. She will have to pay, you know that.'

Clara interjected, 'Why don't you tell us Michael,' she slowly inched forward, the space between them diminishing, hoping and praying he wouldn't suddenly turn.

'She left me like the others, treated me with contempt. They thought they could sneak back into my life, pretending to be someone else. Pretending they didn't know me. Liars, they had to die. They were going to take it all from me, my home, my room. They didn't deserve to live, not after the way they treated me. But God spoke to me, he had a plan,' his right hand moved in front of him. A kitchen knife pulled from his jacket pocket gleamed under the new spotlights above. His red jumper warming his torso underneath. Thunder could be heard crashing across the skies outside. 'She'll never speak again.'

'Michael, wait! She isn't Grace,' Jeremiah shouted.

He slowly turned to face them, his hand clutching the knife with desperation.

'I remember Grace, her hair was long just like Georgina's, but it wasn't brown Michael. She had long blonde hair. This isn't Grace.'

He looked down at the woman tied to the table, then back up at Clara. His brows furrowed as he tried to process what Dubois was saying.

'You're wrong, I remember what she looked like. Stop trying to play mind games with me.'

'Michael, put the knife down gently and walk towards me,' Agent Strong insisted.

'I need to finish my game.'

Chapter Thirty-Two

Sheriff Harris sped off towards Butler Library. Officer Dawson and Asher had informed him Georgina Miller's home was empty. The weather was worsening, intermittent strong gusts of wind blew into the side of his police vehicle. Lightning striking at every opportune moment.

Seeing his police cruiser parked, Harris pulled over next to it, entering the library. As he sidestepped across the parquet floor of the foyer and set foot inside the main room, a huge bolt of lightning struck the top of the building. The sudden increase in voltage from the power surge, overloaded the library's circuit board, causing a sudden blackout in the new extension.

'Shit!' Clara reached for her maglite, switching it on she saw he was gone. Georgina's lifeless body still tied to the table. 'Phone for medics, stay with her,' Clara raised her weapon, rushing back into the main room.

She could hear someone else in there. 'Agent Strong don't shoot, it's me Sheriff Harris.'

'His gotten away.'

'Nobody passed me on the way in so he must still be here. I'll go back to the front entrance and take the first floor.'

She agreed, taking the stairs to the second. The main room towered to roof height, while the first and second floors sat around the edges, creating mezzanines with their wooden balconies.

Clara knew this library. Her elementary school outings consisted of tours around the building, trying to encourage students to take up reading. The place was the same, nothing had changed. Taking the last step to the second floor shining her light in front of her, she could see shadows. Statues were situated in different sections of the library, casting shadows, playing tricks on her eyes.

'Michael, it doesn't have to be like this, I know your parents treated you badly, I know what that feels like,' she didn't expect an answer.

'You don't know what pain feels like. No one does,' his voice sounding choked with anger.

'You're wrong Michael. I feel pain every single damn day of my life. It hurts and it's cruel. Listen Michael, we can talk about this together. Have a proper conversation. Just you and me,' the sound of a door slamming indicated he had gone. 'God damn it!' Bookshelves were situated every ten feet, adjacent to the balcony. She peered into each small reading hub, which allowed visitors to read and admire the view of the grand building. *Where the hell are you?*

There was a door to the end of the second-floor mezzanine, Clara opened it slowly then pointed her weapon inside. Another set of stairs led back down to the first and ground floors. She descended a few steps. 'Michael, I want to help. We all want to help.'

She heard footsteps advancing from below her on the stairs. 'Stop!'

'It's me. No luck?' Harris asked.

'I thought he came this way. Check again. I'm going to head back to the second floor.' Opening up the doorway, passing shadows, she saw a tall figure leaning against the balcony. 'Michael?' He didn't answer. Her weapon poised, her light shining on his body, she slowly walked over to him. Keeping a little distance between them. He had his back to the balcony, his demeanour looking defeated. He knew he was cornered.

'Don't come any closer Miss Agent.'

Her heart sank, remembering that name he had called her back in the parts store.

'You've ruined my game. I was in front all this time.'

'Your gaming skills Michael have messed with everyone's minds. You had us all running around in circles. You planned it beautifully; I'll give you that. How did you manage to trick us into believing it was all the other people?'

He sniggered but with a sorrowful expression. 'You just have to be patient. Executing those moves took time, planning. It's easy when you have the run of people's homes, decorating, building. Stupid people, too trusting. It was too easy. Constructing Joseph's new wall was the icing on the cake,' he put his hand up with the knife, 'Don't come any closer!'

'I won't, I promise.'

'He left the house open; I needed in and found his studio, took the items to help me with my moves. Same at Eleanor's house, they were at school teaching, leaving me to put new posts in on their jetty. Stupid gullible idiots. Johnson wanted his kennel fixed and painted so I took his traps, went back later when he was on the road driving his big truck, pretending I had forgotten some things, and his stupid drunken wife didn't even ask questions. That's when I planted the acrylics and blue rope on his property, when I realised you were on my trail. I had to befriend that mutt to get past, but it didn't like me, I had to tie it up on a short piece of rope, bloody dog. David's office was easy to access. One rip of an invoice and it would make him look guilty. They were all coming for me. Evan riled me up the wrong way in his bar, I recognised him, he thought he got away with it, pretending to be some hotshot bar owner. I knew it was Elijah. When I did some work for him his mother-in-law even said she was fed up with the way he was treating her daughter, wishing he would mysteriously disappear.'

'What about putting the knife down and we can talk some more?'

'No. I think I'll hold onto it for a while longer,' he smiled, looking at the knife, caressing it with both hands. 'Eli was just weak. I planted the blue rope in his shed, replaced the old one's he had. Then I made him out to be guilty of never being around, always taking time off especially the days after I had killed. The chains were an easy lift too, purchased some Longleaf pine panels for a job, using the leftovers to create my masterpieces and there they were, just looped around in a circle on the ground ready to be used on a job. People only see what they want to see.'

'What ever happened to your parents Michael?' Agent Strong asked, figuring out a way to end this situation.

'Don't know. One minute they were there, the next they were sitting on my mantle. Authorities couldn't find my siblings, so the house was given to me. They must have got wind of it and colluded with each other over the years to take it away from me. I couldn't let it happen. So here I am.'

'It's over Michael, you know that.'

'I know. Before you take me in, would you read to me, just a few chapters from a book behind you. Please?'

Clara knew she should be taking him down, arresting him for the atrocities he had committed but her instincts told her to comply with his unusual request, and then she could arrest him without anymore consequences. 'If I do then will you come quietly?'

'You have my word, Miss Agent.'

She didn't take her eyes off him. Instead, she reached her hand back and fumbled for a book. She grabbed the first one and brought it forward, lifting it slightly so the book and Michael were in line with one another.

'What's the title Miss Agent?'

Flicking over to the cover, hands unsteady as she looked, 'Walking since daybreak.'

'Who is the author?'

Her hands shook trying to hold her maglite, weapon and book. 'Modris Eksteins.'

'Can you read me something, even from the back, then I will let this all be over.'

'A story of Eastern Europe, World War II, it's an autobiography. He's a professor of history,' her eyes were still fully fixed on the killer. 'A Latvian Canadian historian. Eksteins finds a doorway to his subject in his own family history. He begins with his maternal great-grandmother, Grieta Pluta, born in 1834. Grieta is seduced by her lover, a Baltic-German Baron,' Agent strong looked up at Michael. He was crying. She thought if she cooperated with his wants, she would get her own results. 'Do you want me to stop?' Sirens were heard in the distance. The storm had eased. *Please let Georgina be alive.*

'Please continue just for a few more minutes.'

'The Baron leaves Grieta while she is,' she paused.

'She is what? Pregnant? There's a surprise,' he guffawed.

'I can get another book. This one seems to be upsetting you.'

'Miss Agent, I'm not upset, these are tears of gratitude because for the first time in my life I feel like someone is listening to me, being my friend. You have taken the time to read to me, I feel extremely humbled and grateful. I have planned this day for years, this isn't the way I thought it would end, but I'm okay with that. Now God won't visit me and give me my new life because I never completed his game, his moves. I have dreamt of standing on that winning podium for years, but this balcony will do instead. There's only one way to finish it, I see that now. If he won't come to me then it looks like I will have to bestow myself upon him in his kingdom,' Michael's smile radiated warmth and she could see he was ready to take his next step. He perched himself on the wooden balcony and dropped the knife to the floor near her feet.

'You know Miss Agent; my surname means Eagle Power, ironic really.'

Agent Strong dropped the book and ran forward to grab him.

His eyes stared at her as he rocked himself off his podium, his body falling backwards landing on the library floor, taking him to his new life.

The sounds of the sirens approaching the scene overrode Clara's thoughts. She shone her light. His body lay on the wooden floor, his blood splatters reaching some of the fictional bookshelves. He was no longer suffering. He was dead.

Clara had to carry on, she needed to check on Georgina. Reaching the ground floor the same time as the medics arrived, she pointed to where Georgina and Dubois were. The main lights switched on. Sheriff Harris stood in the doorway. They glanced at the body on the floor not saying a word.

Deputy Dubois came from the extension seeing his friend lying face up on the floor. He stepped forwards, kneeling down beside him. He took his coat from his back and placed it over Michael's body. 'You should have spoken to me; I could have helped you.'

Clara rested her hand on Dubois's shoulder. 'He isn't suffering anymore. He can rest in peace with his God.'

Jeremiah turned to face Clara not understanding what she meant. 'I want to give him a proper burial.' She nodded, feelings of every emotion stirring within her. *The victims, their families, Michael. All of them suffered because of life's injustices.*

The medics wheeled a stretcher past the three standing by the corpse. 'How is she?'

'She has lost a lot of blood; we need to get her to the hospital fast,' the woman medic carried the oxygen bottle as the other two pushed her to their rig.

Clara and the two police officers pulled out chairs from under the library desks and sat in silence. A phone buzzed. It was Clara's. *Now what!* She answered.

'Miss Strong, it's Butler Hospital. I have your name down as next of kin for Mrs Alice Strong. I'm afraid I have some bad news.'

Epilogue

He wore his favourite suit with the buttoned-up waistcoat to match. His corpse lay on white satin cloth, which complemented his blue outfit. Jeremiah Dubois made sure his friend would be taken care of until he reached his new destination. Michael's funeral consisted of Dubois, Strong, Harris and Pastor MacArthur. It was a basic traditional ceremony, which included a religious ritual, followed by a procession to the burial ground situated to the side of the church. Pastor MacArthur finished off with a few words at the graveside, remembering his new church goer's words a few days ago about having a seat in the front pew, next time he visited.

As Clara was about to walk out of the cemetery, she placed some flowers on a grave. She knelt down and looked at the headstone. 'Your secret goes with you mama. If Grayson is with you, say hi from me,' she stood up and looked around.

She knew people were talking about her, attending a funeral of a killer. She didn't care. Clara was doing it for Jeremiah Dubois who needed some sort of closure to this tragic story that unfolded before their eyes.

Agent Strong, Sheriff Harris and the police department of Butler also showed their respects to each person that fell victim to Michael Arnold's killings. Crowds gathered outside the churches of their denominations, then laid a plaque beneath the confederate statue outside the courthouse in their memory.

'You'll be heading home then?' Harris spoke up, as they walked away from Michael Arnold's funeral.

'Yes, have to get back to the office, see where my life stands. It's in the hands of my boss,' she was too tired to think about it.

'I had a phone call this morning at the police department. Sarah Johnson's dog has disappeared. You wouldn't know anything about that?' He laughed, 'Of course you wouldn't.'

'That reminds me, could you drop JD and myself off at the train station?'

'He's going in the trunk on the way there!' He was becoming fond of the mutt, just didn't want to admit it to her.

They drove over to the police department so she could gather up her things and JD. Hannah had volunteered to dog sit, she hated funerals.

They walked through the main doors of the courthouse; the aroma of paint was still lingering in the air. The corners of her mouth slightly curled up; as much as it pained her to think of the ending, she had done her job. She just wanted to get home now, see Perez and Frank.

As she walked into the department she was greeted by the team. Officer Hannah Young was the first to say something. 'We are definitely going to miss you around here Ma'am. Stay in touch.'

'If there is ever a job going at the FBI in Durant in a couple of years, I'll give you a shout,' Hannah's face blushed.

Saying her goodbyes, Jeremiah Dubois walked her back out. 'Thanks Agent Strong, maybe we could meet up again sometime, have a proper chat over a coke and ice?'

'I would love that, Jeremiah. Apparently, there are apps on your cell now to help, so I was told,' she winked at him and headed outside to get a lift to the station.

Explaining to the ticket clerk the dog was a trained animal, top of its game in the FBI and they were on official duty, he reluctantly agreed to let him travel, moving them both on so they wouldn't cause a queue.

'It's a long journey so rest yourself,' he snuggled his body against her legs under the carriage table, then laid down to sleep on her feet. She looked outside and thought about the past couple of weeks. A cacophony of events had gradually unfolded before her, but she pushed through them, resolving each one with everyone's help. She had hopefully found the inner strength to turn her back on the booze, she knew it wasn't the answer. It would take time, there maybe times she might relapse, but she would continue to dig deep, fight those demons if they ever arise. Her thoughts drifter to the three victims and Georgina who was sent home yesterday from hospital. Her life would never be the same, just like the families of Evan, David and Eleanor.

Clara lifted her cell and flicked through it, reading different people's studies on how people affect one another's thoughts, feelings and behaviours, the understandings of behavioural psychology, studies that helped predict how humans behave, and the mental processes and brain functions of humans. Everything she read was complex and not straightforward or clear, yet her curiosity was heightened to learn more. Instead of fighting against her feelings, she had a newfound sense of embracing them and learning what they all meant.

She closed up her phone and thought about her mama and the attorney who was looking for her to read the Will, but she couldn't face anymore drama at present.

The train pulled away and JD gave a little whimper, settling down again and no doubt dreaming of freedom. She sipped on her coffee, looking at her bag. Pulling out a vanilla-coloured file, she placed it on the table and opened it, making sure other passengers weren't in eye shot of the contents.

Dr Patrick Cameron had kindly photocopied some of the findings from Michael Arnold's home. He had slipped a note in to say he couldn't record all the details as there were too many. She wanted to explore to a greater degree, why he was pushed into acting out such heinous acts. Clara had a little understanding, but she wanted to probe deeper, educate herself more about his behaviours. Adam had inspired her, and she needed a new focus. Apart from JD.

Her heart was broken by the photos displayed in front of her. The games on his shelves from his basement had been removed and placed into boxes. Wrapped up and ready to be distributed to Zachariah Jackson's children's charities. The contents of the cupboard, concludes they belonged to the victims, no questions.

She picked up sheets of written notes and glared at the inscription. It was samples from Michael's game plan he had penned. Reading some of the paragraphs brought unsuspecting tears to Clara's eyes. *He was a child, left behind by his family and society. He had no one to help him.* She read a passage from the beginning of his plan, and it saddened her. "I believe in the Lord God, as he is my only hope. He has spoken to me and told me he would make my life complete. He listens to me, speaks to me, notices that I am alive. He has asked me to do his work here and I will be repaid with eternal peace and life."

Her heart tightened, she turned to another sheet. Michael had planned this for 6 whole years. Every detail of how he was going to master his moves were right in front of her.

Of course, she was thinking about the victims that had succumbed to their deaths, she would be heartless not to, but she couldn't help thinking about how a lot of people's traumas from such a young age turn into tragedies as adults. Her head was full of information, she couldn't process anymore, she was too exhausted. She closed over the file, placing it back in her bag and slowly drifted off to sleep.

***

Frank was sitting in his Honda outside the station, waiting for his best friend. Hoards of people poured out of the building and greeted their loved ones. His eyes scoured through the crowds. He couldn't believe his eyes. She appeared from behind a group of young girls who were laughing and joking on their cells.

'A dog!' He mused to himself.

She tried to wave to get his attention, but the dog's leash was wrapped around her legs, creating chaos. Frank got out of his car and went to help her. JD saw the man approaching and jumped up to greet him. 'Aww he likes you!'

'A dog?'

'JD meet Frank,' she was pleased to see they were bonding at their first meeting.

'Whose dog is it? Tell me it's not yours Clara Strong.'

She smiled and raised her eyebrows.

'But you live in a stuffy apartment and work 24/7.' She gave him a kiss on the cheek. 'No! Definitely not. A bar is not a place for a four-legged animal.'

'It's only temporary. It's about time I found myself a new place, if Assistant Miller doesn't sack me.'

'You and Perez have just cracked a case, why would he get rid of you?'

'I believe he just doesn't think I'm cut out for this kind of work, he knows I'm carrying baggage and he's testing me.'

'But look at you after a couple of weeks away, you are practically a new woman,' he said with a slight hint of admiration in his voice.

'I know going home has made me think starting my journey in life from scratch is the answer.'

'I'm always a good listener, I have missed you Agent Strong.'

'You too Frank,' they leaned in closer after they stopped talking. He stroked her hair with his fingers, she winced.

'What? What did I do?'

She turned around, showing her shaven head. 'It'll grow back.'

'You never stop surprising me,' his face beamed, expressing tenderness towards her.

'Can I ask you a favour?'

He nodded, 'Ask away.'

'Can we call in somewhere before I go home, it's on the way?'

Frank drove Clara to her destination, she jumped out the car, JD followed. 'You can't come in boy,' before she could knock, the front door opened. 'Emily!'

'Agent Strong, it's so good to finally meet you properly. Come in please.'

'I just need to throw JD back in the car.'

'Aww no, he can come in. Hello boy,' she bent down and gave him a playful stroke.

They walked through to the kitchen at the back of the house. Emily's parents sat at the breakfast bar eating.

'I really didn't mean to intrude. I was passing and I wanted to see how you were doing?'

Emily introduced Clara to her parents. They both got up from their seats, approached Clara and took it in turns to hug her tightly. 'You are always welcome,' her mother said, tears rolling down her red cheeks.

Clara heard the patio doors sliding open. She turned around and saw Emily playing with JD in the large back yard.

'She is seeing a specialist. Nighttime is the worst time for her. We're trying to keep her busy, doing everything we think is necessary to get her through this,' Emily's Father said, out of the blue.

'That's the happiest I have seen her since...,' her mother found it too emotional to finish off her sentence.

The three stood in the kitchen watching the two run around the garden. JD full of life, enjoying Emily's company. They suddenly came racing in, 'Do you want some water?' She scuffed up his fur on his head. 'Can I give him a drink?'

Clara nodded, watching the two establish a friendship. Her heart fluttered at the obvious enjoyment taking place in the kitchen.

Her father hunted through the cupboards for an empty container. JD sat at his feet, waiting. 'There's a good boy. Has he a name?'

'JD. I adopted him a couple of days ago. I don't know anything about him just that he was treated badly and needed rescuing. 'He really has taken to you Emily.'

Her father looked at Clara, raising his eyebrows and smiling, she knew exactly what he was asking, without saying a word.

Her future was to have something to look after, concentrate her energy on, anything to take her mind off the booze. Looking at Emily she could see her future was going to be harder than hers to navigate back to some normality. She looked back at the teenager's father and nodded. His face lit up with pure gratitude. Clara felt mixed emotions about leaving her new companion behind, but he hadn't even come near her since visiting Emily.

'Emily, the thing is JD really needs a place where he can run around, release all his energy and my pokey apartment is far too small ….'

'Yes! Can I daddy, please?' She interjected before Clara could finish, running back outside with him before her father could answer.

'Thank you Agent Strong, you have given her a positive focus.'

'Please call me Clara.'

'We would love you to come back anytime and see how they are both doing, we know she would love to see you as much as you can, it will hopefully help with her recovery and healing process.

She always talks about what you did for her. A 14-year-old shouldn't have to start life with psychological traumas, but she is a determined young thing, and we hope she will overcome any obstacles she encounters. We can never repay you, but our doors are always open,' tears fell as Marcus, Emily's father, opened up his heart to her.

Clara thought of her own battles and felt a sudden closeness to Emily. She fetched JD's bowls from Frank's Honda and said her goodbyes. JD was happy to be running around free, playing with someone who actually cared. *Everyone deserves someone,* Clara thought.

Frank drove her home and parked outside her apartment block.

'I'm proud of you Clara, that was a great thing you just did.'

'I'll just have to find a new companion,' holding her stare with Frank. He slowly leaned across, holding her face in his hands. The gap between them shortened. Just as he was about to kiss her for the first time, her cell phone buzzed in her pocket. His lips met her forehead as she looked down to see who was calling.

'Miller!'

Frank left her to talk and got her things from the trunk of his Honda, waving her goodbye as she listened to her boss on the other end of her cell. She walked to the main doors of her apartment block, turned around and mouthed a silent thank you, which he smiled at.

'Agent Strong, it's Miller. Are you back in Durant?'

'Just arrived Sir. Just walking through the door as we speak. How's Agent Perez? I want to drop by and pay him a visit.'

'He's awake, up and eating. Good sign,' Miller was a man of few words. 'Good job down in Butler. Sheriff Harris commends your work. That's the reason I'm calling. I have another case I need you to take care of. It's not here, it's in Alexandria, down in Louisiana.'

'What's happened?'
'Two teenage boys have gone missing.'

Printed in Great Britain
by Amazon